The *Backdoor* Billionaire's Bride

USA Today Bestselling Author

ROZLEE

Ford
&
Becky Jean
(The Backdoor Billionaire's Bride)

ROZ LEE

ISBN: 978-1-966224-12-9

DEDICATION

For Terrell. Thanks for making me laugh.

ACKNOWLEDGMENTS

I have many people to thank for bringing this story to life.

First, I have to thank my family for putting up with me and my neurotic mood swings when I'm writing. That includes our rescue dog, Bud, and our rescue grand dog, Scout, who made sure I got plenty of cold, fresh air during the long days that went into writing this story.

A special thanks to my husband for helping me plot the story on one of our long drives. P.S. – This one is done. We need to take another road trip!

The Backdoor Billionaire's Bride might never have been completed without the New Jersey Romance Writers who cheered me on during JeRoWriMo. I needed someone to hold my feet to the fire as much as I needed to know I was not alone in my struggles to get words on paper. For all of my fellow 30K'ers, I owe you one.

To Karen and Diane—thank you both for reading and giving me your honest opinion. It fills my heart to know I have friends I can count on.

Many thanks to Talina Perkins at Bookinitdesigns for the beautiful cover. I spout nonsense and you translate it into a work of art.

To my editor, Laura Garland at Wizards in Publishing, thank you for knowing where the commas go.

PART ONE

A successful marriage is an edifice that must be rebuilt every day.
Andre Maurois

CHAPTER ONE

K. Ford Adams ran his fingers along the edge of the massive wooden desk. Generations of Adamses had run an empire from this very spot, and now it was his turn—whether he wanted it or not. And, he definitely did not want.

His father was gone. Kenneth Adams had appeared in good health up until a few days ago when a heart attack had taken him from his family, his business, and his town, at the young age of fifty-eight.

Butte Plains, Texas, would miss the elder Adams. The third generation born and raised in the small town, Ken Adams had been loved and respected by everyone.

As the single-largest employer in Butte Plains, the town had been built around his family's factory generations ago, so naturally, the employees would be curious about the person taking the helm. At least that's what he told himself as he looked around at more than a century of memories cluttering the office. Nothing much had changed over the years. Each Adams to sit at the desk added their own achievements to the collection, but none had ever removed anything.

Everything from a yellowed photograph of his great-grandfather breaking ground on the original building, to a plaque declaring his father as Employer of the Year in Butte Plains, an honor bestowed only one month ago, lined the walls. What would become of it all once he sold the business? All the memories would need to be packed away and, most likely, stored in the attic of the family mansion along with all the other junk collecting dust there.

He didn't want to think about what would happen to the stuff once his mother passed. Three years her husband's junior, Helen Ford Adams, hopefully, had many more years on earth. He'd leave worries of what to do with the house and its furnishings for later. He had enough things on his plate—like figuring the company's value and finding a buyer. The sooner he converted the assets into cash to provide for his mother's remaining years, the sooner he could return to his own life— and get the fuck out of Butte Plains. Again.

Nothing remained for him here. Never had been.

An image popped into his head—a woman dressed in a trim black suit, a smart hat complete with some sort of net veil shielding the left side of her tear-ravaged face as she listened to the preacher's softly-spoken graveside prayer for Kenneth Adams's eternal peace. She'd looked familiar, but then again, he'd once known everyone in this town. It could have been anyone from his past, though he couldn't think of a single female with as much beauty and grace as the mystery woman possessed.

It didn't matter if he knew her or not, her tears had been genuine, marking her as someone special in his book. Ford didn't want to follow in his father's footsteps, but he had loved and respected the man. Ken Adams had been an excellent father, instilling values, passing on wisdom, and encouraging his son to follow his dreams, even if they took him away from Texas and the family business.

Ruthlessly shutting down thoughts of the mystery woman and how she knew his father, he turned his attention to the one modern thing in the office—a state-of-the-art computer. He remembered the day, a few years ago, when his father mentioned the new office manager had insisted he learn to work the computer system. The year before, all the company's records had been converted to digital files, and this new employee had been determined to drag Ken into the present century. The man had gone along reluctantly, but, from later accounts, he'd taken to the new technology with an ease that spoke of his intelligence.

Since the desk dated back to a century before computers, Ford put the keyboard in his lap, and pushed the Enter key. A password prompt appeared on the flat-screen monitor. Ken Adams's greatest weakness, if he had one, was his love for his wife and son. Every pass code, from the factory's alarm system to the keypad for his home garage-door opener was one of two words. Ford smirked as he typed his mother's name in the blank box.

"So much for security," he mumbled as the blank screen gave way to a program his father had left open. Chuckling to himself, he swiped at tears blurring his vision. When his sight cleared, he leaned back in the chair and moved the next card on the deck to its appropriate place on the Solitaire board. He couldn't stay in Butte Plains and run his father's company, but he could finish this last game for the man who had taught him to balance work and play.

~~~

Following the touching graveside service for her boss, Becky Parker couldn't bring herself to drive up to the family's mansion for the traditional wake. She'd had about all the heartbreak she could stand for one day, and confronting K. Ford Adams today wouldn't do anyone any good. Everyone she talked to seemed confident the heir would embrace the family mantle and come home to steer the helm of Adams Manufacturing. She knew he would not.

Ken Adams had spoken of Ford often, and with great affection, but he'd also known his son had no interest in the family business. Ford was an only child, so, following family tradition of passing down from father to son, the place had become his—whether he wanted it or not. Which meant the company would go on the auction block. Or worse—Ford
~~~

could flat-out close the plant. Butte Plains was struggling enough. Closing the factory would be the last nail in the coffin lid for the small west Texas town she loved so much.

Out of respect for the other workers' grief over losing a beloved friend and employer, Becky had thus far kept her Negative Nellie thoughts to herself. But if she came face-to-face with Ford in the mood she was in, she didn't think she'd be capable of keeping her mouth shut. She'd been brought up better than to cause a scene at a wake, so she'd wait until she had Ford alone before she told him what she thought of a man who would turn his back on his neighbors.

Steering her car in the opposite direction of the Adams's home, she headed toward the one place she knew she'd be alone today—her office. The plant had been shut down so all the employees could attend the services, but she still had work to do. Payday was coming up, and she needed to figure out how to go about transferring funds into the payroll account. There would be legal wrangling to get it done since Ken had always handled money transfers himself. Ford could probably do it, but she didn't want to bother him yet. It might be days—weeks—before he decided to see about disposing of his responsibility, and the factory workers couldn't wait until he got his shit together to be paid.

She absolutely refused to believe this paycheck might be the last any of them would receive from Adams Manufacturing.

Pulling into the vacant parking lot, she eyed the barren planter boxes dividing the rows. The daffodils would be poking their heads up soon, followed closely by the tulips and those other flowers she could never remember the name of. She made a mental note to contact the landscaper and see about having fresh mulch put down before the weeds got out of hand. She parked in her usual spot, extricated her purse from beneath the hat she'd worn to the funeral then exited the car. Approaching the front door, she froze. The seam between the double-glass doors sat off-kilter. Certain she'd secured it the night before, she glanced over her shoulder. Someone had unlocked the door, but her car was the only vehicle in the lot.

Had one of the other workers come by and forgotten to lock up when they left? It certainly wouldn't be the first time the building had been left open. Everyone in town knew there wasn't anything worth stealing in the place, no money, and very little with any resale value—so not worth the trouble if a person meant to make an easy buck. The real, but very small, threat was vandalism. The machinery inside had all been custom built to do what it needed to do. Replacing any part would take time and money. Wholesale destruction would put them out of business. Becky made a mental note to remind everyone with a key to make sure they locked up next time then reached for the door handle. No need courting disaster, especially since disaster already loomed over their heads in the form of one K. Ford Adams.

After locking the door behind her, she made her way through the silent lobby to the hallway leading to the executive offices. She turned the corner, stopping cold at the sight of light shining from the open doorway at the end of the hallway. From Ken Adams's office. Only one person—besides her— had the right to be in the boss's office, and he was receiving mourners at his mother's home across town.

Who the hell would invade a man's office on the day of his funeral? Remembering the empty parking lot, she sighed. *Whoever it is, they're gone. Might as well see what damage they've done.*

Stopping in her office next to Mr. Adams's, Becky noted nothing out of place. Her computer sat in its usual place. If they'd burgled, they'd done a piss-poor job of it. Leaving her purse, she rounded the corner into the adjacent office and came to an abrupt halt.

"Holy crap!" Her hand flew to her chest to calm her runaway heart.

The last person she'd expected to see sat behind the ancient desk. At her exclamation, he glanced her way then tossed the keyboard on the blotter and leaned back in Mr. Adams's chair. Other than catching a glimpse of him at the funeral, she hadn't seen the younger Adams in over a decade, but she'd recognize him anywhere. Ford was the spitting image of his father, and—holy cow—sexy as hell. Her image of him as Ebenezer Scrooge faded fast. "Ford," she gasped. "I mean, Mr. Adams. What are you doing here?"

He scrubbed at his face with both hands in a gesture that spoke to the strain he must be under. Dropping his hands to the desktop, he glanced around the room. No matter what he decided to do with the company, the man had just lost his father and it showed in the lines bracketing his eyes and mouth. Her heart softened toward him. "In case you haven't heard, I'm the new owner."

"Yes. Of course." She willed her breathing to even out. "I meant…. I assumed you'd be at the house."

"I could only take about five minutes, then I had to get away." He gestured absently. "Figured no one else would be here."

Becky nodded. She could relate. When her father passed, she'd hated every minute of the wake. If she'd been able to find a way to escape, she would have. She gave Ford props for doing what he needed rather than bowing to antiquated traditions.

She tossed aside her plan to get a head start on the payroll situation. She'd leave him to deal with his grief. "Oh. Well. I'll go, then. Didn't mean to interrupt." She took a step backward.

"Becky Jean?" He unfolded from the chair.

She didn't remember him being so tall—over six feet, she guessed. He'd shed his black suit coat and rolled up the sleeves of his white dress shirt. A black-and-silver striped tie hung loose, drawing her attention to the triangle of golden skin his open collar exposed. Her mouth watered. An image flashed in her brain of her slowly licking him there.

Becky licked her lips instead then bit her lower lip, just to be on the safe side. If she remembered right, Ford had been sort of nerdy in high school. *There's nothing nerdy about him now. Not. One. Damn. Thing. God, what is wrong with me?* She hadn't had much experience with instant lust, but she knew it when she felt it. And boy, did she feel it from the roots of her hair to the tips of her toes—and in every erogenous zone in between. Even if the man hadn't been her new boss, he'd still just lost his father—a man he loved. She couldn't think of a single thing more inappropriate than lusting after Ford. Drawing a mental line, she shoved her wayward thoughts behind it.

"Don't go." Her body responded to the baritone command, freezing in place, melting at the core. "It is Becky Jean, isn't it?"

"Um… it's just Becky now."

Though his eyes still looked sad, his smile appeared genuine. "I knew I recognized you! Saw you at the service." His smile dimmed. "Thanks for coming, by the way."

"It was the least I could do." She meant the comment with every fiber of her being. She'd started with the company in high school, working afternoons and weekends boxing products for shipment in order to save for college. As an undergrad, she'd spent her summers on the assembly line, a jump in pay she needed to continue funding her degree. A week after her college graduation, her father had been diagnosed with inoperable lung cancer. Her family needed her. And with her brother, Colin, a sophomore in high school, she'd had no choice but to put off looking for a job in marketing in a big city. She'd returned home, and to the assembly line to help pay her father's staggering medical bills. Soon after, Ken Adams learned about her situation and offered her the job of office manager. The pay hadn't been enough, but it went a long way to easing her family's burden. In her eyes, Ken Adams had been a saint, and she would not let her attraction to his son get in the way of doing what she could to keep his factory open.

"Hey. What are you doing here anyway?" he asked.

God, even the way his eyebrows knit together was sexy. *Snap out of it, Beck. Now.* "I… uh…. Payroll has to go out this week. I thought I'd… you know, get the ball rolling."

"You work here."

"I manage the office."

He turned his gaze to the desktop. He flicked the keyboard keys with his index finger. "You're the one who got

Dad on the computer."

She counted bringing the elder Adams into the twenty-first century as one of her major accomplishments. Remembering the struggle, she smiled. "Guilty as charged."

When Ford returned his gaze to her, pain clouded his eyes, but a tiny smile lifted one side of his mouth. "I tried for years to get him online. I'm grateful you managed to convince him. We kept in touch via Skype and email."

"I didn't know about the Skype."

Ford shrugged and went back to flicking the keys. "Doesn't matter."

But it clearly did. He sat, turning his attention to the computer monitor. He seemed to shrink right before her eyes. "I'll look into the account situation at the bank. I'm guessing money needs to be transferred into the payroll account?"

"Yes. By day after tomorrow."

"I'll take care of it." His voice rumbled with conviction and dismissal.

"Thanks." She backed out of the doorway. He looked as if the world rested on his shoulders. "It can wait until tomorrow."

"I'm sure it can, but I need something to do."

"Okay. Well." She bit her lip again. "I'll be in my office. If you need anything."

He glanced at her, appreciation shining past the pain. "Thanks, Becky Jean."

He'd come here to escape the sympathy of others, but she got the oddest impression he still needed to hear it. "He was a good man. Lots of people are going to miss him."

His Adam's apple bobbed. He dipped his chin, acknowledging her comment then turned his focus to the computer screen. Becky slipped into her office, leaving him to deal with his grief in his own way.

CHAPTER TWO

Ford stared after Becky Jean. He'd heard the same sentiment a thousand times since he'd returned to Butte Plains earlier this week, so why did he have the feeling that, coming from her, the eulogy held a hint of warning? Was she implying *he* wasn't a good man? *Why would she think that?*

Chalking the uneasy feeling up to grief and fatigue, he clicked the computer keys. No matter what he did with the factory, the workers needed to be paid. He'd never worked a day in the factory, but he knew how businesses operated. He just needed to figure out which account usually funded payroll and arrange with the bank to make the transfer—then he could get on with gathering the necessary financial statements needed to entice someone to buy Adams Manufacturing.

As he clicked through his father's personal files, his mind kept returning to Becky Jean Parker. He had a hard time reconciling the steaming-hot woman from the cemetery with his long-ago recollections of the girl he remembered from school. She'd been a mouse, sitting at the back of classrooms, never saying a word he could recall. He could count on one hand the number of times he remembered interacting with her, and none of those had been particularly memorable. She hadn't run with any of the popular crowds, hadn't played sports, hadn't attended the high school dances or other social functions. She'd been more of a ghost than a mouse—invisible, but there if you bothered to look.

He hadn't bothered to look.

That's not entirely true. There was that one time….

He'd shown up at the local photography studio to have his senior portrait made and she'd been there. Waiting his turn, he'd peeked to see who had the appointment ahead of him, and been shocked to see Becky Jean perched on a stool, smiling for the camera. She'd been wearing one of those black drape things leaving her slim shoulders bare. Her red hair hadn't yet mellowed to the subdued auburn it was now. The curled ends had lain against her chest, drawing attention to the swell of generous breasts. A Mona Lisa smile graced her glossed lips, and her eyes had sparkled with intelligence.

Only he knew the reason for the slightly pained smile he'd worn in his senior portrait. He'd had a raging hard-on the entire photo session, all because of Becky Jean Parker.

Ford shifted, his dick as hard today as it had been back then. For years, he'd chalked up his response to teenage hormones, but seeing her, talking to her today, proved nothing had changed. She still stirred his blood in inappropriate ways.

As of today, Becky Jean worked for him. He absolutely wouldn't take advantage of an employee. No way.

Another image came to mind—Veronica Ramsey. The younger sister of his business partner, Scott, she was beautiful and sophisticated. They'd been friends and fuck buddies for over a year. When he'd told her his father had passed away and he had to make the trip home for the funeral, she'd expressed her condolences, but hadn't offered to accompany him. He'd momentarily considered *asking* her to but figured if he had to *ask,* then he didn't want her there anyway. He'd begun to question if he even wanted her in his life. When it came down to it, they had little in common. Where he preferred to share a drink with a buddy or two, she preferred a party—the bigger, the better. Born into a life he'd never dreamed of, she'd dazzled him from the beginning, but it didn't take long for him to see past the glitz. Once he had, he'd been surprised to see how empty her friends' lives were. He wanted more for himself, but Ronnie wouldn't take "no" for an answer.

He forced his attention back to the payroll situation. He had no business admiring anything about his new office manager. Becky Jean was his employee. She, and all the others, would expect to be paid this week. His father would kick his ass if he let them down.

An hour later, Ford had learned two things. He couldn't sell the company, and he wouldn't be leaving town anytime soon. Neither realization made him happy. In fact, they pissed him off.

Sitting back in the leather desk chair built to fit his father's frame, not his, he scrubbed both palms over his face. Tension he'd been holding in his shoulders all day felt like cement blocks weighing him down. Why hadn't his dad said something? How had the situation gotten this critical without Ford suspecting? Did anyone know? The employees? If anyone did, it would be the office manager.

Sitting up, he bellowed, "Becky Jean! Get your ass in here right this minute!"

Barreling around the corner, eyes wide, the woman skidded to a halt in the doorway. "What?"

"That's all you've got to say? *What?*" He stood, knuckles digging into the oak desktop. "Where did the money go?"

Her eyes narrowed, her brows knit together. "Money?" One hand white-knuckled the doorframe.

"Umm. The petty cash is in the safe in my office?" Her voice trailed up and off.

"I'm not talking about the petty cash, and you damn well know it. Where. Is. The. Money?"

"I don't... uh.... What?" She swallowed hard, let go of the doorframe, and tugged the hem of her suit jacket down. Squaring her shoulders, she glared at him. "Is there a problem,

Mr. Adams?"

"Fuck, yeah! I mean… yes, *Becky Jean*." He emphasized her name, infusing as much civility as possible into his cold-as-steel voice. Two could play this dignified business game. "There *is* a problem. There isn't enough money in all the company accounts *combined* to meet this week's payroll. I want to know where it went."

All the blood drained out of her face, and she reached for the doorframe again. Her hand missed, but her shoulder caught, preventing her from falling. Ford rushed to her side. Wrapping an arm around her waist, he guided her to one of the green leather visitor's chairs. Hoping his father hadn't broken with Adams's family tradition, he scooted around the desk and opened the bottom left drawer. Seconds later, he pushed a tumbler of Tennessee's finest into Becky Jean's palm. "Here, drink this."

He held the glass steady while she sipped at the amber liquid. Making a face like she'd sucked a lemon, she pushed the glass away.

"Yeck!" She wiped her lips with the back of her hand. "What is that?"

"Whiskey." He finished the two fingers with one swallow and rose to refill the glass—which he downed before returning to sit on the edge of the desk, with yet another two fingers of courage. Ford sipped at his third glass of whiskey, letting the first two work through his system while he studied the woman in front of him. Her eyes looked lost, but at least the color had returned to her cheeks. If she'd known about the company's financial troubles, she did a hell of job playing innocent. Which made his father a better actor than he'd given him credit for. In their weekly conversations, the man had given nothing away concerning the dire financial situation.

"What the hell has been going on around here?" He congratulated himself on sounding close to reasonable—thanks to the alcohol dulling the sharp knife of betrayal.

"I don't know." She seemed fascinated with her hands twisting in her lap. "Is it that bad?"

"Yes. It's that bad." No wonder his father had a fatal heart attack. Ford was about to have a coronary himself. "What happened to the cash flow? From what I can tell, Dad has been dipping into his personal accounts to keep this place running for quite some time." Which meant his mother didn't have a penny to her name. *Shit.*

Becky Jean turned her face up to his. Even her misery didn't dim her beauty. "I swear I didn't know. Mr. Adams— your father—insisted on doing the books himself."

"But the factory is still churning out product, shipping out orders. Or did I miss something in the production schedules?"

"We are shipping orders. Not as many as we did a few years ago, but we have clients."

"How many clients?"

"One."

"One?" Yep. He'd follow his father into an early grave. "What happened to the others? Adams Manufacturing used to be the leading supplier, worldwide, of baby bottle nipples."

She shook her head. "We've been losing market share for a few years. With the movement toward breastfeeding, people aren't buying as many baby bottles as they used to."

Any other time, he would have enjoyed watching her face flame at the mention of breastfeeding, but his present situation had trampled his libido into submission. "What about the agricultural market? Aren't people still milking cows?" For as long as he could remember, their largest contracts had been for the teat cup liners used in milking machines. Not glamorous, but it paid the bills.

"It's China's fault."

"China?"

"We can't compete with their prices. Dairy farmers are just like everyone else. They don't care where the product comes from as long as they save a buck."

Shit. "The agricultural market was the cash cow, so to speak."

"Yes. Farmland Supply didn't renew their contract this year, not for any of the products we supplied them."

He mentally ticked off the products he remembered—teat cup liners, rubber gloves, bottles, and nipples for hand-feeding orphaned and sick livestock and zoo animals. They'd supplied the large farm retailer with those and more for as long as Ford could remember. "So what *are* we producing?"

"Baby bottles and nipples, and not nearly as many of those as we used to."

"China?"

She nodded. "Yep. Your father hired an independent lab to analyze the Chinese products, see what they're made of. He was hoping to launch an advertising campaign to undermine consumer confidence in their products and shift the public back to products made here in the U.S."

It was something, but without the agricultural component, Adams Manufacturing was doomed to fail. "Whose idea was that? The lab thing?"

"Mine." She sighed. She'd appeared sad at his father's graveside. Now, she looked defeated. "It was too little, too late, wasn't it?"

"Yep." He finished off the rest of his drink, savoring the smooth burn making its way down. He stood, circled around to his father's chair, and sank into it. From the moment he'd comprehended the scope of the problem, he'd known what he had to do. He forced himself to say the words. "I'll float the payroll out of my own pocket until I can figure out what to do with the— What's left."

"You're going to close the plant." Her voice held resignation rather than surprise.

He stared into the bottom of the empty glass then set it carefully in the center of the desk. Raising one eyebrow, he asked, "What choice do I have?"

"I don't know. It's just so many people depend on their jobs here. The whole town depends on Adams Manufacturing. This is going to hurt so many people." She made it sound as if he'd said he planned to kick every puppy in town and drown all the kittens, too.

"I don't want to, but unless you can come up with a way

to keep this place running, and to turn a profit then I don't see I have any choice. It's already bled my father, and his widow, dry." Visions of his mother moving into his spare bedroom formed in his head. *Good God.* "If I let it, it'll do the same to me. I don't see what the difference is between closing in a few weeks and closing a few months down the road when I run out of money, too."

She brightened. "You've got enough money to keep the plant open?"

"Hold on a minute." He held his hand up in stop-right-there signal. "I've worked damn hard for my money, and I'm not going to throw it down a dry well and hope it turns into water. I'll contact the few remaining clients we have and negotiate final production numbers to get us out of our contracts. Once we fulfill those orders, we'll shut down for good."

She deflated, but at least she didn't look like she might faint this time.

"I have to think about my mother, Becky Jean. I've got to salvage whatever I can of all this"—he swept his arm out to indicate the business—"for her." He had to be careful or they'd both be wearing paper hats and flipping burgers before the year ended.

"What about the employees? The people who work here don't do it because it's the most fun they've ever had. They do it because they have families to feed."

"I'm not a puppy kicker, Becky Jean!" Fuck, he was back to shouting. He cleared his throat and tried again. "If I could see a way to make this place turn a profit, I'd do everything in my power to keep it open."

"No, you wouldn't." She straightened her spine. "You had every intention of selling this place, or closing it down when you came here. Don't even try to deny it. I'm not stupid. You were looking for an excuse, and you found one." She stood, her outrage making her seem taller, and, damn his libido, sexy as hell. "Go ahead. Shut the plant down. Put all these hardworking people out of a job. This town is hanging on by a thread anyway. The Adams family built Butte Plains. It's only fitting an Adams be the one to cut the last thread."

Pausing in the doorway, she drew her shoulders back and, lifting her chin, delivered her parting shot with the precision of a sniper. "You'll find a pair of scissors in the center drawer."

He jerked the drawer open, found the scissors—a big, sturdy pair, at least a century old. Holding them aloft, he worked the handles, enjoying the metallic rasp of the blades sliding against each other. "Snip snip," he said loud enough to carry to the next office. She answered with a disgusted groan, followed by a door slammed shut.

Dropping the weapon of mass destruction to the desktop, he buried his face in his hands. He'd never seen a more alluring sight than Becky Jean with her panties in a wad. He'd be wise to keep an eye on sharp objects when she was around, but the probability of her doing him bodily harm didn't keep him from imagining all her passion channeled into more pleasant activities.

This is so not the time, ole buddy. Once again forcing his thoughts away from Becky Jean and the way her shapely ass looked as she'd beat a hasty retreat, he made a mental note of all the things he had to accomplish before he could close the doors on Adams Manufacturing and get back to his life.

Grabbing his suit coat off the back of the chair, he called out as he passed the office manager's closed door, "I'm going to the bank. I'll be back." With a little luck, his father had another account not listed on the company computer system. Maybe he'd set up a trust for his wife, or invested funds in something. Maybe he had a safety-deposit box full of cash. Stranger things had happened.

CHAPTER THREE

"You're positive?" he asked the stout man who'd been his father's banker for decades. "There are no hidden assets?"

"No, son. I'm sorry. I argued with your father many times over the last few years regarding his use of personal funds to keep the plant running, but he was adamant the place needed to stay open."

Why? Ford couldn't begin to follow his father's train of thought—beggaring himself so the few remaining employees could keep their jobs.

"I refused to lend him money, hoping he'd come to his senses and close the place down, but he was determined to forge ahead. Said he was working on the problem and it was only a matter of time before he had what he needed to turn the place around."

The lab reports on the Chinese products. Too little, way too late. "He had a plan, but I'm afraid it wasn't much of one."

"I'm truly sorry, Ford. Your father was the best of men." He shook his head. "He was my friend as well as my client. This town is going to miss him."

Ford fought the tears threatening to fall and cleared his throat. "That's very kind of you to say." He stood on weak legs and extended his hand across the solid oak desk. "Thank you for taking the time to see me today, Mr. Wheeler."

They shook hands. "If there's anything I can do for you…?"

Ford paused at the office door. "Lend me a few million?" he asked with a smirk.

"Anything but that," the banker said.

So much for hidden assets. The extent of Ken Adams's savings appeared to be the jar on the corner of his dresser where he deposited whatever change he found in his trouser pocket at the end of the day. Rough estimate—ten dollars, minus the fee the bank would charge to count and roll it.

Retracing his steps back to the factory, three blocks south then four blocks east, Ford paid little attention to the businesses he passed along the way. His stomach rumbled, reminding him he'd missed lunch and he'd had no appetite for breakfast. Thinking to grab a sandwich at Marge's Diner, he stood on the sidewalk, stunned, looking in the window at the vacant interior. The establishment had been a fixture in Butte Plains dating back to his grandfather's days. Seeing it gutted, the familiar lunch counter and Formica tabletops gone, shook him almost as much as finding out his parents were on the brink of bankruptcy.

Turning from the disturbing carcass of a once-thriving business, he glanced up and down the block. Many of the stores he'd taken for granted as a kid were empty shells. With most of the shops closed, the place began to look like a ghost town.

What the hell happened?

Forgetting everything except his empty stomach for a minute, he made a left instead of a right, hoping to find another of his favorite eating establishments still in business. He almost jumped for joy when he spied the neon *Open* sign in the window of the Hanson's Bakery. His mouth watered for one of Mrs. Hanson's ham-and-cheese croissants. As he pushed the door open, his stomach growled again. Perhaps he'd have two of the delicacies.

Mrs. Hanson smiled at him from behind the ancient counter. Nothing had changed here, which he immediately recognized as part of the town's problem. People were drawn to new and shiny, not outdated and dull, no matter how good the food.

"Ford," the older woman said, her sympathy grinding against his last nerve. "I'm so sorry about your father. He was a good man."

"The best," he answered automatically. Hoping to change the subject, he pointed to the top shelf in the display case. "Can I get two of the ham and cheese, and a soda? To go." He could eat and walk at the same time.

She grabbed a square of waxed paper and reached into the display case. "I couldn't make it to the funeral—didn't have anyone to mind the shop. I sent some pastries up to the house, though."

"Thank you," he said.

"Mr. Hanson passed three years back, and our Bobby and his family moved to Dallas. I'm thinking of closing up and moving, too. I miss my grandkids something awful."

Bobby graduated a year behind Ford, as he recalled. "Why'd Bobby move?"

"Not much need for electricians around here." Mrs. Hanson talked while she bagged his food. "He got a degree in electrical engineering and went to work for Matthews Electric." Ford recognized the name. They operated out of a big warehouse about a mile from Adams Manufacturing.

Pausing with her hand in the cooler, she asked, "Regular or diet?"

"Diet."

"He looked for work around here after Matthews closed, but—"

"Matthews Electric closed?" They'd been the second-largest employer in Butte Plains in their day.

"Been nearly two years, I guess." She pushed buttons on

the ancient cash register. "A lot of people left town, looking for work. 'Course your father took on as many as he could, but he didn't have much use for electricians and such."

That explained the heavy payroll numbers he'd noticed a few years back in the records. The numbers had evened out as, he supposed, most of those people found other jobs or moved away. Like Bobby Hanson. "Are those turkey and cheese?" he asked, pointing at the display again.

"Yes, and I've got one pepperoni left."

"Give me one of the turkey ones, too. And another diet soda." Talk of his failing company reminded him Becky Jean had arrived shortly after he had, which meant she probably hadn't had lunch either. If she didn't want a croissant pocket, he'd eat it himself.

Butte Plains had always seemed so stable. Staid and dull, but stable. He'd never thought of it declining the way it obviously had. There wasn't a damn thing he could do to turn it around, but the idea of the idyllic, yeah, it had been a great place to grow up, town disappearing made him sad. It must be doubly hard for someone who lived here to watch it happen.

He knocked on Becky Jean's office door, trying the handle before she had a chance to answer. Pissed off as she'd been, at least she hadn't locked him out. Stepping inside, he took it as a good sign she didn't attack him with a letter opener. Instead, she turned hopeful eyes his way. He set a firm look on his face and shook his head. "No go. No hidden accounts. No safety-deposit box full of cash." He held up the bakery bag. "However, Mrs. Hanson had some stuffed croissants left. Ham or turkey?"

She pushed some papers to the side. "Turkey."

He tossed one of the parchment wrapped delicacies her way, unwrapping the other for himself. "Diet okay?" He set a bottle on her desk blotter. "Did you know Matthews Electric went out of business?"

"Uh-huh," she said around a mouthful of pastry. "Along with Roma's Pizza, the skating rink, the bowling alley, and the Majestic."

"Shit. The Majestic?" He'd taken his first date there to see *The Matrix*. The outing had been his first and only date with Katelyn Roberts. The girl had zero appreciation for good films.

"Among others. Those are the ones I can think of off the top of my head." They ate in silence for a while. "Remember Herschel's Appliances on Main?" she asked.

Ford nodded. "Closed?" he asked, though he already knew the answer. He'd seen the empty retail space earlier.

"Walter Construction?" She took a bite of her stuffed croissant.

"Closed?"

Becky Jean took a sip from her soft drink then swallowed. "Yep. You remember Scooter's Plumbing, don't you? They had those trucks with the cartoon characters on them?"

"They're closed, too?" *Fuck.* "What hasn't closed? That might be a shorter list."

"Hanson's Bakery is still open." She glanced at the grease-stained bag on her desk with the familiar logo printed on it.

"I hate to tell you, but she's thinking about closing. Wants to move closer to Bobby. Apparently, he has a wife and kids now. Did you know about that?"

"He married Chrissy Matthews."

His eyebrows rose. "Didn't her dad own Matthews Electric?"

"Yep. Didn't make any difference. There wasn't enough business around these parts to keep the doors open, so he was left without a job, just like everyone else." She wadded up her empty wrapper and tossed it in the bag. "I'm sorry to hear about Hanson's. I'm going to miss that place."

"Me, too." What was he saying? Unless she closed up in the next few weeks, he wouldn't be around to miss the woman's tasty concoctions.

Becky Jean finished off her soda, collected all their trash, and tucked it into the wastebasket behind her desk. She rocked back in her chair with a sigh. "So, what's next?"

"Damn if I know." He leaned forward, resting his elbows on his knees. "I can't think right now. I arranged to move enough funds out of my personal savings to cover this week's payroll. Tomorrow, I'll call my wealth manager and see about converting some investments into cash. I'll need to see all the accounts receivable and a summary of what we owe—taxes, utilities—anything else you can think of."

"You look beat. Why don't you go home, try to get some rest?"

He stood and made his way to the door. He couldn't ever remember being this tired. "See you tomorrow?"

"I come in at eight."

Noticing he'd left the lights on in his father's office, he reached for the switch. "Damn. Forgot to turn off the computer." Visions of an electric bill he couldn't pay danced before his eyes. He'd just powered down the system when he glanced up to see Becky Jean standing in the doorway.

"I didn't see your car out front when I came in. How did you get here?"

"Walked." Christ. Why did she have to be so damn beautiful? He caught himself looking at her left hand. No ring. No husband. No fiancé. *Not my business.* Which reminded him he needed to call Ronnie and tell her he wouldn't be back in time for the museum opening she had her heart set on attending. Maybe Scott would accompany her. He made a mental note to ask his best friend if he could fill in for him.

"Come on. I'll give you a ride."

He vaguely remembered she lived on the opposite side of town from his parents. "It's out of your way. I can walk."

She headed toward the front of the building. He followed, admiring the way her ass swayed from side to side with each step she took. "Nope. Remember the Wilsons? They moved to Florida. I rent their house."

He knew the house she spoke of. It sat at the base of the hill his parent's house occupied. "They moved to Florida? When did this happen?"

"About the time you graduated from college, I guess. Bobby Hanson rented it for a while."

"Then he lost his job and moved to Dallas."

"Yep. I moved in when the Hansons moved out."

For a town that never seemed to change, it seemed everything had changed. With opened eyes, he noticed what he hadn't seen before. Businesses boarded up, weed-covered parking lots, broken out windows, and *For Sale* signs in front of empty houses were like pickets on an ancient fence—close together and falling down.

"I'm staying in the gatehouse," he said as the car wound up the long drive.

"Why?"

He glanced at the woman driving. "Seemed like a good idea at the time. Besides, I brought work along." Or he hoped he had. The 3D printer he'd had shipped should have been delivered today. He'd planned to use the time away from the office to work on some ideas of his own. With everything going on, he doubted he'd have time. Getting his mother out of the financial pit she didn't know she was in would take all his time in the foreseeable future.

"What kind of work do you do?"

"I design things for people."

"What kind of things?" She stopped in front of the gatehouse, put the car in park, and turned to face him.

"People come up with ideas, things they want to build but don't have a clue how to go about it, or don't have the resources to create a prototype. I work with them, take their concepts, and turn them into reality." He liked what he did— he'd actually made a shit-ton of money at his job. But it kept him so busy he rarely had time to do what he wanted—to develop ideas of his own. A few days with nothing to do but help his mother put her life in order and sift through offers to purchase the company had sounded perfect.

"You can make a living doing that?"

He smiled. "I've made more than a living at it. Lots of times, inventors don't have capital to pay upfront for my services, so I take a percentage of sales once the product goes to market. If the item sells well, it can be extremely lucrative."

"Wow. I went into the wrong line of work."

"Office managers don't usually bring down the big bucks." She certainly hadn't. He'd noted her salary in the payroll records.

She shrugged. "My degree is in marketing, but my dad got sick and had to leave his job. So when I graduated, I stayed home to help out. Your father promoted me from line supervisor to office manager. The boost in salary allowed me to help my parents. I've been there ever since."

"How's your dad?"

Her shoulders sank, and he knew before she said the words. She'd lost her father, too.

"He passed away last year. His life insurance paid off the house. Mom still has her part-time job at the nursing home. It's enough for her to live on."

"I'm so sorry."

"It gets easier," she said, though her body language said she was lying through her teeth.

He tried to recall her parents, but if he'd ever met them.... Not a single memory surfaced. "I doubt that," he said, turning to look out the passenger-side window. A large cardboard box sat on the front step—the perfect excuse to end what had become an awkward conversation. "Looks like my package arrived." He reached for the door handle. "Thanks for the ride."

"Not a problem." She cranked the engine before he had both feet on the ground.

"See you in the morning," he said as he closed the door. She made a neat three-point turn and disappeared around the curve in the drive. He made a mental note to stay away from the subject of her father's passing. There had to be a story there, he was sure of it, but he had enough problems of his own to solve without borrowing more.

After lugging the printer into the house, he placed a call to his office in New York. Scott's disappointment rang through the line when Ford informed him he needed to stay in Texas for a month or more. Fortunately, his friend understood obligation to family and agreed to take his sister to the museum opening in Ford's place.

Ronnie had been less pleased to hear his news than her brother. Who would escort her here or there? Fuck if he knew. He had *real* problems to deal with. Ford didn't tell either of the siblings the extent of his financial troubles. Scott would have understood, but Ronnie wouldn't. He often wondered how the two could be related. Scott had no intention of relying on his trust funds for the rest of his life. He had talent and drive, where his sister simply… didn't. Scott possessed enough tact not to ask questions, and Ronnie appeared too busy worrying about her social calendar to think to ask him why. Soon, the whole world would know why he'd stayed in Texas, but he hoped by then he'd have better news to impart.

The thought of the big, old building his great-grandfather had built no longer bearing the Adams's name hit him hard. The feeling didn't make any sense. He'd known all along he wouldn't keep the company. Selling would be ideal, but that option no longer existed. He might be able to unload some of the machinery once they closed. He made a mental note to check into the possibility in the next few days. Maybe there was some kind of auction house he could contact to handle the sale for him. If not, the scrap value of the metal inside the plant had to be considerable. He could keep a few of the employees on to dismantle the equipment.

He added *call salvage yards* to his mental to-do list. Surely, someone would haul the scrap off for a cut of the value. *Then* he could put the buildings up for sale, but given the number of empty storefronts in Butte Plains, his kids, if he ever had any, would still be paying taxes on the property long after he'd departed the planet. He made another mental note to see what the taxes actually were, and if he could get them reduced once the place fell into disuse.

Before turning in for the night, he called his mom. He knew he'd been a shitty son, leaving her to deal with the swarm of mourners on her own, but of the two of them, his mother had the social skills to handle the situation. The daughter of one of the wealthiest families in the county, she'd been born to play hostess to throngs of people. She fussed over him, worrying as usual about her only child instead of focusing on herself then informed him she and her sister Florence would be fine alone in the house overnight. He wished her good night then slipped into bed.

Instantly, an image of Becky Jean Parker flashed into his brain. He'd made the mistake of mentally undressing her earlier, and the image refused to go away. Every time he closed his eyes, he saw her shapely body on display. Physically, the two couldn't be more different. Ronnie liked to tell people her tall, lean form and small breasts attributed to her runner's body, even though her idea of running meant hurrying to grab the last barstool in a crowded restaurant.

Ford considered himself something of an artist. He created drawings and models in his mind and on paper then turned them into sculptures. Useful sculptures, but the point remained, his brain saw what his eyes couldn't. He didn't need to see Becky Jean undressed, his brain calculated the information his eyes collected and translated it into an image he knew would be pretty damn close to the actual thing.

Given the proportions of the image, his body couldn't help but respond. He'd have to be dead not to react to large breasts, a trim waist, and a heart-shaped ass. God, how he'd love to get his hands on her ass. His palms itched to feel her soft, pliant skin beneath his hands. He'd take his time, committing the details to memory then he'd part her— *Shit!*

He could not be thinking about what he wanted to do to Becky Jean's ass. He had other things he should be thinking about, like figuring out how to tell his mother she couldn't afford the luxuries she took for granted.

Helen Ford had come from money and married into money. The Ford family fortune had taken an unfortunate turn back in the 80s when her father and brothers had sunk, literally, everything they had into an offshore drilling rig. A good portion of their money, in the form of twisted metal, constituted a man-made reef at the bottom of the Gulf of Mexico. It had become quite the attraction in recent years for the scuba diving set. What money hadn't sunk with the drilling platform had gone to clean up the oil spill, and to settle the resulting lawsuits. Only Ford's trust fund, set up by his grandparents years ago, had escaped untouched. If it weren't for the tax issues involved, he'd sign it over to his mother. The interest on the principle had paid his college tuition and given him a start in life, but he'd never relied on the money for his day-to-day living. Shortly after graduation, he and his roommate established their own business. In less than a year, he made enough to live on. The following year, he requested the interest on the principle be put back into the account instead of being paid out to him.

He'd managed to accumulate considerable wealth on his own. He didn't need his trust fund. He made another mental note to ask his wealth manager about the possibility of transferring the trust to his mother. But that would have to wait until the factory had been dealt with. No way would he let hungry creditors have access to his trust fund if he could help it. Nope. It would be just fine, right where it was.

CHAPTER FOUR

Becky had always wanted a house with a porch, and now she had three outdoor living areas to choose from. The house she rented might not be the prettiest residence in Butte Plains, but it suited her perfectly. The wraparound porch began in the front, traversed the south side of the house, ending on the east side outside of the kitchen. She enjoyed nothing more than watching her backyard come alive each morning while she sipped her first cup of coffee. The birds and squirrels going about their business usually held her attention, but not today.

She'd had a difficult time getting to sleep the night before, and when she'd finally succeeded, her dreams had bordered on nightmares. Her life was changing, and once again, she had no choice in the matter. She'd had no alternative but to help her parents and younger brother get through her father's illness. The decision had been the right one at the time. Staying in Butte Plains after her father passed away had been easier than trying to start over. Too much time had passed since her college graduation to try for a job in her chosen profession— or so she told herself. Colin had graduated from high school and announced he wouldn't be going to college. He'd packed his guitar and a duffel bag of clothes and hopped the first bus to Nashville, where he'd achieved his dream of being a musician, and more. He'd written a couple of hit songs for other artists and sang lead for a band that was building momentum daily.

She didn't begrudge him his success, but on days like today, she wished fate and circumstances hadn't taken her choices away from her. If not for her father's illness, she might have found a job in a big city, become something more than office manager for a failing company. Becky faced the harsh reality.

In a few months, she would be out of a job, and nothing remained for her in Butte Plains. Her mom would be fine, but if she wanted, she could move, too. She wouldn't have any trouble finding a job in a nursing home in a big city.

What will I do? Office managers are a dime a dozen in big cities.

I could look for a job in marketing.

Yeah, and start at the bottom with all the kids with their shiny new degrees and probably a couple of summer internships under their belt.

As much as she wanted to blame Ford for her predicament, she couldn't. He'd done what she had wanted to do—he'd made a life for himself outside of Butte Plains, and she understood why he would want to get back to it. Maybe if the factory had been in good financial shape, she could have talked him into letting her run the place, but, under the present circumstances, he had no choice but to shut down. If she were in his shoes, she'd do the same thing. But understanding the situation didn't stop her from wishing for a way to keep the place open. She would survive, even if it meant moving to a big city, but concern plagued her about the other employees.

Manufacturing jobs were drying up across the country as businesses outsourced production to China and Mexico. Most of their workers had lived in Butte Plains all their lives. They had extended families to consider, too. She couldn't help but think about the head of their shipping department, Todd Carver. His elderly mother lived with him, and she knew for a fact his neighbors helped keep an eye on her while he worked. Moving would be a major upheaval for Todd and his mother.

The more she thought about it, the more determined she became to convince Ford to keep the plant open as long as possible. There had to be some way.

Practicing her impassioned plea in her head, she wished the birds pecking at the birdfeeder a good day and went inside to get dressed.

~~~

Her new boss pulled into the parking lot as Becky got out of her car. She chalked his punctuality up to his desire to put Butte Plains in his rearview mirror as soon as possible. Waiting beside her car for him to join her, she thought about the man who had starred in her dreams last night. Sometimes he'd been the sexy seducer, making her body sing, then he'd be the monster raining terror on her quiet little world.

If she were to draw the man of her dreams, he'd be Ford Adams. She'd always been drawn to tall, dark, testosterone-overloaded men. If he had an ounce of compassion in his bones for his new employees, she might consider acting on her attraction, but he didn't, so she wouldn't. Then there was the part about him being her boss. She'd checked for a wedding ring, and his father would have mentioned his son becoming engaged. So, unless he had a girlfriend back home….

The expiration date on their professional relationship couldn't have been stamped in more indelible ink, so there wouldn't be any *real* harm in sleeping with him. It wasn't like he could promote her from unemployed to employed. Only her scruples stood in the way of a fling with the sexiest man in Butte Plains.

She didn't do flings. She'd had a brief relationship with a guy she'd met in the library her sophomore year of college. The chemistry between them had been off the charts, but David had been immature, skipping classes in order to party. He'd flunked out of school the spring semester and moved home to
~~~

Colorado. Last she'd heard, he'd become a ski instructor at one of the smaller resorts in the winter, living off his parents the rest of the year.

Her scruples were there for a reason—to protect her from doing stupid things.

Damn scruples.

"Good morning." She shaded her eyes from the morning sun with a hand to her brow.

"I don't know what's good about it."

She opened her mouth to say it was a good day because she'd woken up on this side of the grass—an old joke her grandfather on her mother's side had been fond of—but thought better of it before the words passed her lips.

Unlocking the door, she ushered Ford in ahead of her. She punched in the alarm code then flicked on the overhead lights. "Someone's grumpy this morning." He had a right to be. He'd buried his father yesterday, and today he had to begin the steps to shut down the business his ancestors had built. Nothing to be happy about in either of those things.

"Didn't sleep well." He stalked off in the direction of his new office.

His grumbled remark gave her the opening she'd been hoping for. She caught up with him as he sat down at his desk. "Did you come up with any ideas to keep the plant open? You know, a lot of good people are going to lose their livelihoods. Families are going to suffer. People are going to have to move to find other employment. Kids are going to have to change schools. And—"

"Forty years of darkness! Earthquakes! Volcanos! The dead rising from the grave! Human sacrifice, dogs and cats living together… mass hysteria!" He powered up the computer while he ranted. "I get it, Becky Jean. I really do, but I'm fresh out of ideas."

She shook with the need to pummel him. How dare he make fun of the situation? She clenched her fists at her sides and unclenched her jaw. "I can't believe you're quoting *Ghostbusters*! You might think this is all a joke, Mr. I've-got-plenty-of-money, but I can assure you, the people who depend on their jobs here will *not* think closing the plant is funny."

Slamming her office door didn't bring the satisfaction she'd anticipated. Becky crumpled into her desk chair and lowered her forehead to her arms folded on the desktop. She didn't know what came over her, but when he'd begun quoting from one of her favorite movies, applying a scene she'd always thought hilarious to the present situation, she'd lost it. Every bit of civility she possessed flew right out the window.

So, so stupid.

She revisited the last few minutes, wondering how she could have prevented the scene from happening. Things had started out on an even keel. A pleasant good morning from her. A not-so-welcoming reply from him, making his mood apparent.

She'd goaded him. Poked the bear, and the beast had lashed out.

Great. Just great.

She owed Ford an apology. Just, not yet. Her outburst couldn't have improved his mood, and it hadn't improved hers, so waiting awhile—a year or so—would be a good idea. Give them both time to cool off.

~~~

Ford stared at the empty doorway. His ears still rang from her tirade, and his brain remained fixated on the image of her ass, walking out the door.

"Down, boy," he cautioned his cock. "Can't have her."

He'd lain awake most of the night, contemplating his next moves, trying to come up with another solution to his problem besides shutting down operation of the factory. After finally drifting off to sleep in the wee hours of the morning, he'd dreamed of making love to Becky Jean and woken with a boner he'd had no choice but to take care of in the only way available to him.
~~~

He hated to start the day jacking off, but the hand job and a cold shower made it possible for him to function. He'd been celibate too long, and he'd had a thing for Becky Jean in high school, even if had only lasted a day or two.

Well, a week. It had taken him a week to shift his lust to Cindy Price. She'd offered to give him a hand job behind the castle on the seventh green at Put Around Mini-golf. He'd taken her up on the offer and escorted her to prom in payment. They'd called it even after getting it on in the backseat of the limo on the way home. Last he'd heard, Cindy had gone to junior college in the next county and married some cowboy she'd met when the rodeo came to town.

Ford shook his head to clear it. He owed Becky Jean an apology. He'd let yesterday's revelations overwhelm him, and in so doing, he'd forgotten how this would affect her. No matter what happened, he had a job to go back to, but she wouldn't. She'd thought highly of his father, her tears at the funeral were proof enough, and even though her job was just as temporary as everyone else's, she seemed more worried about the other employees than about herself. She had a college degree, and she seemed reliable enough. She'd find employment somewhere. Most likely she'd have to leave Butte Plains. She'd blame him, but hell, none of this was his fault.

He'd do the best he could for her, and for all of them. But he wouldn't make promises he couldn't keep.

He picked up the phone, intending to call the office next door to remind Becky of the reports he needed. When his door opened and she stepped inside carrying an armload of folders, he set the receiver back in its cradle. "Ms. Parker."

"Mr. Adams." She placed the folders on his desk and stepped back. "I'm sorry. I was out of line earlier." Backing toward the door, she continued, "Those are the reports you wanted. They're on the server, but I thought you might need them printed out for… the bank?"

He offered her a weak smile, accepting her apology and her peace offering. "Thank you." He thumbed through the stack, opening the one marked Accounts Payable. "This will be very helpful.”

“I don't know what this month's utilities will be, but I included copies of our bills for the last three months to give you an idea.”

“Becky. I owe you an apology, too. Quoting a silly comedy, under the present circumstances, wasn't appropriate. My only excuse is I'm under a lot of stress. The words just came out. I'm sorry.”

“It was my fault. I pushed your buttons. I understand you're focused on the immediate need to shut down, but I wanted you to see the broad picture, too. I was insensitive. You're dealing with the loss of your father—now, all this.”

“We're both under a lot of stress. This can't be easy on you, either. I appreciate your concern for the workers, and believe me, if I could do anything to prevent this from happening, I would.” He shook his head. “I lay awake last night trying to come up with options.”

“Nothing?”

“Nope. Not a thing.”

Becky Jean bit her bottom lip, and her eyes glistened with unshed tears. *Fuck.* Time to get her out of there before he did something stupid like try to console her. Recalling the dream he'd had once he'd fallen asleep last night, touching her wouldn't be a good idea, not even to offer comfort. He cleared his throat. “Thank you for these.” He tapped the stack of folders. “I'll look them over before I have to leave.”

She nodded again. “The reading of the will at two o'clock?”

“Yes. How did you know?” He'd gotten a phone call this morning from his father's attorney notifying him of the reading.

“Mr. Trumble called a few minutes ago. He said I should be there.”

“Why?” He couldn't imagine why she'd be invited. Wills were private, to be shared only with the interested parties.

“He didn't say, and I was too shocked to ask. Maybe it has something to do with the running of the company. It's the only thing I could think of."

Ford shrugged. "Could be. And since you're the office manager…." He didn't believe her excuse for a second. A cold sliver of unease slid along his spine.

She shifted her feet, her gaze landing everywhere but on him. "Umm." She bit her lip again, and a sudden and unwanted urge to taste her lips hit him. Ford mentally pushed the thought away.

"Something else, Becky Jean?"

"Yes, sir. Everyone else is here—all the office staff."

He sat back. He knew exactly what she wanted. Nothing good could come of telling the employees how temporary their jobs were. "There's no need in stirring the hornet's nest just yet, do you think? Let's keep this to ourselves until we have a plan—a day or two at most. No use in everyone panicking before we have something concrete to tell them."

"You're right, of course. A couple of days won't make any difference in the grand scheme of things."

"My thoughts, exactly." Only a day or two could make all the difference—he should know. Look at all that had happened to him in the last few days. He'd gone from a successful business man in his own right to a puppy kicker and dream destroyer in the blink of an eye.

Becky Jean backed out of his office. He braced for another slammed door. Hearing nothing, he relaxed. If he planned to get this thing done, he needed her on his side, or at least not fighting him.

CHAPTER FIVE

Ford saw his mother off with a kiss to her tear-stained cheek. Aunt Florence would see her safely home. They all needed time to process what had just occurred in Mr. Trumble's office. He couldn't imagine what his father had been thinking when he'd drafted his will, but he damn sure needed to find out. Turning to his car and the woman waiting next to it, he clenched his jaw to prevent making rash statements he'd hear repeated back in court proceedings later on. Who was Becky Jean Parker to his father? Ken Adams wouldn't have done what he'd done for just anybody. Several possibilities ran through his head—none of them acceptable or fathomable. His father wasn't that kind of man. He just wasn't.

Calling on his best manners, he held the passenger door while Becky Jean slid into the passenger seat. She remained quiet on the ride across town, giving him time to run through his options. The will stipulated the factory had to remain operating for one year before it could be sold. They'd need money to make payroll, purchase supplies, pay utilities and taxes. He had some savings, but not enough to last an entire year unless they scaled staff and production back to the barest minimum. The will hadn't said anything about what capacity the factory had to run—just that it had to run.

Becky Jean would be pissed about laying off employees, but unless she paid the extra wages herself then the cuts would be made. The way things stood, her salary would be coming out of his pocket which, in his mind, meant she had zero say in who he fired in order to keep her ass out of bankruptcy. Which brought him back to how he was going to come up with the necessary funds.

If push came to shove, he could sell his house in New York. Since he'd restored the historic home, he'd been approached more than once with offers. He'd bought it because it reminded him of the house he'd grown up in, only in need of repair. Half a million dollars later, the property had turned into a showplace. Letting go of it would hurt, but he could always buy another house. Thoughts of selling brought him around to the house in Butte Plains he owned 50 percent of—the one his mother lived in. He couldn't sell it out from under her, but he could mortgage it. He'd have to tell his mother the precarious nature of her financial situation in order to get her signature on a mortgage, but it might not come to that. For the moment, he'd prefer to keep her out of the loop. Mired in grief, he didn't need to distress her more with things she couldn't do anything about. There had to be another way. He'd start with trying to find a way to turn a profit.

"When we get back, get me a sample of every item we currently have in production, and every item we have produced in the past... say ten years. No. Make it twenty-five years."

"What for?"

"We have to keep the factory operating for the next twelve months. In order to do that, we need to turn a profit, even if it's only a dollar. Maybe if I see what we've got to offer, I can come up with a way to make us profitable." He nearly bit his tongue off on the word *us*, but until a court decided differently, he had to include Becky Jean in the equation.

"Tell what's her name in receivables to get on the phone.

We need to collect every outstanding invoice owed us. Start with the most recent and work back from there."

"Her name is Angela."

He'd met the rest of the office workers before he and Becky Jean left for the reading of the will but couldn't remember their names. "Doesn't matter what her name is. What matters is cash flow. We need income. Anything over six months old, tell her to discount it by 10 percent if they pay in the next ten days."

"Okay."

"Thanks to Dad draining every account he had, our payables are in decent shape. We can't afford to piss off our suppliers. No supplies equals no production. No production equals no income."

"I get it."

He ignored her snide remark. He didn't have time to soothe hurt feelings, not if he meant to prevent this Titanic from sinking and taking them all down with it. "Just get me those product samples, ASAP."

"Yes, Your Highness."

Ford braked hard at the stop sign, taking his anger at her snippy tone out on the brake pedal. Eyes focused straight ahead, he unclenched his jaw enough to speak. "Unless you have come up with a way to get us out of this mess then I'd appreciate you not getting your panties in a wad over the direction I'm taking. At least I'm doing something." He might be high-handed, but he didn't see he had any other choice but to take charge. He let up on the brake then applied slow, steady pressure to the accelerator pedal when he'd much rather smash it to the floor and drive until Butte Plains, Adams Manufacturing, and Texas disappeared in his rearview mirror, becoming nothing but an unpleasant memory.

Becky shifted in her seat. Her heated gaze seared like the West Texas sun on an August day. "You make it sound like I'm not doing anything," she huffed. "I've done everything you asked so far, haven't I? And, in case it hasn't occurred to you, I can't afford for this company to go under. It was one thing to lose my job when it closed. As part owner, if it closes now, I'll lose everything. I'll do whatever it takes to keep the place running for the next year. I don't see as I have any choice."

No, she didn't, and neither did he. They were partners in this mess until a court decided otherwise, and the legal process could easily take more than the year they needed to stay in business. Like it or not, he needed her help for the next twelve months.

"Glad to hear you're onboard." He actually liked the way she'd found her spine. He'd been worried about her—the quiet, devastated woman she'd become following the bombshell bequeath wasn't the Becky Jean he'd come to know. "Do we have a marketing person?"

The shift in the conversation caught her off guard. She faced forward again, though the vacant look from before had vanished. "No. I've sort of been doing the job—what little there is to do."

"Congratulations, Ms. Parker. You've just been promoted to marketing director. I'd give you a raise if I could."

"But…. I…. What?" She huffed out a breath, and her pale cheeks colored.

How would her other cheeks look with a bit of color? *Don't go there, Ford. She's your business partner. Remember the lawsuit she's likely going to file. A sexual harassment complaint won't help you any.*

"We have to sell our product. Since we can't lower our prices to compete with foreign manufacturing we're going to have to come up with a marketing plan to convince retailers and consumers our product is worth paying more for."

"We haven't gotten any results back from the lab we hired to analyze the foreign-made products."

"Cancel the lab report. See if we can get a partial refund. We'll—*you'll*—have to think of something else to convince people to buy our product."

He pulled into the parking lot and followed Becky Jean inside. At the reception desk, she went straight ahead instead of turning down the hall to their offices.

"Where are you going?" he called out.

"To the factory floor. You want product samples, I'm going to get you pr—" As she opened the heavy steel door, noise from the production line nearly drowned out her last words.

He spun his key ring around his index finger then pocketed his keys and headed toward his office. The contrast of her soft curves surrounded by the industrial machinery shouldn't be so intriguing, but it seemed everything about Becky Jean Parker intrigued him.

~~~

Becky grabbed a sound-muffling headset off the rack by the door and put it on. She'd welcome the din of machinery in motion, but drowning out the racket going on in her head wasn't worth losing her hearing over. She'd have to find another way to silence the turmoil of the last few days.

On the heels of the shock of her boss's sudden death came grief and the stress of being at the helm of Adams Manufacturing until his son arrived to take over. Seeing Ford again after all these years had been another shock. He'd been good-looking—in a geeky sort of way—in high school, but man, oh man, had he changed! The last decade had been good to him in a way it hadn't been with most of their classmates. Riding in the car with him had been a mistake. There had been no escaping his scent in the confines of the sporty rental. Not even the smell of melting rubber and heated plastic on the factory floor could drive the memory of his woodsy, all-male scent from her nostrils. Lord, she'd wanted to strip naked and rub herself all over him. Still wanted to. Damn it all to hell.

Then, to top it off—Kenneth Adams had left her half of his half of Adams Manufacturing! Heaven only knew what Mrs. Adams thought. And Ford. Did they think something had gone on between her and the late Mr. Adams? By the way the lawyer had looked at her when he read the part of the will pertaining to her, he'd certainly thought so. Neither Ford nor his mother had said anything, but they must have been thinking it. Hell, she'd be thinking it if it were anyone besides her in this
~~~

position.

She had to find a way to assure them she hadn't been carrying on an affair with Kenneth Adams. He'd been kind to her, for sure, but he'd never… and she'd never….

No. She wouldn't go down that road. It was just too weird to think about. Ken Adams had been like a father to her, giving her a job when she needed one, never once asking for anything but a solid day's work from her. She'd loved him, but not for the reasons his lawyer seemed to think.

Touched beyond belief Mr. Adams had thought to include her in his will, she couldn't credit the position she currently found herself in. Part owner of Adams Manufacturing. An equal partner with Ford Adams. Well, a minority partner given he controlled his mother's 50 percent, too. Once again, her life had taken a path she hadn't chosen for herself.

One year. Twelve long months before they could sell or close the business. Which meant they had to keep it running, because God knew, her share of the business's debts far outweighed her personal assets. She had to do everything possible to keep the factory going, and, at the moment, that meant hitching her wagon to Ford's, no matter which direction he decided to head.

She grabbed an empty box from shipping then made her way through the warehouse, dropping one of each style product into the box. Waving to the dozen-or-so people hard at work, she made her way to the front offices. After replacing the hearing protection back on the rack, she stood for a minute, welcoming the sound of normality before opening the door and stepping back into the chaos her life had become.

At the sound of Ford's voice, heavy with frustration, Becky halted short of his office. "Can we talk about this later?" A short pause. "Because I'm busy."

Torn between wanting to drop the box of products he'd requested over his head and not wanting to pry into his personal life, she faltered in the hallway then headed toward her own office.

"You think I want to stay here for a year? Fuck, Ronnie.

You know me better than that."

Becky stopped cold. *Ronny? Who the heck...?*

"Listen, I really am busy. The sooner I get this figured out, the sooner I can come home." He'd lowered his voice so, giving up all pretense of not eavesdropping, Becky leaned closer to hear his next words. "Yeah, yeah, I know. I'll call tonight, and we'll talk about it then."

Ford's gay? What the hell? It would certainly explain why he'd chosen to live so far away from where he'd grown up. She imagined it would be easier to start over someplace new than to explain to the people he'd grown up with. There were some narrow-minded people in Butte Plains, but they were the minority. Still, she could see where it would be easier to live an alternative lifestyle as little fish in a big pond instead of a big tuna in a goldfish bowl.

Her arms ached, reminding her of the reason she stood outside his office to begin with. In light of her new knowledge, the thoughts she'd been having in regards to Ford's hotness seemed ridiculous. He was taken—and gay. She laughed at the old cliché? All the good ones were either taken or gay. Just her luck. Not that she had ever had a chance with the man—or wanted a chance with him. Boyfriend in New York or not, Ford would be leaving as soon as possible. In the meantime, they had to find a way to keep Adams Manufacturing running for the next year.

Fear gripped her gut, and she leaned against the wall, willing the pain in her belly to go away. Ford and his mother would sustain huge losses over the next twelve months if the factory didn't show a profit, but she would lose everything. And like it or not, and unless she found a way to decline her inheritance, she had little choice but to help Ford turn the company around.

After taking a few deep, calming breaths, Becky straightened her shoulders and stepped forward.

CHAPTER SIX

"Here."

Ford sat back while Becky Jean placed their current and past products in a line across the front of his desk. She was pissed, still or again, he didn't know which. Did it matter? Not one little bit, he decided. It didn't even matter if she was pissed at him or her situation or both. She could stand in line with everyone else in his life wanting to tear a strip of hide off him. Neither Scott nor Veronica had taken his news well. They both wanted him back in New York. He could handle all his obligations to his east coast business from Texas, but, for the next year, Ronnie would be on her own, socially. Her brother would do his duty as escort for the most important events, but Scott didn't enjoy the social whirl the way his sister did.

He didn't want to think about what Ronnie would do without him there for the next year. A beautiful woman, she had a need for others to prove it to her on a regular basis. They'd never agreed to be exclusive—not that he cared if she slept around. It would take a stronger man than he to keep Veronica in line. He wasn't up to the job, and he knew it.

Fuck. He had needs, too. The next twelve months would be hell—in more ways than one. Forcing his attention back to the woman in his office, he studied her. Her movements were jerky— telegraphing her anger—yet the emotion looked good on her. Her cheeks bloomed with color, and her eyes sparked with fire.

She had passion best channeled into something besides anger. He knew what he'd like to channel it into, but since he had no intention of bedding her, he'd settle for getting her ass in gear to keep him, and his mother, from bankruptcy. He didn't want to admit it, but he couldn't do it alone. He needed Becky Jean's help. But before they went any further, they needed to talk about something else. He'd seen the look on the lawyer's face, knew deep down what the man had been thinking. He should have called him out on it, but without knowing absolutely for sure....

He leaned forward, got down on eye level with the assortment of baby bottles, nipples, and flashlights. "What happened to the flashlight business? Everyone needs a flashlight."

"Can't you guess?"

"China?"

Placing a hand to her chest, she sighed dramatically. "I feel so much better knowing my business partner is such a genius." Tossing the empty box into the corner of his office, her glare dared him to make something of her smart remark.

He reminded himself she had plenty of reason to be angry and let it go.

"Anything else?" she snapped.

"Nope. Just the things we talked about in the car."

"You mean the things you ordered me to do? *Those* things?"

Studying the array of basic items lined up on his desk, he nodded. "Yes, those things. The sooner we implement our plan, the better."

"You mean the less of your own money you'll have to put into the company."

"I could demand you put in 25 percent, but since you don't have it…. Or am I mistaken?" If she were a cartoon, there'd be a thundercloud hanging over her head. The blush of anger on her cheeks grew to an inferno. His question may have been a low blow, but he could go lower. He *would* go lower. She stepped back from his desk. "One more thing before you go."

"What?" She practically vibrated with anger.

He dove low, went in for the kill. "Were you sleeping with my father?"

The blood drained from her face, and, for a second, he thought he might have to leap over the desk to catch her before she hit her head against the chair standing between her and the floor. Coiled to move, he relaxed when she pinched her lips tight, straightened her shoulders, and torpedoed him. "Fuck you, Ford Adams."

Turning on her heel, Becky Jean strutted out of his office, her perfect heart-shaped ass swaying like a sailboat on rough seas.

Bang!

The pictures on his wall shook. If she kept slamming her office door, he'd have to call someone in to reinforce the door and the walls of his office.

Well, there's your answer. She hadn't been his father's mistress—not that he ever really believed his dad would cheat on his mom—but others would think it. Did think it. He'd make a point to set Mr. Trumble straight the next time he saw him, and, as soon as he could, he'd find a new lawyer. One who knew what the word discretion meant.

With the image of Becky Jean's ass burned on his retinas, Ford turned his attention back to the products on his desk. They were all serviceable and essential to different segments of the population at various times. Demand for the items certainly hadn't dropped. As far as he knew, babies were still being born, human, bovine, and otherwise. Breastfeeding craze aside, water and juice didn't come from breasts, so mothers were still buying and using bottles and rubber nipples.

He picked up one of the bottles, turned it over. Nothing on the bottom. Everything made outside the U.S. had to be stamped with the country of origin. He remembered a while back a big movement to buy products stamped *Made in America*. It wasn't much, but they could capitalize on the trend. Maybe even get a mention on the morning talk show behind the story. He made a note on the legal pad at his elbow to see about having the label added to the bottles and their packaging. His new marketing director could put some feelers out to the news networks, see if they could run a story. He smiled, realizing he'd just added public relations to Becky Jean's new duties. She'd fume about the added work, but she'd do it.

Imagining her tuning up to rip him a new one had him hard as a post. Again. He glanced up from his notes, and his gaze landed on the giant nipples designed for hand-feeding livestock. His gaze traveled down the line to the teat liners for milking machines.

A chill chased up his spine. He grabbed both items, studying them with new interest. "Huh." He slipped the teat liner over the giant-sized nipple then set his creation on the desk. Maybe he'd been approaching this from the wrong angle. Instead of trying to push the products they already had, maybe they should consider a *new* product. Something nearly everyone he knew had at least one of.

People were still having babies. Which meant they were having sex. And everyone knows, *sex sells*.

He reached for his legal pad, ripped off the top sheet of notes, wadded it into a ball, and tossed it toward the empty box in the corner. Opening the center drawer, he pushed aside the scissors earmarked for cutting the last thread holding Butte Plains together, and found the set of drafting pencils his father always had at hand.

When he finally looked up from his drawing, he realized how quiet the office had become. The low hum and rumble from the machinery had ceased. He strained his ears for the sound of voices in the other offices. Nothing. He glanced at his watch, noting the late hour. Everyone would be gone, and he should be, too. He'd promised to visit with his mother this evening, and since he'd been scarce ever since the funeral, he needed to fulfill his promise to her.

Grabbing his suit coat, he shoved his inspiration into one of the pockets then picked up the pad containing his sketches. He'd have plenty of time later tonight to transfer his drawings to his laptop. And, if he had any luck, he'd get to try out his new 3-D printer this evening. They'd need a prototype in order to make an injection mold for the new product.

He shut off the lights in his office and headed out. A thin band of light showed beneath Becky Jean's door. He tapped lightly then turned the knob.

"You still here?"

Becky glanced up at the man filling her doorway. It had taken most of the afternoon for her to calm down, but seeing him standing there smiling at her as if he hadn't accused her of having loose morals a few hours ago, brought the anger back to the surface. "Apparently," she said through gritted teeth.

"Look, I'm sorry about earlier. You had to know I would ask. And just for the record, I never, not even for a second, thought you and my dad…. Well, he wouldn't have, and, in the little time I've known you, I'd come to the conclusion you wouldn't have either."

"You insulted me, and your father, Ford. I don't know which made me angrier."

"Both, I hope. Once word gets out about his will, others are going to think it."

The blood drained to her toes again, leaving her light-headed. She dropped her forehead to the desk, silently begging the room to stop spinning.

"Becky Jean. Are you okay?" Ford's big hand rubbed a circle on her back. Jiminy, his touch shouldn't feel as good as it did.

"I'm fine." She managed to sit up. He removed his hand and sat on the corner of her desk as if he owned it. "Your mother doesn't think…?"

His eyebrows knit then relaxed. "No. I'm sure she doesn't. She and my dad were always thick as thieves. Admittedly, I haven't been around much in the last ten years, but I'm sure nothing changed. They always had a marriage I envied. A love like theirs doesn't come around often."

"I couldn't bear it if your mother thought—" She shook her head. "The others don't matter."

"They matter to me." The words were spoken so softly, she couldn't be sure she heard right. Before she could ask him to repeat them, he bounded off her desk and headed to the door. He stopped and turned to her. A big smile on his face, he looked like a kid who'd just found a stash of cookies.

"What?" she couldn't help but ask.

"I've got an idea. It could be something big."

His excitement reeled her in. She wiggled in her seat, anticipation chasing away all other thoughts. "Well? What is it?"

"Can't tell you yet. I will. Soon. Gotta Go."

Becky stared at the empty doorway. How dare he dangle hope in her face then leave her hanging? Grabbing the nearest item on her desk, she held her stapler aloft, poised to throw it through the door. When his head then his body filled the space, she sighed and put the missile down.

"Hey? Do you cook?"

"Y-yes. A little. I'm no Julia Child, but I can boil water." She narrowed her eyes. "Why?"

"'Cause I need to eat. If you'll cook tonight, maybe I'll let you see what I'm working on later. Deal?"

She tried to picture Ford in her little kitchen, sitting at the table she'd found at the Methodist Church thrift store, and just couldn't do it. "You want to come to my place for dinner?" she squeaked.

"No. You come to mine. Bring food. I don't think there's much in the fridge. Anything will do. I'm not picky. See you in say, an hour?"

"Um." If there could be anything worse than him being in her kitchen—it had to be her in his.

"Good. Great!"

Once again, Becky Jean stared at the vacant doorway in disbelief. What had she just agreed to? "Don't forget to turn the lights off when you leave," Ford shouted from the end of the hall.

Becky raised her middle finger. "Fuck you, Ford Adams."

She would need to wash her mouth out with soap if this kept up. She'd used the F word twice today *and* made an obscene gesture. Neither was her style, yet she couldn't really regret either transgression. They'd fit the situation, which went to prove how different her circumstances were today from all the previous days of her life.

~~~

Elbows on the granite countertop at the Adams's gatehouse, Becky stuffed a forkful of spaghetti in her mouth and chewed. Since her arrival, she'd exchanged less than a dozen words with Ford. He seemed to be in geek heaven, typing on his laptop computer, muttering under his breath, and occasionally letting go with some choice curse words. She'd fixed a simple meal of spaghetti and meatballs with a salad and garlic bread then proceeded to eat by herself.

She swallowed then spun her fork in the long noodles again. "Are you going to eat? You know, I could have stayed at home and done the same thing."

Ford turned his intense gaze on her. "A few more minutes, Becky Jean. I've almost got it."

"Got what? Are you going to tell me what this is all about?"

"In a minute. Trust me, Becky Jean, this is good. Stupendous. Best idea I've had in ages." He returned his gaze to the computer. Having no clue as to the quality of his previous ideas, she had nothing to judge this one by—provided he ever got around to sharing it with her.

Becky took another bite then washed it down with a sip of some very good wine she'd found in the wine rack above
~~~

the sink. When she'd asked Ford about opening it, he'd answered with a grunt, never even looking up. Surely no one would leave a special bottle of wine in a rarely used gatehouse. But, what did she know of rich people's habits?

Shrugging, she refilled her glass. It turned out to be damn good wine and shouldn't go to waste.

"Voila!"

At Ford's triumphant shout, Becky nearly jumped out of her skin. "Geez, Ford. Give a girl some warning. I almost spilled my wine."

"Pour me a glass, will ya? I'll be right there."

She reached for the glass she'd set out for him over an hour ago. "Are you going to tell me what's going on?"

He had moved to the kitchen table where he'd set up a 3-D printer. "Soon, Becks. Real soon." He slid a memory card into a slot on the printer. With his index finger poised in midair over a red button, he smiled at her. "Here goes nothing!"

As soon as he punched the button, the printer whirred to life. Fascinated, Becky watched as the machine spit droplets of black goo onto a small platform. She'd heard about 3-D printing technology, but she'd never seen it in action. "What are you making?"

He admired his creation in the making for a few seconds then joined her at the eat-in bar. Nodding at her almost-empty plate, he asked, "Any left for me?"

She obviously wasn't going to get any answers until Ford decided to give them, so she filled a plate and slid it in front of him. He dove in, eating like a starved man. While he ate, she kept her eye on the object slowly taking shape across the room. Like playing *Wheel of Fortune*, she needed more clues before guessing. After a few minutes, Ford slowed to a normal pace.

"We've been looking at this all wrong, Becks."

"How do you mean?"

He sipped from his wine glass then set it down. "We've been trying to figure out how to make a profit by selling products we already have."

"We can hardly make a profit selling things we don't

have," she pointed out.

"True enough. But I'm talking about new products. Something we can retool for at a minimum cost, and be ready to ship in less than two weeks' time."

"What makes you think we can sell this mystery product and make a profit?"

"Ah hah!" He stabbed his pointer finger toward the ceiling. "Not we." He turned his index finger toward her. "*You*. You're our new marketing director. You're going to sell it. Leave the profit making to me."

The fine hair on the back of her neck stood up. If he'd been sure she would go along with this, he would have come right out and told her his idea instead of being so secretive. She glanced at the printer. The object remained unidentifiable. "What, exactly, do you think I'm going to sell?"

CHAPTER SEVEN

"The first-ever, lock-in-place butt plug!"

Her insides turned to ice while, inexplicably, heat infused her skin. She didn't need a mirror to know her face had turned tomato red. Her gaze automatically went to the printer dripping plastic droplets onto an ever-growing pile. Could the item really be…? She had no idea. She'd read about their use in a few steamy romance novels, but she had no firsthand knowledge of the devices.

"You can't be serious." Needing to steady her nerves before she went ballistic on her business partner, she reached for her wine, brought the cool glass to her lips, and drained it.

"I'm dead serious, Becks. It won't take much to retool one of the machines to make them. We'll keep packaging to a minimum—a plastic bag with a cardboard header. We'll earmark the first five hundred as free samples, which you'll send out, worldwide, to wholesale adult toy distributors. I tell you, this will work. People will buy this product."

"Are you insane? First, this is Butte Plains. If we start making… those *things*"—she nodded toward the printer—"all our employees will quit. Second, I don't know anything about the adult toy industry. I wouldn't know where to start if—and that's a very big *if*—I were to agree to your ridiculous plan and we could convince our people to produce the… things."

"First," he mimicked her not-quite-business-like shrieking voice, "our employees will make what we tell them to make if they want to keep their jobs. If they quit, then what is the unemployment rate in Butte Plains? Ten? Fifteen percent? We'll replace them. Second, you're a smart woman. I'm sure you've heard of the Internet. It shouldn't take you more than a few hours to acquaint yourself with the major adult toy wholesalers."

She barely heard what he said after he called her smart, but evidently, her subconscious had been listening. She caught up quickly. "Even if we could accomplish a miracle turnover, do people buy those *things*?"

"The adult toy industry is huge, Becks."

"I wouldn't know." She forced her thoughts away from the cute pink vibrator she kept in her nightstand for those times when she needed release in order to remain sane. Ford might be right about sex selling, but she'd never in a million years let him in on how lonely she'd been since returning to Butte Plains. Some things a girl had to keep to herself.

"Trust me, sex sells."

"Even if it does, what makes you think your… *item* will sell?"

"Mine locks in place. It's a huge improvement over anything on the market today." He got up and crossed to where the printer put the finishing touches on his creation. "There will be some assembly required before packaging. I've already contacted Scott about the locking mechanisms. He designed one a couple of years ago for a project that never went anywhere. He's willing to let us use it for a few pennies royalty on each unit sold. He's sending me a case of them by special messenger to try out. They'll be here tomorrow."

"Who's Scott?"

"My best friend and business partner. He's an incredible

designer in his own right. Luckiest day of my life was the day we were assigned as roommates at MIT."

"Oh." Did Ronny know about Ford's relationship with Scott? Maybe they had a three-way going on or something. *Not my business.*

Becky gathered the dirty dishes and put them in the sink. Leaning back against the counter, she gazed at her insane business partner's back. He had one thing right—they needed to do something different, but did they have to dive ass first into the adult toy manufacturing business? Turning, she rinsed the dishes and put everything into the dishwasher. When she spun back around, Ford stood in front of the table, his new creation in his hand.

"It doesn't look any different on the outside. The locking mechanism will be what separates it from the run-of-the-mill variety." He flipped the item over, examining it from every angle.

"I just don't see it working, Ford."

"Have you ever used a butt plug?"

Heat rose to her cheeks. "No. I've never even seen one."

"You through there?" He nodded toward the kitchen prep area.

"Yeah. Why?"

He set the plug on the counter. "Come on. It's time for us to take a field trip."

"Where are we going?" she asked, sinking into the soft leather seats of his luxury rental car.

"Don't ask."

"I don't like this, Ford." She reached for the door handle.

"Okay, okay." Before she could bolt from the car, he cranked the engine and drove down the driveway. "There's an adult store out on the Interstate. I saw it when I drove in from the airport."

She knew the place—by sight only. "You can't be serious."

"I wish you'd quit saying that. I'm dead serious, Becks. I appreciate what you and my dad were trying to do, but the fact is we need to change course, and fast. We're headed straight for the iceberg. If we hit it, we're all going down. You, me, my mother, all our employees."

He painted a grim picture, but, in truth, she'd seen the same one hanging on the wall. But there had to be another way.

"If you've got a better idea, this is the time to speak up."

Damn him for being logical. "No. Sadly, I don't have any idea at all, much less a better one."

"Then give me the benefit of the doubt here, Becks." He pulled into the blessedly empty parking lot and cut the engine. "There are thousands of these stores across the country. They're springing up in malls and respectable neighborhoods, too. Many are women-owned businesses. You should like that."

"Impressive." *Not.*

"Come on. Let's go inside."

"No."

"Come on, Becks. Consider this your first class in Marketing to the Adult Toy Industry 101."

She rolled her eyes at him. "What if someone sees us? What will they think?"

"I hope you do see someone you know. It will help convince you normal people are buying this stuff. As for what they'll think… well, I suspect they'd wish they could help you with whatever it is you're buying tonight."

"I'm not buying anything."

"Just wait until you see what they have to offer. You might change your mind."

"I hate you."

"No, you don't."

"Yes, I do." She reached for the door handle. "I'm going to go inside, but only so I can gather enough information to point out the errors in your plan."

Ford placed his hand on the small of her back and guided her through the aisles toward the back of the store where a flashing neon sign said *Anal Play.*

"It's okay to look around, Becks."

"I don't want to look around."

"Sure you do. This is the kind of place you can't *not* look around. It's like an old-time carnival—filled with oddities you're drawn to even though you know you shouldn't be."

Damn. Why did he have to be right all the time? She'd already spotted several things she wouldn't mind taking a closer look at, but Hell would freeze over before she'd admit being curious. "Let's just do what we came to do and get out of here."

"Sure you don't want to look around?"

"Positive."

They stopped in front of a wall display covered with butt plugs of every size and color imaginable.

"They're identical to the one you just printed." *Except for that one. And that one.*

"Yes, they are." At the sound of Ford's voice, she tore her gaze away from the one with electrical wires attached. He took one down for closer examination.

He held it up, end first. "See? Where this one is solid on the end, mine has a hole in it. The locking mechanism will go right there."

She scanned the wall. "None of these have locks?"

"Nope. A design flaw I'm going to correct."

"Seems to me, if a lock was such a good idea, someone else would have come up with one. And, have you considered there could be a reason none of these have locks?"

"Like what?" He took a large pink one down.

"Like, it's a bad idea, for reasons I can't even begin to think of."

He turned his gaze to her and smiled. Something inside her flared to life. She took a step back. *He has a boyfriend. He has a boyfriend.* Maybe if she reminded herself enough times she'd believe it.

"You've never tried to keep one of these things in, have you?"

No. "Have you?" God, she did not want to go there, not with Ford.

His smile turned to a smirk. "I plead the fifth. But I can see I need to convince you of the superiority of my product." He reached for a shopping basket from the stack of them in the corner.

"You'll need something small at first." He dropped a package containing a slim, pink plug in the basket.

"Ford!"

Two more, in successively larger sizes landed in the basket. "Look, Becky Jean, if you don't believe the product is the best on the market, you won't be able to convince the buyers to give it a try. This is Market Research 101—know the competition."

Damn. Why did he have to be right? Again. "I didn't say I would market this thing."

"You will. Once you try it, you'll see." He tossed in two more styles then headed off down another aisle. Becky followed, cringing when he stopped at the section containing personal lubricants. She pretended not to read the labels while he searched the shelves. Eventually, he picked two different ones and added them to his shopping basket. "One more thing," he said, moving off again.

He stopped in front of a rack near the checkout counter. "Cleaner," he said, tossing a large bottle with a pump-style lid into the basket. "Anything you want to look at while we're here?"

"Absolutely not," she lied. She eyed an interesting display of vibrators nearby. While Ford paid, making small talk with the cashier, she pretended not to look at the various battery-operated boyfriends. She'd ordered hers years ago from an online retailer, but she wouldn't mind having one of these new high-tech ones.

"All set," he said, coming up behind her and putting his hand on the same spot it had been before. Heat radiated off his palm to the small of her back. The gesture felt intimate, and so good she almost forgot to be mad at him.

He ushered her to the car and opened the passenger door for her. She climbed into the seat, relieved to have gotten in and out of the store without being seen. As Ford went around the back of the car to get to the driver's side, another car pulled into a parking space a few over on his side. Becky sank as low as possible and thanked the universe for poorly lit parking lots. To be on the safe side, she turned her face away and hid behind her hand.

Hurry. Hurry. Hurry. The sooner they got out of there, the better.

"Hey, Mr. Boggs. Nice to see you again." Ford's voice pierced the car door.

Crap! Mr. Boggs had been the principal at the high school forever. Everyone in town knew him, and he knew everyone. Thank Heaven she'd made it to the car before he drove up!

"Good to see you, too. How's your mother doing?"

"She's holding up. Thanks for asking."

"Sad thing, your father going so young. We're all praying for you, and your family, son."

"Thank you, sir."

"Gotta hurry," Mr. Boggs said. "It's our anniversary this weekend. Gonna pick up something special." His voice got closer as he approached Ford's car parked directly in front of the entrance to the Adult Emporium.

"How many years have you been married?"

"Twenty years since Sharon said, 'I do.' Gotta keep things fresh, you know? Well, of course you know. You're here, aren't you?"

"My regards to Mrs. Boggs, sir."

The driver's side door opened. Ford slid into the seat and tossed the shopping bag into her lap. "Coast is clear. You can sit up."

"Did he see me? Do you think he knows?"

"No, he didn't see you, unless he has X-ray vision, and what, exactly, would he know?"

Once they'd cleared the parking area, she sat up and fastened her seat belt. "Not funny," she said, tossing the bag to the backseat.

"Look, he didn't see you, and he has no idea what I had

in my bag." He chuckled. "I bet Mrs. Boggs is going to have a mighty fine anniversary. Don't you?"

"I have no idea."

"You do realize they have sex, don't you? They have three kids. Or is it four?"

"Five."

"You don't say? How old is the youngest?"

"Two."

Ford's laughter filled the car.

No longer in danger of being discovered, she could see humor in the situation. "Okay, so they've had sex."

"At least five times in twenty years," Ford added, helpfully.

"Okay. You win. People have sex, and some of them buy… toys. But I'm still not convinced this thing of yours will sell."

"You'll sell it, Becks." He parked at the curb in front of her house and reached in the backseat. He plunked the heavy shopping bag into her lap. "Try the smallest one first. See how long you can keep it in doing normal stuff."

Nothing she could say would sway him, so she changed the subject. "My car is at your place."

"I'll pick you up in the morning. No use both of us taking our cars to work since we live so close."

He had a point. Besides, as long as he paid for the gas, why should she argue? She opened the door and prepared to step out. "What time?"

"Seven thirty okay? We can pick up breakfast at Hanson's and you can fill me in on how your market research is going."

"I'm not going to try these." She clutched the bag in her hand as she got out. "See you in the morning."

Before the door closed, Ford said, "Lube, Becks. Lots of lube!"

~~~

If he'd ever thought about what Alice must have looked like when she hit the bottom of the rabbit hole, he now knew.
~~~

The expression on Becky Jean's face when she stepped inside the Adult Emporium had been comical. She appeared ready to turn and try to claw her way back out. Only his hand on the small of her back kept her from doing so.

Oh, and her expression following his conversation with Mr. Boggs? *Priceless.* Becky Jean riled so easily, and damn, if pushing her buttons hadn't been the most fun he'd had in years.

At the gatehouse, he set his prototype on the dresser in the bedroom while he undressed and showered. As he passed by later on his way to bed, he picked it up. He'd made it a good size. Not small, but far from being the biggest on the market. Silicone would make it light and pliable, adding to the comfort while allowing the stretch needed for the locking arms to work properly. It would be easy enough to make it in a variety of sizes, even one small enough for a beginner.

An image popped into his head of Becky Jean wearing his invention. He didn't have anyone else in Butte Plains he could trust to test the prototype, so she'd be the first to try it out. He imagined turning the key, locking the plug in place then examining the device to make sure it seated properly. God, he wanted to help Becky Jean with the plug, and more, but he couldn't. Maintaining a professional relationship had to be a priority. He'd get Adams Manufacturing back on its feet, then they could sell it. He'd go back to his life, and Becky Jean would move on. If they made something of this new product, perhaps her 25 percent would amount to enough to set her up in a new life away from Butte Plains.

Thinking about Becky Jean dating—getting naked—with some guy made Ford grind his teeth. For Christ's sake, she'd never used a butt plug! What did she know of the world and the perverts inhabiting it? She needed someone to lead the way, show her the delights to be experienced without destroying her moral compass. It couldn't be him, though, so he'd best put those thoughts out of his head.

He admired her loyalty to the employees and to the town as a whole. The success of his recovery plan depended on her sense of responsibility and her desire to help the people she cared about. She would do her best to market his invention, but in order to do so, she had to understand how revolutionary it was.

When he'd stopped by to see his mother earlier, she'd given him his dad's phone, and he'd transferred the contacts he'd deemed essential over to his own. He'd made sure to transfer Becky Jean's first. Picking up his phone from the nightstand, he searched out her number and made the call. It rang several times before she answered, sounding breathless.

"I hope nothing slipped out when you ran to catch the phone," he said, easing into his favorite tease-Becky-Jean mode.

"What do you want?" she asked, her tone indicating she hadn't forgiven him for taking her to the sex-toy shop.

"I wanted to see if you needed any help with your market research."

"I'm doing just fine without your help."

He smiled at the admission she let slip.

"I told you I wouldn't try the… products, and I'm not."

He swallowed the laugh bubbling up. He'd let her have her little deception. "You're not, huh? Do you think it's too difficult to insert them on your own? Because, if you do, I stand ready to assist. All you have to do is ask."

CHAPTER EIGHT

Becky slid gingerly into the passenger seat of Ford's fancy car, acknowledging his chipper greeting with a grunt. Their shopping adventure the previous evening, plus her embarrassing experience with a few of the items they'd purchased made him the last person she wanted to see.

"I need my car back." Somehow, knowing she had the means to put distance between them whenever the mood struck mattered a lot this morning.

"You can pick it up this evening."

She didn't expect him to be so agreeable. After he'd called last night while she'd been trying out the smallest of the items he'd purchased, and having little success keeping it in place, she figured he'd be hammering her with questions this morning. The fact was, he hadn't made her uncomfortable.

"What's wrong?"

"Nothing's wrong."

"Something is. I thought you'd want to know the results of my market research, but you haven't even asked."

"Nothing is wrong. You hung up on me last night, so I

thought it best to drop the subject."

"You don't want to know if I tried one of them or not?"

"I know you tried at least one. You know as well as I do, in order to judge our product against the competition, you are going to have to try all of them. You *could* ask someone else for their opinion, but I don't see you running around town asking people to fill out a survey in regards to their experiences with butt plugs."

That he knew her so well didn't make her any happier. "You know darn well I'm not going to survey anybody. For your information, I tried some of the competitors' products, and you were right, they don't function as well as one would expect them to."

"How are you going to sell butt plugs when you refuse to say it?"

"You still have to prove to me you have a superior product. Until then, there's nothing to sell."

"Point taken." He parked then walked around to open her door. "I printed two more last night." He held up a plastic grocery bag. "As soon as I get the shipment of locking mechanisms, I can show you how this is going to work."

Unlocking the front door, she entered with Ford on her heels. She disengaged the alarm and followed him down the hallway to their offices. He paused before entering his. "The locking mechanisms will be here today. In the meantime, I'm going to get Owens in the machine shop working on a mold. The sooner we turn out a complete unit, the better."

"I suppose so." She still wasn't sold on the idea of a new product, especially given the nature of the item Ford had come up with. "I'm going to see how Angela is doing with the receivables then go over our outstanding bills with Carla to see if we can prioritize the bills. Maybe we can delay paying some of them. If need-be, I can call some of the creditors, explain about Mr. Adam's death. It could buy us a little time. We've paid well in the past, so we have that going for us."

"You could check out wholesalers, too. I'd like to see a list of places we can approach to carry our new product. The sooner we get it in their online catalogs, the better."

She might just get through this crazy partnership if they kept things on a professional level. "I'll see what I can do."

Sometime later, Ford popped his head in her office door. "Come on! There's someone I want you to meet."

He hurried off before she could question him. Shaking her head, she glanced at the clock on the corner of her desk. She'd been working steady for over three hours.

"Break time," she mumbled, pushing away from the desk. Raised masculine voices floated down the hall, drawing her out of her office.

Ford and another man she didn't recognize stood in reception, beaming at one another like loons. She hung back, watching the obvious reunion. Who was this man? She knew everyone in town, and if he'd attended Butte Plains High School, she would recognize him. He appeared to be Ford's exact opposite. He was blond where Ford had dark hair. His skin had the flawless quality of a Norse god where Ford's skin leaned more toward golden sunset. Her partner dressed to the nines—suit and tie every day—where the newcomer wore aged denim and a NY Giants T-shirt. Equal in height to Ford, the man was undeniably handsome, but she had no trouble tearing her gaze away from him.

In the week since Ford's return to his hometown, he'd had little to smile about. Seeing his face transformed in genuine pleasure damn near took her breath away. His eyes sparkled with life, and the laugh lines bracketing his mouth made her knees weak.

"Ah, man, it's good to see you."

"You, too," the god replied. "Ronnie said to tell you to get your ass back, ASAP."

Ford's smile dimmed. "I'll be back when I can, you both know that."

"Yeah, we know."

"I miss my life there." As if he willed the sad thoughts away, his smile returned. He clapped the newcomer on the shoulder. "I'm damn glad to see you, though."

Stepping forward, Becky cleared her throat.

"Becky Jean!" Arm around his friend's shoulders, her partner turned to her. "Look who I found!"

The Giants fan punched Ford's midsection. "Who found who? I'm the one who flew halfway across the country to see what the hell is taking you so long."

Becky squirmed under his appreciative gaze.

"And now I know."

He separated himself from Ford and approached, hand outstretched. "I'm Scott Ramsey, and you must be Becky Jean."

Ford's business partner. Not what she expected, though she couldn't say exactly *what* she'd thought the man would be like. He was too pretty and in too good a mood to hold his scrutiny of her body against him. She took his hand. "Nice to meet you. You're the partner I've heard so much about?"

"He's been talking about me?"

"Truthfully?" She raised one eyebrow.

"By all means. Tell me what this reprobate has been saying." He glanced over his shoulder.

Leaning against the reception desk, arms crossed, Ford smirked.

"Well, he's hardly mentioned you."

The newcomer laughed. "I knew it! Out of sight, out of mind." He leaned in and placed a kiss on Becky's cheek. "It's a pleasure to meet you, Becky. We've heard a lot about you."

"We?"

"Me and my sister, Veronica—Ronnie. Ford told us all about you, but I see he left out the part about you being gorgeous." He glanced over his shoulder at her new partner, who shrugged off the criticism.

Ronnie. Not Ronny. A woman.

"Enough." Ford straightened. "Did you bring the locks?"

So much for giving the newcomer the third degree. She had no business prying into Ford's personal life anyway. She'd learned all she needed to know—Ford was taken. Did it make any difference his significant other turned out to be a woman instead of a man as she'd incorrectly assumed? It shouldn't, but it did. Whatever fledgling thoughts she'd had about her sexy new partner were inappropriate in more ways than one.

"I did." Scott motioned to a box on the corner of the reception desk. "Decided to bring them myself instead of trusting them to an overnight carrier."

Ford scooped the box into his arms. "You didn't have to go to the trouble, but I'm glad you did. Come on. Let me show you what I'm working on." He led Scott toward the factory floor. "I'm dying to see if this works."

The roar of machinery filled the air as the two men disappeared through the door like two little boys with a new toy, leaving Becky behind shaking her head.

"Are there more like him in New York?"

Becky startled at the other woman's voice. She'd all but forgotten about the girl seated behind the high desk. "You mean, Mr. Ramsey?"

Carolyn had been manning the front desk at Adams Manufacturing during the day and taking night classes at the county community college since she graduated from high school three years ago. Lord knew what she would do if she lost her job. Becky Jean's gaze lingered on the door the two men had disappeared through and sent up a silent prayer Ford's idea would work.

"Holy cow, Ms. Parker. He's gorgeous."

Becky wasn't at all surprised by the receptionist's remark. Other than Ford coming home, this Ramsey fellow had to be the first fresh bait to swim in the Butte Plains pool in forever. The sharks would be circling him in no time. Innocent little Carolyn didn't stand a chance.

Becky resisted the urge to roll her eyes. Yeah, the man was good-looking, but his Scandinavian genes had nothing on Ford's Texan ancestry. "Wipe the drool off your chin and finish up the time-sheet logs, will you?" Becky turned back toward her office.

"Sure thing."

She did roll her eyes at the exaggerated sigh the girl let out.

Geez.

When Ford appeared in her doorway, she glanced at the clock, surprised to see she'd worked through lunch and most of the afternoon. "Did you need something?"

He stepped inside and shut the door. "I have something for you." He set a butt plug on her desk then stepped back. "Ta da! The first-ever, lock-in-place butt plug!"

Up until the moment he set the lump of molded plastic on her desk, she'd been in a state of denial about the new direction he wanted to take the company, but with the evidence front and center, those days were over. She pasted a smile on her face. "Wow! You work fast."

"Not me. Owens is a genius. The man can make anything, I tell you. I gave him the prototype first thing this morning, and voila! Here's the finished product." Pete Owens kept the machinery running, sometimes by miraculous methods. He either deserved a raise, or to be drawn and quartered. She didn't know which.

Becky stared at the obelisk. She hadn't given its size much thought when she'd seen his prototype, but she'd never worn one, either. With the experience behind her, she viewed Ford's new invention with trepidation. "I didn't remember it being so large."

"It isn't as big as some of the ones we bought last night."

True enough, but she hadn't tried any of the larger ones. She'd been uncomfortable enough with the ones she had tried, and since they all appeared to be constructed in much the same way, she saw no point in trying the others. "I'm not putting that thing inside my body."

"Yes, you are." He picked it up, turning it so she could see the protruding end of the device. "Let me show you how it works."

"No need. I'm not going to test it for you."

He'd produced a small key from his pocket and inserted it in the lock embedded in the base. "Once it's fully seated, just turn the key." He continued to talk, completely ignoring her protests. "This lock Scott designed is genius, and this is the perfect application for it. See the way the arms on the lock expand outward creating a shelf-like effect?" He made a ring with his thumb and index finger, encircling the smallest part. Becky shuddered, imagining the thing inside her.

"Once the lock is engaged, the only way to remove the device is with the key." He inserted the key again and turned it. The locking arms retreated and the plug returned to its original size. "Come on. Let's go home. I can't wait for you to try it."

"I'm not trying it."

"You are trying it." He picked her purse up from where she'd left it on the corner of the desk, stuffed the sinister-looking device inside, and headed toward the door. He acted like an overgrown child sometimes—there was no reasoning with him.

Becky closed the file she'd been working on and rose. "I want my car back."

"Sure thing. We'll go to my place, you can put the plug in there. I'm can't wait to hear what you think of it."

She knew where she wanted to put the plug, and it wasn't where Ford thought. Besides, she didn't really need to try it, did she? The difference appeared obvious, and in theory should work. She hoped it would be enough to convince people to buy it.

"What did you do with your friend?"

"Scott? Said he was tired. He's chillin' at the bed & breakfast over on Maple Street."

"Roseanne Meadow's place?"

He shot her a look she couldn't decipher then went back to watching the road. "The Yellow Rose? I thought Roseanne and her parents moved to Florida when we were in high school."

"They did, but her grandmother left her the old Victorian, so she came back, fixed it up, and turned it into a B&B. She's been having a tough time of it, like everyone else in town. If things don't pick up, she'll probably have to close the doors soon."

"I remember. You two were friends back in the day, weren't you?"

"Yeah. We stayed in touch, sort of, after she moved. It's been nice having her back in town."

"I'm sorry her business isn't doing well. I dropped Scott off earlier. It looks like a nice place."

"It is. She used to serve high tea there on Sunday afternoons, but she stopped about two years ago, I guess. Times have been hard on the town."

Ford grunted a response. What did he care if the town folded in on itself like an armadillo? In a year's time, maybe less if they got the plant turning a profit, he'd go back to New York where his biggest problem would be deciding which restaurant to eat at before he and his girlfriend took in a Broadway show.

They pulled into his driveway, and Becky made a beeline for her car. "See you in the morning," she called out, fishing the keys out of her purse.

"Wait! Aren't you going to come in, give the new product a trial?"

"No. I'm not. I told you I wouldn't, and nothing has changed my mind." She climbed in her car, tossed her purse into the passenger seat, and cranked the engine. As she pulled away, she caught sight of Ford standing next to his car, watching her drive away. She absolutely would not do what he'd asked her to. No. Way. In. Hell.

CHAPTER NINE

Determined not to dwell on thoughts of Becky Jean trying out his new invention, and all the process entailed, Ford walked up the long drive to his mother's house. She'd called earlier and invited him to dinner. He'd explained about his friend being in town, and requested a rain check, but when he'd called to see what time to pick Scott up, he'd said the owner of the B&B had offered to fix him something so he could call it an early night. If Roseanne was anything like Ford remembered her from a decade ago, he figured his buddy had more going on than a quiet dinner and early bedtime. The guy definitely had a way with women.

Even though Ford had begged off earlier, his mother wouldn't turn him away. Helen Adams always prepared for company.

He had a few things he needed to ask her in regards to the estate, and he wanted to hear her reaction to finding out her husband had left a significant portion of the company to a young, female employee. He knew beyond a shadow of a doubt nothing had been going on between his father and Becky Jean, but no matter what assurances he'd given his new partner, he wanted to make sure his mother agreed. He had yet to come up with a tactful way to broach the subject when his mother solved the problem for him.

"How are things going with Becky? She seemed shocked at the reading."

Ford searched his mother's face for any sign she harbored ill will toward Becky Jean and found none. "That's an understatement. I take it you knew all along?"

"Your father discussed it with me years ago when her father became ill. I agreed it would be a nice thing to do."

All kinds of possible reasons for the bequeathment to be the right thing to do flitted through his mind—none of them good. God, could Becky Jean be a half-sister? *Shit!* Given the thoughts he'd been having about her, the idea made him sick to his stomach. "What do you mean?"

"It means just what it sounds like."

He sure as hell hoped it didn't, but he kept the thought to himself.

"I had been dating Jess Parker when I met your father. In fact, if he hadn't brought me to a dance at the Community Center, I wouldn't have met your father. Kenneth and Susannah were there together. I took one look at Kenneth and knew I would marry him one day. Jess took one look at Susannah, and practically forgot my name. I left with your father and Jess left with Susannah."

He'd never heard the story of how his parents met, or if he had, he didn't remember. His father and Becky's mother? Becky Jean and he were the same age. It didn't take a genius to figure it out. He couldn't understand how his mother could be so nonchalant about the fact her husband had recognized an illegitimate daughter in his will. Appetite gone, he dropped his fork and sat back.

Helen Adams pointed her butter knife at him. "Ford Adams! I know what you're thinking, and you'd better get it out of your head this minute." His mother's scolding voice shook him out of the funk he'd sunk into. "I led your father on a merry chase, but Jess and Susannah married right away. They didn't have Becky Jean until years later. Your father said he could never repay Jess for taking me to the dance. Providing for his widow and daughter was the least he could do, and I agreed."

Ford dabbed at the sweat dotting his brow then placed his napkin back in his lap. Several years ago, leaving Becky Jean a percentage of the company would have been a nice thing to do, but today, not so much. Ken Adams had set out to do something good and inadvertently destroyed any chance Becky Jean had of financial success—unless Ford pulled a miracle out of a hat—or shoved one up the ass of every adult in the United States. More than ever, the pressure to turn Adams Manufacturing around weighed on him.

"She's a lovely young lady, don't you think?"

He recognized the tone of her voice. He'd have to nip his mother's matchmaking in the bud if he wanted to have any peace. He cut his mother a look meant to squelch her meddling. "I'm sort of seeing someone, Mom. Besides, Becky Jean is a business partner."

"Who is the person you're seeing, and why haven't I met her?"

He spent the next ten minutes dodging his mother's bullets. He'd never once considered bringing Veronica home to meet his mother. They didn't have a meet-the-parents kind of relationship, but he'd gladly throw his fuck buddy under the bus to shut his mother up.

He sighed with relief when, halfway through dessert, his phone rang. Glancing at the screen, he excused himself from the table. "Gotta take this—work." Out of earshot, he accepted the call. "Hey, Becky Jean. Everything alright?"

"No. Everything is not alright. Get down here. Right. This. Minute." Her angry tone immediately conjured an image of her cheeks flaming with color, her blue eyes shooting lasers at him.

"Where are you?" Visions of the plant going up in smoke filled his mind.

"My house. Now, Ford. If you aren't here in five minutes, I'm going to hunt you down and murder you with my bare hands."

Okay. So the plant hadn't burned to the ground. "What's going on? I'm having dinner with my mother."

"I don't care if you're having dinner with the queen herself. Get here, pronto."

Ford pulled the phone from his ear. How had she managed the equivalent of an old-fashioned phone hang-up with her touch-screen cell phone?

"Neat trick." He stuck his head in the dining room. "Sorry, Mom. Gotta run. Something's come up." Before she could protest or inquire as to the nature of his emergency, he headed for the door. Not bothering to stop at his place, he took off down a path he'd frequently used as a kid when he walked or rode his bike into town. Where the driveway wound back and forth up the grade, the path cut a straight swatch down the face of the butte, ending up on the alleyway running behind the houses on Becky Jean's street. Without thinking, he knocked on her back door.

"Becky Jean? It's me, Ford."

He heard her stomping through the kitchen then the door swung open. He'd seen hornet's nests look less volatile. He took a precautionary step back.

"It's about damn time you got here." She grabbed a hold of his sleeve and pulled him inside, slamming the door shut behind him.

"I came as soon as I could." True. Nothing short of a jet pack strapped to his back would have gotten him there sooner. "What's wrong?"

"I'll tell you what's wrong, mister. This thing you invented is wrong!" Her face red, her shoulders drawn up tight, she looked ready to explode.

"Calm down." He reached for her, intending to guide her gently away from the kitchen and the block of knives on the countertop, but she jerked out of his reach. For the first time, he noticed the pink Texas Rangers T-shirt and denim cutoffs she wore. Damn, he'd never found the wholesome girl-next-door style to be sexy before, but she rocked the look.

"Don't touch me!"

Hands in the air, he tried his best to appear harmless. "Why don't you tell me what's going on? I can't fix what I don't know."

"The thing you invented," she said through gritted teeth.

"The butt plug?"

"Yes, you idiot. The…. It's stuck." He thought it impossible for her face to get any redder, but he'd been wrong.

"Stuck where?"

She crossed her arms in front of her and tapped her bare foot. Her cotton-candy-pink toenails momentarily distracted him. "You know where." Her voice came out so small he surely misheard.

"You mean?" He glanced down to her hips then back up to her face. Tears tracked down her cheeks and her bottom lip trembled.

"Yes. I got it in, but once I removed the key, I can't see to get it back in. I tried and tried…."

All humor gone, Ford stepped tentatively forward, arms open. She flung herself against his chest. He closed his arms around her, holding her while her tears soaked his shirt. "I tried to call Roseanne, but she's not answering her phone."

"There, there. It's going to be all right." He rested his chin on top of her head and patted her back, inhaling her intoxicating scent—simple and clean—not even a trace of the expensive perfume Ronnie favored, and often made him sneeze. He had no business being attracted to Becky Jean. She wasn't his type, but the more time he spent with her, the less it seemed to matter. Knowing he would soon see and touch her ass set his blood to a slow boil.

"Why couldn't it just slip out like the others?"

Grateful they were back to talking business, albeit sex-toy business, he smiled at the confirmation his design worked. Gloating, however, didn't seem like a good idea. "Is it uncomfortable?" Severe discomfort could explain her panicked state and signal a design flaw that would end any chance of his plan working. But the opportunity to see her ass made the experiment worthwhile.

"No. It's…. I…. When Roseanne didn't answer, I didn't know who else to call." She sniffed and hiccupped at the same time. He gave in to a crazy impulse and kissed the top of her head.

"Give me the key."

"I don't want to."

"Not ready to take it out?"

She socked him in the ribs.

"Ouch! Why did you hit me?"

"You deserved it for putting me in this situation. I hate you."

He was dying a slow and painful death—torn between wanting to gloat and howl at the success of his invention and wanting to see what he had no trouble at all imagining. But first he had to calm his test subject down. "No, you don't. You hate the position you're in, and I completely understand."

"This is all your fault."

Ford rubbed his chin on the top of her head. "I take full responsibility for your predicament." He held her for a few moments, waiting for her to calm. If she didn't stop trembling, he'd never manage to fit the tiny key into the lock mechanism, and he figured he'd only get one shot at it before she murdered him.

"You can't tell anyone about this."

He knew men who liked to talk about their conquests, but he'd never been one of them. The way he saw it, if a woman let him see or touch any part of her, he owed her the favor of keeping the details to himself. "I promise. Not a word to anyone."

"Okay, then."

When she didn't move out of his arms, he asked, "Where's the key?"

She loosened her hold on him and stepped back. Without making eye contact, she turned and headed down the hall. "I left it in the bathroom. Come on."

Ford filled his lungs, holding the air in as long as possible before letting it out in a *swoosh* before following her sexy ass down the hallway. This sure beat the hell out of dinner with his mom.

She led him through a bedroom he presumed to be hers to a large, modern bathroom. Someone had updated the century-old house to include the trendy en-suite. They'd done an excellent job blending vintage and modern together. Knowing how difficult the effect was to accomplish, he appreciated it even more. "Nice," he said.

Becky Jean glanced over her shoulder at the bathroom. "Oh. Yeah, Bobby and Chrissy put this in. I love the way they used modern touches but kept the vintage feel of the house."

"Me, too. If I didn't know better, I'd think it had been here since the house was built."

"I didn't ask you here to admire my bathroom."

Ford laughed. "Sorry. I recently finished a complete remodel on my house in New York. I did something similar there." She didn't share his amusement. He wiped the smile off his face and held out his hand. "Key?"

She dropped the tiny piece of metal into his palm. "No looking at anything else. Don't touch anything you don't have to. Are we clear?"

"Perfectly."

She dropped her shorts and bent over the counter, providing him with his first up-close-and-personal view of the ass that inspired him to create the plug in the first place. The sight of those perfect globes were enough to bring him to his knees, but add in the three-inch strip of black plastic wedged between them, and he held onto his good intentions by the thinnest of threads.

"Are you going to use the key today?"

"Huh?" He jerked his chin up. Their gazes met in the mirror and held, and, for a second, the ground beneath him shifted. Her contradictions baffled him. Brave and confident, yet vulnerable. The urge to make her his in the most elemental way hit him in the solar plexus. He sucked in a sharp breath.

"Ford!" Her gravelly growl had to be the sexiest thing he'd ever heard, but it snapped him out of the lust-filled haze he'd become lost in.

He took a step forward. "Yeah. One sec."

His fingers were numb, probably from lack of blood since most of his supply had diverted to his groin the second she dropped her drawers. He fumbled around trying to get a grip on the tiny key. "We need to make the heads on these keys bigger."

Becky Jean made a sound—part sigh, part groan—and wiggled her butt. "Just get on with it, will you?"

"Okay. Got it." He dropped to one knee behind her. "Is it okay if I touch you? I mean… I need to part… can't see."

"Just do it!"

Ford willed his hands not to shake. As careful as a man handling a bomb, he parted her cheeks enough to see the lock mechanism. "Here goes." With a little push, he slid the key home then turned it 180 degrees counterclockwise. "There."

Rising, he wiped a bead of sweat from his brow. "All done. You can do the rest yourself, can't you?"

"Yes."

He made it as far as her bedroom before he had to stop and lean against the wall for support. It had taken every ounce of self-control he possessed to walk out of Becky Jean's bathroom without doing something monumentally stupid. Like remove the plug and replace it with his cock. He managed to hold onto his control, but the feel of her skin and the erotic image of the toy he'd created with his own hands seated between her cheeks would stay with him until his dying day. And, at the rate his heart raced, he could die any minute.

The sound of running water reminded him he needed to get the hell out of his partner's house, but his legs were in no shape to carry him anywhere just yet. Besides, he'd feel like the worst sort of human if he didn't hang around long enough to make sure she hadn't suffered any ill effects from the untested device. Thinking he could have caused her harm sent a bolt of fear through him. Eventually, the door opened and Becky Jean stepped out. Other than a rosy flush to her cheeks, she appeared to be fine.

"You okay?"

She slicked her hands down the sides of her denim shorts. "Fine. I'm fine. No harm done. Sorry I panicked."

Relief loosened the glue holding his feet to the floor. He pushed away from the wall and smiled at her. "Understandable, under the circumstances."

"I suppose so. At any rate, your device works." Her gaze darted around the room as she spoke, eventually coming around to land on him. "You know what you said about making the key bigger?"

"Yeah." He held up his hand, fingers spread. "It's a little small for someone with big hands."

"Well, I got to thinking, what if we made a key with a flat head on it, sort of a thumbscrew design that would stay in all the time. So, if someone used the device solo, like I did, they wouldn't have the issue of trying to get the key back in. All they'd have to do would be turn the thumbscrew."

After all she'd been through, she still had the wherewithal to find a way out of the situation she'd found herself in. Amazing. "I think it's a great idea. I'll ask Scott to design one as an option."

Becky nodded. "Good. Good. It would solve the problem, then."

He didn't want to leave. He wanted to pull her into his arms and hold her, tell her how special she was, do all the things to her he'd envisioned over the last few days. But he couldn't. They were business partners—a fact he'd do well to remember. "I'd better be going."

She walked him to the back door.

"See you in the morning."

Every step back to the gatehouse was pure torture.

CHAPTER TEN

"Where were you last night? I called the B&B and your cell phone and got a recording." Becky eyed her best friend across the antique oak table in the kitchen of The Yellow Rose.

"Sorry. Ford's friend is staying here. He's… demanding." Roseanne picked a potato chip off her plate and snapped it in two. Something seemed off about her friend, but Becky couldn't put her finger on the change. Usually attentive to every detail, today she seemed… distracted.

"So demanding you couldn't answer your phone? What if it had been an emergency?"

"Was it?" She jerked her gaze to Becky as if checking for visible injuries.

Becky shrugged. "It seemed like it at the time." She'd never forget the moment she realized she couldn't get Ford's invention out of her body without help. When she hadn't been able to reach Roseanne, she'd contemplated calling her mother and dismissed the idea as beyond insane. For a brief moment, she'd considered driving to the twenty-four-hour emergency clinic, but scrapped the idea as soon as she realized she'd have to sit in the car in order to get there. Ford had been her last, and only, resort.

"Everything's okay?"

"Fine. Just fine." *Ford has seen my ass, up close and personal, but, no biggie, I'm good.* She'd come over on her lunch hour to vent to her best friend, but for whatever reason, she wanted to keep what had happened the previous evening to herself. The night had been embarrassing, but the way Ford had handled the situation made her want to hoard the moment. Once she'd calmed down enough to tell him why she'd demanded he come over, he'd been wonderful—tender and not at all condescending, as she had expected him to be. After she'd bent over the bathroom counter, he'd inserted the key, disengaged the lock then left her to remove the plug herself. The expression on his face when she found him lounging outside the bathroom door had been… complicated. She'd lain awake most of the night trying to decipher what it had meant, and come up with absolutely nothing. Until she made sense of it, she'd rather keep the incident to herself.

"Tell me about this Scott guy. He didn't seem like the demanding sort when I met him yesterday."

"Hon, you have no idea."

Becky finished the salad she'd brought for her lunch while her friend listed off the demands made by her Yankee guest. None of it sounded particularly out of line to her. Water on the bedside table, turndown service. Other than the request for a specific brand of coffee, it all sounded like things any guest might expect from a Victorian B&B. She didn't say it out loud, of course. She'd never tell her friend how to run her place of business any more than Roseanne would tell her how to make baby bottle nipples. Instead, she let her friend vent. Scott Ramsey couldn't be the first demanding guest Roseanne had played hostess to, and he wouldn't be the last.

Besides, Becky had her own problems, of which she couldn't speak. She and Ford had yet to tell the employees the severity of the situation, and until they did, she had to keep the details to herself. She trusted Roseanne not to say anything, but the woman clearly had enough on her plate without worrying about the last major employer in town closing its doors. And, lord knew, she didn't want to talk about what had happened the night before. If Roseanne had answered her phone, it would have been different. Ford's involvement would have ended with him asking her to try out the plug—something she could explain away as the crazy idea it had been. Even if the plug turned out to be the best thing to ever happen to the adult toy market, she didn't see how it could to save Adams Manufacturing. How many could they sell, anyway?

As soon as she'd finished her lunch, Becky snapped the lid back on the plastic container she'd used to transport her lunch and pushed back from the table. "As lovely as it is here, I've got to. Things to do, you know?"

"What's Mr. Ramsey doing here, anyway? Is Ford leaving soon?"

Becky couldn't tell her about the locking mechanism without mentioning Ford's big idea to save the company, so she settled on a version of the truth. "They're working on some sort of project together. As to Ford leaving, I don't see that happening anytime soon."

"Why not? You were so sure he wouldn't hang around."

She shrugged. "He has no intention of staying a day longer than he has to, but things are… complicated."

Roseanne narrowed her eyes. "Define complicated."

What the heck? It'll be common knowledge soon enough. The terms of Mr. Adams's will would become public through probate proceedings, and the struggle to keep the plant open wouldn't go unnoticed by the employees. "Mr. Adams left me 25 percent of the company."

"What?!"

"Calm down." Becky held up a staying hand.

"How can I calm down? You're rich!"

"Whoa! Whoa." She shook her head. "I'm on the brink of losing everything, and so are Ford and his mother. The company is broke."

Her friend's enthusiasm hit the proverbial iceberg.

"What's going to happen to all the people who work there?"

"Unless Ford pulls a miracle out of his hat, we're all going to lose our jobs, but I'll also be on the hook for my share of the debt. I know Mr. Adams intended to do something nice for me, and, a few years ago, it would have been. But for the last year or so, we've been holding on by a thread. I only found out yesterday how thin the thread really is."

"And there's nothing you can do?"

Becky explained the terms of the will and how she had no choice but to go along with whatever idea Ford came up with. "Ford has an idea for a new product he thinks might at least keep us in business for the next year, and he asked Scott to help him with it. If we survive the year? Who knows?"

"Wow."

"Tell me about it. My life's become one long, crazy roller coaster ride."

"That's what you wanted to talk to me about last night? I'm so sorry I wasn't available to you. I feel like a jerk."

"No, please. Don't give it another thought. I was just feeling a little down last night." She pasted a smile on her face. "I'm better today. Talking to you helped."

"Is there anything I can do?"

"No. Just keep this to yourself for a while, okay? No need upsetting everyone in town until we've explored every avenue open to us."

"My lips are sealed." Roseanne stood and began to clear the table. "Any idea how long Mr. Ramsey is going to be here?"

"As long as it takes, I guess." Becky stood. "I've got to get back."

Roseanne wrapped her in a warm hug. "Call me if you need anything."

"I will."

~~~

Becky sorted through the stack of message slips she'd picked up from reception on her way in. They couldn't hold
~~~

off telling the employees much longer. It had been weeks since they'd shipped out the first batches of their new product to suppliers around the globe, and they hadn't heard a peep out of any of them. She'd put off everything she possibly could to cut costs to the barest minimum, including ordering the mulch for the parking lot dividers. The spring bulbs had done their thing and been replaced by knee-high weeds. If not for the cars parked there daily, passersby would think the place abandoned. *Great curb appeal.* She pitied the Realtor who had to sell the place looking the way it did.

Something had to change—soon.

The first three messages were from suppliers they'd delayed paying, no doubt wanting to remind her the three-week deferral they'd requested would end soon. She'd have to ask Ford about providing more funds. Confident orders for his toy would come in, Ford insisted on continuing to produce the item, in an attempt to save face with their employees and the town, she'd named the *Safeguard Backdoor Locking System.* As a result of the aggressive production schedule, they were running desperately low on materials, and unless they paid their suppliers, they'd be shutting down *all* production soon.

She set the dun calls aside and read the last of the messages. Recognizing the name of one of the largest wholesaler's they'd mailed product samples to, her heart tripped and her skin tingled. Could this be it? Could they have actually made a sale? Ever since the night she'd had to ask Ford to help her remove his invention, she'd known he was right— it would revolutionize the butt-plug industry. *If* they could get anyone to buy it, and so far, she'd had no success in that area.

It had to happen. Ford had poured money into the project for additional molds and to retool several of the machines no longer in use to churn out their new product. Everyone but a skeleton crew assigned to complete the last orders of baby bottle nipples were assembling and packaging products for which they had no orders.

Scott, Ford's friend and business partner from New York, had sunk a lot of money into the project, too, providing the locks free of charge in hopes of making his money back, and then some, once the product began to sell. He'd offered to train the people on the assembly line, and for reasons Becky couldn't fathom, remained in town. *Probably waiting to see if any orders are going to come in.*

Becky read the short, uninformative message again. Maybe they just wanted to ask questions. She opened a file folder, pulled out the sheet she'd prepared with all the talking points for their new product. "There's no time like the present." Lifting the receiver, she dialed the number listed on the pink message slip.

~ ~ ~

"Ford?" Becky knocked on his open office door then stepped inside. "Got a minute?"

He put down his pencil and rocked back in his chair. "Sure. What's up?"

He'd been working on a new design the last few days, and seemed to have lost track of routine things—like shaving and combing his hair. *He looks like he just climbed out of bed.*

She had no business thinking about a sleep-tumbled Ford. They had a purely professional relationship that, due to the nature of the business, included him seeing her naked ass on one occasion—but it had been a one-time occurrence, and an emergency to boot. Nothing remotely similar would happen again. Becky wouldn't be seeing his adorable disheveled countenance across the bed, so best to quit imagining it. Besides, as soon as they put Adams Manufacturing back on an even keel, Ford would start looking for a buyer for the share of the company he controlled. He'd been clear from the beginning about his desire to go back to his life in New York, and she couldn't blame him. Butte Plains didn't rate a dot on most maps. The nightlife here consisted of high school football games in the fall and catching lightning bugs in the summer. The pace of life was two steps behind slow and getting slower with each passing day.

She closed the door and approached his desk. "I have good news and bad news. Which would you like first?"

"Might as well start with the bad." He sighed and held his hand out for the paper she extended to him. "Don't make me read it, just tell me."

"We're running extremely low on raw materials. If we don't pay some of our suppliers, we're going to have to scale back our production of the *Safeguard Backdoor Locking System.*"

"Bottom line?"

She named a figure that made him whistle. He dropped the paper on his desk. "And the good news?"

"We *need* more raw materials."

His brows knit as he stared up at her. "Isn't that the same as the bad news?"

"No. It's the opposite of the bad news." She could barely keep the smile off her face, but she loved turning the tables on Ford. "See?" She handed him another sheet of paper. As he read, his face relaxed then his lips curved upward in a tentative smile.

"Tell me this isn't a joke."

"No joke. I just got off the phone with the head buyer. They want fifty-thousand units as soon as we can ship them. I promised ten thousand a week for the next five weeks with a promise to fill the order faster if we could manage it."

A giant smile split his face. "You did it, Becky Jean. You really did it!" He jumped up, rounded the desk, and threw his arms around her, lifting her off the ground with a whoop they probably heard in Dallas. She laughed right along with him.

After printing out the purchase order the buyer had emailed to her, she'd danced around her office until she'd been able to control her expression. Seeing Ford this happy filled her with joy. She laughed and hung on as he spun her around until she became dizzy.

"This calls for a celebration." He set her down then went back to his desk. Chest puffed out, he produced a bottle and two glasses from a lower drawer. "Tennessee's finest," he said, removing the top.

She laughed and accepted the tumbler with a splash of amber liquid.

Ford lifted his glass in the air. "Out with the old, in with the new," he said. "And, to the latest incarnation of Adams Manufacturing."

They tipped their glasses together until a crystal-clear *clink* rang out. Becky sipped at her drink while Ford finished his in one gulp, then refilled it and downed the second helping. They were a long way from being out of the woods, but this first order did warrant a celebration. She tipped the rest of her drink back. Coughing as the liquid burned its way down, she held her glass out for a refill.

"We did it, Becky Jean." They'd done significant damage to the bottle of Tennessee's finest. Ford had called Scott to let him know, then drank a toast to his best friend whose locking mechanism was the true success behind the new product. Never mind it had taken Ford's genius to marry his design with a lock with no other practical application. Several drinks later, he'd waxed poetic about Becky's marketing skills.

If anything reeked of donkey doo-doo, his statement did. She'd named the product, slapped a bunch of them into boxes, and shipped them off to adult toy suppliers then prayed they'd see what Ford saw—the chance to make a fortune.

She still didn't believe more orders were imminent, but Ford thought differently, and for the time being, she chose to believe him. For the first time since the reading of Mr. Adams's will, the doom of bankruptcy seemed less certain.

"To butt-plug wearers everywhere," she said, lifting her glass.

"Here! Here!"

PART TWO

Marriage is an adventure, like going to war.

Gilbert K. Chesterson

CHAPTER ELEVEN

Four months later....

"It's a good idea, Ford." Becky paced in front of her partner's desk and refused to back down. "The *Home Shopping Network* is huge. They've proven the marketing strategy works."

"So, why not let *them* sell our products? I don't see why we need to stick *our* necks out."

"I thought you were all about innovation. This should be a no-brainer, partner of mine. Thanks to your creative mind, we have several products on the market, and more on the drawing board. Our Internet sales are through the roof on our site, and on the sites we distribute to."

"If sales are so good, then I don't see any point in expanding into something we know nothing about."

"Sales are good, but they could be better." Becky planted her feet and glared at her stoic partner. "Ever since the *Safeguard Backdoor Locking System* hit the market four months ago, we've become known for our innovation in the adult toy market. Internet stores are a dime a dozen. Everyone with a computer and a garage to stock inventory has one. Yes, those are profitable for us, but think about it. We would have our own cable network where we sell our own brand directly to the public. We could sell advertising to all those Internet stores, as well as to the brick-and-mortar stores. I don't see a downside to it."

Ford rocked back in his chair, a sure sign he was softening. Since becoming business partners, she'd learned to read him well. Becky tamped down her enthusiasm. The biggest hurdle would be getting Ford to agree to establish the first-ever adult cable shopping network and, in her estimation, by far the easiest task ahead of her, given her plans.

Elbow braced on the arm of his chair, he brushed the knuckle of his index finger over his bottom lip. She would not allow the unconsciously sexy habit to distract her as it always did. This was too important.

"You're talking about a huge monetary investment. We'd have to hire studio space, professionals to produce the show, spokespersons to sell the products, plus we'd have to set up a fulfillment center separate from our current wholesale distribution center. None of which would be cheap. Can we afford it?"

She had answers to all his concerns, but with Ford, she had to take it one step at a time or he'd dig in his heels. She shifted the focus back on him. "Don't you even read the reports I put on your desk?"

"I'm supposed to read them?"

Shaking her head, she plopped into one of the twin leather guest chairs facing his desk. Lord, he could be exasperating sometimes. "I read the ones you put on *my* desk."

"I don't write reports." The samples of various plastics, notebooks, and drafting supplies strewn across the top of his desk testified to the truth of his statement. The crumpled grease-stained sandwich wrapper occupying one corner could have been today's lunch or from last week. She made a mental note to sneak the cleaning staff in as soon as possible.

"Yes, I know. However, when you come up with a new product, I at least take the time to look at it." She'd also personally tried every one of his inventions, but she'd keep the information to herself.

"I don't have time to read every report that comes across my desk, Becky Jean. I trust you to inform me if something needs my attention, but otherwise, I don't want to be bothered. I'm happy with my role as head of product development." He lifted a sketchpad then dropped it. Becky blanched at the particles of dust dancing under the glow of his desk lamp.

Ever since Ford's former college roommate turned business partner had returned to New York two months ago, Ford had focused his attention on designing new, innovative products. "Is Scott coming back?"

"I don't think so. Why?"

"Just wondering. He stayed longer than necessary the first time, which made me think he had other reasons for hanging around." Reasons like Roseanne Meadows. The town grapevine had buzzed with rumors about those two the entire time Scott had stayed at the B&B. Becky had asked her friend more than once about her guest, but Roseanne always shifted the conversation to Ford and Becky, and since she had no intention of discussing her obsession with her new business partner, what little she knew about the Yankee and the owner of The Yellow Rose was stained with grape juice.

"He needed to get back. We have clients, plus he wanted to hire someone to take my place for a while."

The reminder of Ford's temporary residence status plunged an ice pick straight into her heart, but she masked the hurt with a smile. "You mean you're replaceable?"

"Apparently. Or so Scott believes." He waved the insult away. "We've been thinking about hiring an apprentice, somebody straight out of college. This is as good a time as any."

"Well, we all appreciate you stepping in here, and your dedication to the company, but it's important to stay abreast of our financial status, don't you think?"

"Like I said, if we have cash flow problems, I'm sure you'll let me know."

She added hardheaded to her list of Ford's personality traits. "To answer your earlier question—yes, we can afford to undertake this new project. In fact, I don't think we can afford not to. Someone is going to do it. It's only a matter of time, Ford. It's a natural move for the most innovative company in the adult toy market."

He sighed again and rocked forward to cross his forearms on the desktop. Becky hid her victory smile and waited for confirmation of what she already knew. She had him.

"What do you need from me?"

Yes! She did a mental fist pump. "I'll have the documents on your desk tomorrow at the latest. Sign them and get them back to me. That's all I need." *For the time being.* She'd spring the rest of it on him once she'd sealed the deal and he couldn't say no.

"Okay." He reached for his drafting pencil. "Can I get back to work?"

"Sure." As she stood, their gazes met and held for a breathless moment before she remembered he was her partner and the spark of interest she thought she saw in his eyes had to be her overactive imagination. Forcing her mind back to business, she straightened before heading toward the door. Recalling the reason she'd come to see him in the first place, she gripped the doorframe and faced him. "Thanks, Ford. This is the right thing to do. I know it." He waved her on her way with a grunt indicating he'd already shifted his focus back to his drawing—further proof her eyes and her mind had been playing tricks on her. The only thing Ford was interested in was whatever deviously naughty toy he was designing.

She hadn't lied. His innovative designs had catapulted Adams Manufacturing into the adult toy market with the force of an all-out assault. Their competitors had scrambled to come up with products to gain back market share and failed miserably. They could no longer sit on their well-padded asses. If they did, the competition would catch up and eventually overtake them. She had no intention of letting that happen.

When *Home Shopping Network* had come to her with an offer to feature their products in an exclusive late-night showcase, she'd been flattered, but she'd also seen the possibility in the idea. If the popular home shopping network thought they could sell their products, then there was money to be made. Why not make it themselves?

She'd done her research before presenting the idea to Ford. It would be less expensive to rent studio space, but they already had an entire building not being used. The red-brick structure she had in mind had been the original home of Adams Manufacturing and had been deemed structurally sound by the people from the state historical society who had come out to see if it qualified for listing on their registry. Renovating the space would cost them up front but, in the long run, would be an investment in the future and a feather in the cap for Butte Plains. Once completed, the building could be home to a new state-of-the-art studio with plenty of room for offices and the distribution center Ford had correctly listed as an expense. Removing the cost of land and constructing a new building out of the equation made the start-up bottom line a nice shade of pink instead of bright red.

Until the new studio could be completed, she planned to begin production in the conference room in the present building. Some soundproofing would be necessary to prevent rumblings from the factory bleeding into the sound feed, but the renovation wouldn't cost much. Besides, she fully intended to start small. No sense dumping a lot of cash into what she had to admit could be a bit of a risky venture. No one had ever attempted to sell adult toys on television. The concept might be a complete flop, but she didn't think so. She knew marketing, and the success of various niche home shopping networks told her this one would be well received by the buying public.

Especially if you had a sexy-as-sin person hawking the wares. And Ford Adams was *sexier* than sin.

~~~

Ford had to admit the conference room turned studio looked pretty good. Not fancy, but thanks to the magic of television, the viewing public would never know. The part of it they would see had clean lines, and above all, looked classy.

"Is it worth all the noise you had to endure the last few weeks?"

Ford hadn't gone along with the idea of launching their own adult toy shopping show easily, but he'd seen the miracles Becky Jean could achieve when she set her mind to something. If she said it would work, then it would work. He turned to his business partner. "It looks good."

"That's all you've got to say?"

God, he loved to push her buttons. When riled, she turned a becoming shade of red, and Lord, if the sight didn't set his blood on fire.

He had no business toying with her, though. He'd long since decided their professional relationship wasn't enough to keep him from taking what he wanted, but every time he thought about acting on his desires, something happened to remind him his stint here would end soon. The last time he'd spoken to Ronnie—over a week ago—she'd pumped him for information about when he would find a buyer for the company and get the hell out of Dodge. He'd reminded her Dodge was in Kansas, not Texas. She hadn't been amused.

Truthfully, he'd begun to like it here. He was having more fun than the law allowed, as his dad used to say, designing sex toys and watching his company grow. His company. Not his dad's, not his family's. *His.* Yes, he'd built on the bones of the ones who'd gone before, but in all fairness, there hadn't been much left. He'd take partial blame for the condition he'd found the company in. If he'd returned to Butte Plains after college, he might have helped his father turn the company around before things became desperate. If his father had asked, he would have come. But Ken Adams knew his son, and, in keeping his difficulties to himself, he allowed Ford to seek his
~~~

own happiness.

He'd be eternally grateful for the opportunity. His dad had been one in a million.

So, coming to the realization he wasn't exactly bored with his life in Butte Plains came as a bit of a shock. He'd yet to decide if he wanted to stay permanently. He still had eight months before he could sell out, so he didn't need to make a decision until then. And, if he did decide to keep the place, Becky Jean had proved more than capable of running the entire shebang without him being present. He could design products anywhere in the world. If they needed him in the initial stages of product development, he could pop back in for a while.

Looking around the room once again, he admired Becky Jean's ingenuity. She'd made something out of nothing, and done it in record time. "How deep are we into this project?"

"I put the expense report on your desk this morning." She had, and he'd glanced at the bottom line, but telling her so would make her suspicious. She thought he didn't read the constant stream of financial reports she sent his way, but that wasn't entirely true. He read the bottom line on all of them, if not the details. He'd never told anyone about the second mortgage he'd taken on his house in New York. Those first couple of months had all but drained his personal reserves. Thanks to their success with the *Safeguard Backdoor Locking System*, he'd paid off both mortgages on his home, and he once again had financial reserves. Becky Jean Parker had as much to do with it as anyone. Adams Manufacturing had gained solid financial ground, thanks to her marketing skills and her ability to be everything to everybody. The earning potential of the company was through the roof, the cash flow robust, and their debt low. Now would be the perfect time to look for a potential buyer.

So, why are *you still here?*

He'd asked himself the question a million times, and the only answer remained—he was having fun. He was designing for himself for the first time in his professional career, and he had the means to watch those designs leap from the page, become reality then go out into the world for millions to enjoy. One day, he'd have to go back to the business he'd built with Scott right out of college, but for the time being, he owed it to himself to enjoy the life he'd dreamed of since he drew his first invention at the age of seven.

He glanced at the woman who made it possible for him to do nothing but draw all day. Becky Jean solved problems across the spectrum—from production snafus to missing paperwork. Everyone, including him, relied on her. "You did?"

"You know I did." Her tone made it clear she'd lost all patience with him. He needed to come clean.

"Yes, I know. I read the report. You've kept the cost down on the project, and I appreciate it. I'm not entirely convinced this is going to be a success, but at least we won't lose our shirts on the deal."

"High praise from you," she said.

"It looks like you've got everything under control." He ran a hand over one of the boxes containing lighting equipment that had arrived earlier today. "Your report listed the technical people you hired, but I didn't see a spokesperson. Haven't been able to find anyone?"

It was one thing to stand in front of a camera and talk about cookware or jewelry, and quite another to talk about butt plugs. Not to mention, finding someone to fill the role in Butte Plains seemed an impossible task.

"Uh… no. I mean, yes."

Her stammering made the hairs on the back of his neck stand on end. Everything from the flush of her cheeks to the way she pretended interest in the papers on her clipboard told him she had something to hide—something he wasn't going to like. "Which is it?"

"Which is what?" She wandered around the room until she'd maneuvered a stack of boxes between them.

He hadn't seen her this nervous since the night she'd called him to her house to help her remove the prototype of the *Safeguard Backdoor Locking System*. "Becky Jean."

"It's the right thing to do," she pleaded. "The

demographic research suggests more than 75 percent of all adult toys sold are purchased by women."

He'd read the same statistic somewhere. Probably on one of the reports she'd sent his way. "So? What does that have to do with our spokesperson?"

"Well, it needs to be a guy."

He didn't like the leading way she'd ended her statement. "I don't care if the person is male or female, as long as they can sell our products."

"Good!" She smiled the biggest smile he'd ever seen then made her way out from behind the wall of boxes. "It's all settled, then."

"Wait," he said, putting himself in between her and the door. He could almost feel the weight of the boulder dropping out of the sky, aimed straight for him. "What's settled?"

"Our spokesperson, of course. You'll be perfect."

Wham! Splat! She'd played him like a fiddle. He raised both hands, palms out. "Whoa. Back the wagon up, little lady. I am not going to go on TV to sell butt plugs."

"Well, someone has to, and who knows the *Safeguard Backdoor Locking System* better than you?"

Logic wasn't going to work on him. Not when it came to making a fool of himself. "That's not the point, and you know it. I'm a product development engineer, not an actor."

"Who said anything about acting? Remember when you were trying to sell me on the idea?"

He nodded, recalling how difficult she'd been to win over. In the end, it had been the product, not anything he'd said that had convinced her to jump on the bandwagon.

"You convinced me, and I'd wager the phones will be ringing off the hook with women wanting to buy anything you're selling."

"Don't bet the company on it, Becks." He used his most menacing, don't-fuck-with-me voice. He trusted her judgment regarding their business, would do anything she said—within reason. This was *not* within reason. Not even close.

"I'm not, but even if I did, it's a safe bet. No one is more passionate about your designs than you. Our sales took a noticeable jump after the article about you appeared in *Texas Monthly*. And, at the risk of inflating your already-considerable ego, you aren't bad to look at. The female audience is going to eat you up."

He stored away the fact she thought he was good-looking for another time and concentrated on the more pressing matter. "What about the male audience? Don't they matter?"

"Truthfully? Not as much. Women do most of the purchasing in this country. They're the ones we have to appeal to."

"As a male of the species, I'm offended." *And screwed.* As usual, she knew her facts.

"Get over it, Ford." She glanced over her shoulder at the boxes. "The technicians will be in this afternoon to set everything up. We'll have a dress rehearsal at six this evening. If everything goes well, we'll go live next week."

"Live?" Out of necessity, he'd long ago gotten over his aversion to public speaking, but live television? Not his idea of a fun time.

"For now. If sales warrant, we'll invest in taping equipment, but until we see if this is going to work, our shows will be live broadcasts."

He closed his eyes and counted to ten. He wished he'd put his foot down on this project when he'd had the chance. "What if I say no?"

She huffed out a breath. "Look. You wanted me to keep expenses down, so I have. I've compromised on everything, including the studio I really wanted. On-air talent is expensive."

"How expensive?"

She named an hourly wage he could barely comprehend.

"You're shittin' me."

"I wish I was. Plus, the agents I spoke to all insisted on lengthy contracts. I want this to work, but I'm realistic, too. We're launching to a small, localized market. It could flop, and I don't want to be on the hook for any more than we have to be."

He couldn't fault her for being practical. She was a hell of a businesswoman and a marketing genius. Adams Manufacturing was lucky to have her. *He* was lucky to have her. For better or worse, they were in this together. She'd left him little choice. "I'll agree on one condition."

"Anything you want."

For the first time since she'd sprung her crazy-assed idea on him, Ford smiled.

~~~

I can't do this. Standing on the mark the director indicated, Becky couldn't ignore the testosterone tower next to her. Since Ford had taken to wearing jeans and worn-out MIT T-shirts to work—something she blamed on his friend Scott—she'd almost forgotten how breathtaking he looked in the tailored suits he'd worn when he first returned to Butte Plains. Between his distracting presence and the display of butt plugs on the table next to them, she was as nervous as an armadillo crossing a six-lane freeway during rush hour.

Anything you want, her conscience mocked. *Whatever possessed you to say such a thing?*

"I'm ready. How about you, Becky Jean?" Ford's deep voice held a hint of mockery, too. And why wouldn't it? She'd opened the door, and he'd walked right through, dragging her into the pit of humiliation she'd dug for herself.

"Ready as I'll ever be, I guess." She wiped her sweating palms on her skirt.

"This is a rehearsal. It doesn't matter how you look," Ford said.

Easy for you to say, Mr. Perfect. "Still no reason to be a slouch."

"Just relax," Justin said. The kid just graduated college with a degree in filmmaking, and he was eager to put it to use. The idea of being on the ground floor of something as innovative as the *Adult Shopping Show* appealed to the young
~~~

man. Even the pittance she'd offered him hadn't discouraged him from accepting the job as producer/director/master-in-charge of getting them on the air. "Everything is on the teleprompter but feel free to improvise."

"I think I'll stick to the script," Becky Jean said.

"Not a problem. It gets the message across."

It should. She'd written it herself.

It took over an hour to get through the half-hour segment. Justin continually stopped to adjust the lighting and remind them to relax. Remind *her*, she amended. Despite his initial resistance, Ford proved to be the natural she'd predicted he would be. She was the mess.

"You should do this alone," she said as they wrapped up the second run-through.

"Oh, no you don't," Ford said. "If I have to do this, *you* have to do this."

"I'm worse than Lucy Ricardo trying to sell Vita-Meata-Vegimin."

"You'll be fine," he stated with a finality that said he wasn't going to let her off the hook.

"I'm going to remind you, you said that when social media starts lighting up with scathing reviews of our show." As she stomped off the set, she wished she'd never had the idea in the first place.

CHAPTER TWELVE

Becky Jean had to be the worst spokesperson he'd ever seen, but Ford knew exactly how to fix the problem. He didn't know shit about teleprompters, but, being mechanically gifted, he could figure out most anything. Arriving early to the makeshift set, he disabled the reading device. Without it as a crutch, Becky Jean would be obliged to interact with him instead of just reading scripted lines. She'd never had any trouble telling him exactly what she thought, so, he reasoned, if he could keep her attention focused on him, she'd forget all about the camera and the audience, and things would go much smoother. He hadn't convinced Justin, but the younger man agreed to give it a shot after Ford added another percentage point to the man's commission off sales made through their new 800 number.

"Don't let on you know this is a setup or she'll walk," he cautioned their jack-of-all-things-television.

"My lips are sealed, Mr. Adams."

"Seeing as we're partners in crime, why don't you call me Ford?"

The kid nodded. "Ford it is. You really think your partner is going to be able to pull this off?"

"If there's one thing I know about Becky Jean, it's she can do anything she sets her mind to. Just remember, no matter how mad she gets, keep the cameras rolling."

"Whatever you say, Ford."

Becky Jean breezed in. Earlier in the day, she'd had on a cute dress that reminded him of summer picnics. The suit she'd changed into screamed cock-block. If she buttoned up any tighter, her eyeballs would bulge out.

"Oh, hell, no."

"What?" She stopped in her tracks. "Is something wrong?"

"Where'd you get the Mary Poppins' suit?"

She glanced down at herself. "Nordstrom's in Dallas. Why?"

"It's hideous." Judging by the color in her cheeks, he'd pissed her off and he hadn't uttered a single lie. "Is it the same one Lucille Ball wore in the Vita-Meata-Vegimin commercial?" It damn sure could have been. It was that ugly.

She lifted the skirt thingy hanging over her hips. "Peplums are very much in style, I'll have you know."

"You wearing something under that hideous thing?"

Her mouth opened and closed like a fish as she absorbed the insult and contemplated her answer. "Of course."

Just as he'd thought. Buttoned-up Becky Jean would have more than one layer of armor. "Then take it off. Style or no style, the jacket has to go."

She turned to Justin, silently asking his opinion. The younger man didn't miss a beat. He shook his head. "I'm with Ford. Take it off."

"Well, I never—" She removed the jacket, then hung it carefully on the doorknob. "Satisfied?" She spread her arms wide to show off a silk blouse. It wasn't anywhere near as ugly as the suit coat, but it still screamed uptight bitch, not sexy woman.

"It's not great, but it's better." Ford motioned her over to her spot beside him. They would open with a wide shot of the two of them then narrow to a close-up as the two introduced themselves and welcomed viewers to their new show. Later, they would move to the display table and spend the last twenty minutes talking about today's product—the *Safeguard Backdoor Locking System.*

Becky Jean had done a credible job with the script she'd prepared for the sabotaged teleprompter, but it had nearly bored Ford to death. If they had any chance of this network idea working, they were going to have to grab any viewer's they had by the short hairs and refuse to let go.

He fully understood his plan could backfire. Becky Jean could walk out and leave him there to woo customers all by himself, but he didn't think she would. He needed it not to happen. If he had to subject himself to public ridicule, she would, too. They were partners, after all.

She placed her feet precisely over the X taped on the floor. "Let's do this."

Ford glanced at the clock. Less than a minute to airtime. He exchanged a look with Justin then turned his gaze on Becky Jean. "Hmm. Something is still not right."

"Really? I look perfectly fine. Nobody's going to be looking at me anyway."

Oh, he begged to differ. Yes, the women would be looking at him most likely, but they'd be curious about Becky Jean. They weren't just selling butt plugs, they were selling sex. And though he thought she oozed sex appeal no matter what she wore, present suit notwithstanding, the viewers, all two of them, he suspected, didn't know his partner as well as he did. Therefore, something had to change.

"Which is why we need to do something different. No one wants to buy a butt plug from someone who looks like their ass is so tight nothing short of a jackhammer could drive a wedge of plastic up it."

Color flooded her cheeks, and her mouth fell open in horror. Moving quickly, Ford reached for the top button on her blouse. Despite its tight-ass appearance, the fabric was the softest silk. Under different circumstances, he wouldn't mind feeling it slide against certain parts of his body. His fingers slipped, but he managed to release the top two buttons before Becky Jean recovered from his shocking statement. By then, it was too late. The fabric fell in a soft V from her collarbone to the top of her cleavage. Bedroom ready, he'd call the look. *Perfect.*

"On the air in Three. Two. One," Justin counted down.

Ford faced the camera and plastered a smile on his face he'd used countless times to charm women out of their panties. Slipping his arm around Becky Jean's waist, he tugged her to his side. "Good evening, ladies and gentlemen, and welcome to the ASS—*The Adult Shopping Show.* I'm K. Ford Adams, and this is my partner, B.J. Parker." He smiled down at Becky Jean who looked sexy as sin with her cheeks flushed and her lips parted. He hoped the audience would interpret the anger simmering in her gaze for another sort of passion. Before she found her voice, Ford rushed on with the detailed instructions he'd memorized from the original script. Business was business, and the viewers, if they had any, needed to understand how the ordering process worked.

Keeping his arm snug across her back and his fingers digging into her hip, he ushered Becky Jean to the display table, talking to the camera all the way.

"B.J. and I want you to know every product we recommend has been tested by us and deemed worthy of adding to your bedroom collection. And all our products come with a money-back guarantee. If the product doesn't live up to your expectations, simply return it for a full refund within thirty days of purchase."

He stopped behind the draped table where an array of butt plugs lay artfully arranged to showcase the item from all angles. After the initial release, sales had warranted production of the plug in various sizes from a slim, beginner model to a fist-sized one for the more advanced ass-play crowd. Across the board, the line represented the lion's share of their earnings.

"Tonight, we want to introduce you to a revolutionary

new product—the *Safeguard Backdoor Locking System*."

She was going to kill him. Right there on local television. Becky thanked heaven the projected viewership for the eleven-thirty-to-midnight time slot on the small regional cable network amounted to about a dozen people. With any luck, ten of those had already fallen asleep, leaving only two witnesses, and Justin, to convict her of murder.

Ford's voice droned in her ears as he explained to the camera what made his butt plug better than all the others on the market. No one knew the item better than the man who had designed it, and his expertise came through in his confident tone of voice. Every woman out there would be hanging on his every honey-and-testosterone-laden word. As she'd suspected from the beginning, he didn't need her. They were twenty minutes into the half-hour show, and she hadn't uttered a single word.

"B.J., honey, you've tried the revolutionary new *Safeguard Backdoor Locking System*. Why don't you tell the viewers what you thought of the product?"

What the hell? He didn't really expect her to endorse his butt plug, did he?

Rage washed through her, making her see red. The two viewers who were still awake would know she'd tried not only his invention, but several of their competitors. She really was going to kill him, but first, she'd give him what he wanted.

"Go ahead, honey. How did it compare to others you've tried?"

Remembering her humiliation at having to call him to help her remove the plug, she smiled up at him. "I'd be happy to, Ford." Facing the camera, she began. "Ladies, I have tried the *Safeguard Backdoor Locking System*, and let me tell you, the operative word here is 'locking.'" She picked up the medium-sized sample and pointed the base toward the camera. "Justin, can you get a close-up of this, please?

"There, ladies. See how tiny the key is?" She looked into

the camera lens. "We've all fumbled with trying to fit a key into a lock in the dark, and know how impossible it is even with a key the size of your car or house key. Now, imagine this product is in place, and you want to remove it. There is no way you're getting this out on your own. Once it's in, and the lock is engaged, it isn't going anywhere until your partner inserts the key for you."

"And, there you have it, folks!" Ford took the plug from her hand and held it up triumphantly. "A glowing testimonial from B.J. Parker! Thanks for watching, and remember, the number is 1-800-BUT-PLUG. We're K. Ford Adams and B.J. Parker for the *Adult Shopping Show*, saying good night, and sleep tight. See you next week. Same time. Same channel."

He tugged her close and planted a kiss on the top of her head just as Justin chirped from behind the control panel, "And, we're out!"

Ford's hand slid from where it rested on her hip, and she had to grab the table to steady herself. She hadn't realized how much she'd been relying on him to keep her upright during the show.

"Great job, Ford. And, Ms. Parker, you were awesome!" Justin bounced with his enthusiasm.

"Are you insane?" She directed her tirade at Ford. "What happened to the script?"

"The teleprompter broke just before you got here. We figured you'd have a coronary, so we decided not to tell you and just wing it."

"Wing it?" She might be irrational, but his winging it had gone too far. "How dare you tell the whole world I've tried the… the *System*?"

"I didn't exactly tell the *whole world*, Becky Jean. You said it yourself. The viewership for this time slot is practically nothing. So what if two or three people know? None of them know you."

"They might!" She stomped to the door and grabbed her jacket off the doorknob. Jamming her arms into the sleeves, she faced him. "What if my mother is one of the people who saw the show?"

He shrugged, and she looked around for something to throw at him. Seeing nothing she could easily pick up, she shook her head in frustration.

"For what it's worth, Ms. Parker," Justin piped up, "I thought it went very well. Better than rehearsal, and the sparks flying between you two was awesome. Heck, you had me wanting to call in, and I've already got the samples you gave me."

"Thanks, Justin," she said, ashamed she'd ranted at Ford in front of an employee. "I'm glad you found the spectacle entertaining."

A knock sounded on the door. Becky spun around and opened it. The young woman she'd hired to work the switchboard overnight in case orders actually came in stood there with a worried look in her eyes. "Yes, Camille, what is it?"

"Ms. Parker, ma'am. Uh…. Could you maybe take a few calls? Kim and Lisa are answering calls as fast as they can, but people are hanging up."

"People are calling in?" She couldn't believe it. "How many calls have come in?"

"At least a hundred, and those are the ones I could answer. If this keeps up, you're going to need a bigger switchboard and a lot more order takers."

"We'll be right there," Ford said over Becky's shoulder. "Can you patch calls into our offices?"

"Sure. Just let me know when you're ready." Becky stared at the girl's retreating back.

"We'd better hustle. Justin, can you take a few calls, too?"

"Sure thing." As the technician pushed past her, she thought she heard him say, "Who would have thunk it?"

She sure hadn't.

CHAPTER THIRTEEN

"Whoowee!" Roseanne fanned herself. "Talk about hot. Your show was H.O.T. hot last night, girlfriend."

"Please," Becky pleaded across her friend's kitchen table. "Can we not talk about the show?"

"Why ever not?" Roseanne plunked two sweaty glasses of iced tea on the table to go with the chicken salad sandwiches she'd prepared for their weekly lunch date. "You are gorgeous, always have been, and Ford… well, he's about the sexiest thing to ever come out of this little town. But the two of you together? Bam! The chemistry between you two is explosive."

Becky lifted the slice of homemade multi-grain bread to examine the chunky chicken goodness underneath. Two lengthwise pickle slices, also homemade, topped the mound, just the way she liked it. For someone who'd never had any culinary training, Roseanne had become a fabulous cook. "You saw rage, not lust. You are right about one thing—there was almost an explosion. I came within an inch of blowing my top, right there on set."

"Really? Do tell, my friend."

Becky replaced the bread on her sandwich with a sigh. The crazy number of orders that came in overnight had gone a long way toward calming her anger. Ford had been right, but damn if she would admit it to him. However, she could tell Roseanne. As they downed their sandwiches and cold drinks, she told her friend what had transpired the night before.

"But the show went off without a hitch, or so it appeared from my end," Roseanne said.

"If sales are any indication, then you're right. We're looking at adding more phone lines to handle the calls."

Her friend shook her head. "I still can't believe you sell sex toys for a living. What does your mother think about it?"

Becky shrugged. "She almost had a heart attack when I told her, but she'd rather me sell sex toys than move to Dallas, or farther away, to find a job."

"Your mother always has been the practical sort."

"Yeah, she is. However, she's still after Colin to get a regular job." She curled her fingers into air quotes around the word regular.

"How's your brother doing? Is he still playing at that club in Nashville?"

Becky's younger brother, Colin, had never been interested in going to college—much to their parent's disappointment. Right out of high school he'd packed his belongings and the guitar he'd made in eighth grade woodshop into the beat-up truck he'd saved all his life for and struck out for the bright lights of Nashville. Determined to make it as a country singer/songwriter, he'd lived like a pauper for years before obtaining a measure of success shortly before their father's passing.

Becky rose to place her empty plate and glass in the sink then leaned against the counter. She needed to go back to the office but was reluctant to do so. "Yeah. He signed a record contract earlier this year. According to him, he's on his way to stardom. I guess we'll have to wait and see."

"That would sure be something, wouldn't it?" Roseanne placed her dishes in the sink, too. "Tell him I said hi, next time you talk to him."

"I will. He says he misses Butte Plains, wants to live here when he makes it big. But for the time being, Nashville is his home."

"Well, I hope all his dreams come true. If talent is what it takes, he's got it in spades."

Becky couldn't argue with her assessment. Her brother had always been gifted when it came to music. He was a genius with wood, too. She counted among her most prized possessions a jewelry box he'd made for her in high school. If music didn't work out for him, he could easily make a living as a craftsman. "I'll tell him you said so," she said, heading for the back door. "Thanks for lunch, and for letting me rant. Same time next week?"

Back in her office, Becky sat at her desk doing her best to stay awake when a blur of pink breezed past her door leaving the faint scent of gardenias behind. Even when her husband had run the company, Helen Adams had been an infrequent visitor to the plant, but she'd been there enough times for Becky to recognize her, even if her unique perfume didn't give her away.

"Ford Adams!" Yep, Helen Adams had arrived, and she wasn't happy. Scandalous news spread faster than a brush fire in Butte Plains. "Tell me what I just heard at the Dippity Do isn't true."

Becky imagined her partner leaning back in the new ergonomic desk chair he'd insisted on purchasing. This one didn't creak the way his father's had, but she'd committed Ford's new mannerisms to memory. Sometimes having a steel-trap mind could be a liability.

"Good to see you, too, Mom. Have a seat." Ford's voice carried through their open office doors.

She didn't envy her partner the job ahead, but it had been his decision to not tell his mother about her precarious financial situation or fill her in when things began to turn around. Ford's days of withholding information had come to an end.

"What is the meaning of this, Ford? Do you have any idea what they're saying about Adams Manufacturing?"

"I've got a pretty good idea." She couldn't miss the frustration in Ford's voice.

"Is it true? Are we making…?"

"Sex toys? Yes, we are. And we're making a lot of money. Money we desperately need."

Becky experienced a twinge of guilt for eavesdropping on the conversation, but she wouldn't miss this for the world. Mrs. Adams owned 50 percent of the company. If she pushed Ford to sell her portion immediately, which could be done since her husband hadn't imposed any restrictions on what she did with her shares, everything they'd worked for would be lost—just as it appeared they might survive the year.

Becky had never envisioned herself selling sex toys, but she *had* imagined bringing Butte Plains back to life, and she could see it slowly happening—all because Ford Adams had designed and built a revolutionary sex toy. Since they'd first begun production of the *Safeguard Backdoor Locking System*, they'd tripled the number of people they employed, and many were locals who had been out of work for years. This morning, she'd approved the hiring of a dozen more phone operators. The print shop making the headers and instruction sheets for their product packaging had recently expanded into a larger building and doubled their workforce. Their success was a perfect example of a trickle-down economy in action.

She had to give her partner credit, he didn't mince words with his mother, telling her straight out about the condition he'd found the company in, mentioning that desperate times had called for desperate measures. When she argued the indecency of their products, he argued the indecency of bankruptcy court and seeing his mother move to an apartment complex and flip burgers to pay the rent. Mrs. Adams quieted down after the reality check. Becky's heart hurt for the woman who, other than burying her husband, had never suffered a hardship in her life.

When other women of her generation were out making

their own way in the world, Helen Adams had chosen the path of wife, mother, and social butterfly, relying on her husband to provide for her. If the threat of destitution didn't scare her straight, nothing would do it.

Becky crept to the door to better hear the woman's response.

"But really, Ford. You said it yourself—the company is doing better, so can't we go back to producing decent products?"

"No, we can't." He patiently explained the shift in the market to cheaper imported goods, as well as the decline in demand for the products they'd been making for the last several decades. Then he reminded her of the ways the company had adapted over the last century, pointing out this latest change to be one more of those shifts. "I don't know how much longer I can stay here and do this, Mom. I planned to sell the company from the beginning, but there's no market for a dying industrial plant. To be honest, if Dad hadn't insisted the plant had to operate for a year before I could sell my portion, I would have been gone months ago."

"Why on earth would you want to sell?"

"I think it's the only solution. Scott and I worked hard to get where we are. He's been great about me being here, but I'm neglecting my partnership with him. I need to get back before he loses patience with me."

"Adams Manufacturing is your *legacy*. I can't believe you would consider selling it."

Go, Mom!

"I don't see any other choice. There's nothing for me here."

"I'm nothing?"

"You know that's not what I mean. This town has been dying for ages."

Rustling fabric and the casters on Ford's chair rolling across the rubber mat alerted her to the mother and son standing. Becky hustled back to her desk and ducked her head, pretending to read the report in front of her. A narrow band of pink appeared along the edge of her doorway where his mother had stopped.

"I don't know if I can ever hold my head up in this town again anyway. Maybe I'll go with you when you go back to New York."

"You know you're welcome to come live with me in New York or anywhere else I might go, but this is your home. Your friends are here."

"I can make new friends, but you're the only son I've got."

Becky held her breath as the older woman stormed past her door. She'd had enough experience with parental guilt to make her feel a little sorry for Ford. His mother wouldn't make it easy for him to walk away from what she perceived as his familial obligation. But, unlike Becky, Ford would never cave to his mother's wishes. He'd be out of Butte Plains on the next bus if he found a buyer today.

"You heard?" At the sound of his voice, she glanced up. Shoulder propped against the doorframe, he looked as defeated as he sounded.

"Heard what?"

He snorted. "No need to play innocent, Becky Jean. I know you heard every word."

"Not every word." She had missed a few. Maybe. "I thought you handled it well."

"So well she'll probably end up living with me in my house back East."

"That would be bad?"

He shrugged. "Not bad, but this is her home. She wouldn't know anyone there. She'd be miserable."

"She has a lot to think about. Give her some time to adjust to the way things are."

His lips lifted on one corner. "You're a good person, Becky Jean. My dad knew what he was doing when he hired you."

Becky stared at the empty doorway long after her partner vacated it. She couldn't decide if she adored the man for his kindness to his mother and hated him for his disregard for the company bearing his name, and the town it meant so much to. Every time he talked about going back to his life on the East Coast, a gaping hole opened up in her midsection. His mother would eventually come around, but Ford seemed resolute. He would leave, and Becky would be wise to guard her heart so it didn't go with him.

~~~

Numbers don't lie, but they do tell a story. Of all the things Becky had learned in her economics classes, that one statement stuck in her mind as she looked at the sales reports on her desk. She'd have to speak with Ford about finding a way to increase production of the *Safeguard Backdoor Locking System*. Sales from the initial broadcast had simply floored her, but she'd forgotten about the local network's plans to tape and replay the show throughout the week.

They'd gone live on Wednesday evening. By Saturday, eleven other small markets had called wanting to get in on the action. In other words, they were an overnight success.

Even the astronomical numbers she had before her didn't lessen her anger at the way Ford had manipulated her. Everyone around town called her B.J. these days… then snickered behind their hands. She knew exactly what they were thinking. B.J. stood for blow job. Her humiliation knew no bounds.

Gathering the papers she needed to discuss with her partner, she took a deep breath to steady her nerves. Ford could be incredibly agreeable on some things, but on others… nothing short of dynamite would make him budge. It would be a shame to blow such a nice-looking male specimen to bits, but if it took an explosion….

She knocked on his open door. "Ford? Got a few minutes?"

"For you, B.J.? Always." He tossed his drafting pencil on the desk and rocked back in his chair.

"I've told you not to call me that," she said, plunking into
~~~

one of the old green leather visitors' chairs. She'd thought Ford would want to change everything about his father's office, but so far, he hadn't moved a thing, except to arrange a place to display samples of all their past and present products. He'd said potential buyers would like seeing how the company had evolved over the last hundred or so years.

No doubt their current success would bring a host of interested people to their door. If she sold her share, too, she'd have enough money to start over someplace else. Maybe open a small marketing firm of her own. Not that selling sex toys meant she had the knack for selling anything else, but she had more credibility than she'd ever had before.

"You have to admit, the nickname turned out to be a stroke of genius, Becky Jean. B.J. Parker is a *YouTube* success."

"We're on *YouTube?*" A stab of horror turned her insides to ice.

"Yep. Our first episode has gone viral. I owe you an apology. I never thought this television network idea would work. You're a marketing genius."

"I don't know, Ford. Maybe we should quit while we're ahead." She handed him the latest sales figures. "Sales jumped through the roof this week. I honestly don't know how we're going to meet the demand. And if the same thing happens with the next product we showcase?" She bit her bottom lip as he scanned the reports. "I think we might have bitten off more than we can chew."

Ford tossed the papers on his desk. "Nonsense, Becky Jean. We can handle this."

"Not without adding another shift to the factory. We'd have to hire more workers, including supervisory personnel. Our expenses would increase, too. Longer hours means higher utilities."

"How long would it take to hire and train a second and third shift of workers?"

"*Two* new shifts? Are you crazy?"

"I don't think so, but thousands of people are waiting for their *Safeguard Backdoor Locking System.*" He smirked at the name she'd given his locking butt plug.

"Laugh all you want, but I was right about the name. It adds a level of respectability to the product."

"And it looks good on the new sign out front." He'd insisted on hanging a new sign on the front of the building. *Adams Manufacturing. Home of the Safeguard Backdoor Locking System. Guard your assets with the best.* She'd argued against the assets part, but he'd pulled his majority-shareholder card, and she'd had no choice but to back down.

"I can't even imagine what your father would say if he knew."

"He'd be proud as hell. The Adams family has weathered wars, depressions, recessions, and advances in technology to stay in business this long. We did what we had to do, Becky. He'd be proud of what we've accomplished."

She tried not to read anything into him calling her Becky. From the first day, he'd insisted on calling her Becky Jean or Becks, and then B.J. Never once, until today, had he called her by her preferred name. "He might be proud we found a way to stay in business, but I can't help but think he would have preferred we do it with a more respectable product."

"Careful. You're beginning to sound like my mother."

"She was right, you know?"

"Maybe, but we did what we had to do."

She couldn't argue with his logic. Ford's ridiculous invention had brought the company back from the brink of bankruptcy, and done it in record-breaking time.

"Which brings us back to these orders. We have to fill them. We don't have any choice."

She sighed. She hated admitting he was right. "It's going to cost a fortune to increase production."

He steepled his fingers under his chin and stared at the computer monitor that barely clung to the corner of his desk. Like all the others in the building, the screensaver was a rotating montage of photos depicting the front of the building from various angles. She smiled at the one interior shot of all the employees on the factory floor, smiling and waving at the camera. Already outdated, it would be more so if they added production shifts. Soon they'd need a football field to hold everyone and a drone to hover over to take the photo.

Ford's voice snapped her attention back to their latest problem. "Remember, we make a lot more money off the direct sales orders. The extra cushion will offset a good portion of our investment in running an expanded production schedule."

She nodded and shifted, trying to find a more comfortable position. Would he even notice if she replaced his ancient visitors' chairs with something new? "True, but what happens when we feature another product next week? If we have an equal response, how are we going to meet the demand?"

Ford's gaze bored into her. "I have every confidence in you, Becky. You'll find a way."

The sincerity in his voice washed over her like a warm summer breeze, lifting her spirits and melting her resistance. "I'll ask our new HR person to start calling applicants she has on file. If we can't find enough workers, we'll advertise the positions. In the interim, we can expand the first shift an hour or two. It will cost us in overtime wages, but the increase will be less than the cost of new hires."

His smile warmed her. "I knew you'd find a way. Don't worry about the numbers. The orders are going to keep coming in." He glanced at the latest sales report again. "Have you looked into transforming the original factory building into a home for the *Adult Shopping Show?*"

"I have the plans I'd initially drawn up and a few estimates. The historical society voted to allow most of the interior renovations, provided we don't significantly change the exterior."

"I suppose putting ASS on a sign out front is out of the question."

She sighed at the old argument. "Yes, I'm afraid it is. You'll have to settle for *Adult Shopping Show* on a discreet, street-level sign."

He shrugged off her dismissal of his ridiculous proposal.

"Let's get hopping on those renovations. As I said, your idea is pure genius. It's already exceeded my wildest dreams, and it's only going to get bigger."

That's what she was afraid of. It was time to make some changes. "About the show," she said, placing another stack of papers on his desk. "I think we should find a real spokeswoman to replace me."

He didn't even glance at the headshots the Dallas talent agency had sent over. "Why would we do a fool thing like that? I didn't sell all those units. *We* sold them, Becky Jean. You and me. Look at the comments on *YouTube* if you don't believe me."

"You tricked me into saying those things," she accused.

"Maybe so, but your backhanded endorsement convinced people to buy the product and cemented in their mind that you and I are more than business partners. They want to see more, and they want to hear you endorse the product."

"You expect me to actually try everything we showcase?"

He nodded. "Yep, *and* endorse it. I promised our viewers we wouldn't bring them a product we hadn't personally tried and found to be worthy."

"Don't you mean you promised them *I* would try the products?"

He shrugged. "It's not my fault they assumed we would be trying them out together."

God, if only we were. She squelched the thought. Having those images in her head during a show would render her incapable of speech. "Aren't you even going to look at the models who want the job?"

"It would be a waste of time, and you know it." He dropped the photos in the wastebasket beside his desk. "Which product are we featuring this week?"

"I don't have a clue," she said, rising to leave before she suggested he help her try something out.

"I suggest we go with the *KeyP Me Safe Light.* Increasing production on the tiny flashlights will be fairly easy."

The small personal vibrator that doubled as a key

ring/flashlight hadn't gained the same popularity as the locking butt plug. It could use a marketing push. It amounted to a variation on the flashlight they had been producing with a few add-ons easily outsourced to people in the community to assemble off-site. "I'll come up with a script for the show and get it over to you so you can read it before we go on air."

"Just send me a list of the talking points. We did okay without a script last time."

Easy for him to say. He wasn't the one who'd made a fool of himself, blurting out very personal and private information. "You aren't going to goad me into confessing I've used this thing."

"I won't have to because you *are* going to test it and tell the audience about your experience. If you don't, I'll make something up myself."

She clenched her fists. "You wouldn't!"

"I would, and I will." He picked up his drafting pencil and shuffled papers, searching for whatever he'd been working on when she came in. "Call me this evening if you need help using the *KeyP Me Safe Light*. That's the kind of research I excel at."

She made it to the door before he stopped her. "Oh, and check out the *YouTube* videos. You'll see what I mean."

CHAPTER FOURTEEN

"Is all this really necessary?" Becky eyed the extensive makeup palette spread across her kitchen counter. She should have known better than to ask for Roseanne's help.

"Yes, it is." Her friend rearranged the assortment of paints and creams, most of which Becky couldn't identify. "Amy did a great job on your hair, and the dress we picked out is killer. All you need is a little makeup, and Ford Adams won't know what hit him."

Amy Kilgore, former classmate and present owner of Dippity Do, had done a fantastic job on Becky's hair. The new layered cut made the most of her natural curls while framing her face in the best possible way. Thrilled with the outcome, she'd made an appointment for the following week to have her hair styled before the next show, too. "I don't want to hit him. I just want him to notice me." Becky closed her eyes while Roseanne smeared some kind of lotion stuff on her face.

"Trust me, he's going to notice." She put the cap back on the tube and tossed it aside. From another tube, she squirted a dot of pale liquid onto her fingertip. Brush in hand, she tilted

Becky's head back. "Hold still, will you? We've got to get this done, pour you into your dress, and get you there in time for the show."

"Preaching to the choir." Becky twitched her nose. "That tickles."

"Shut up. Artist at work here."

Aware of the minutes ticking by, she tried to remain calm, but the closer she came to actually carrying out her plan to bring Ford to his knees, the more she doubted she should. "Am I doing the right thing?"

"No doubts, girlfriend. The man deserves to be taken down a peg or two after the way he tricked you on last week's show."

When Roseanne came at her with another brush, Becky closed her eyes again. She didn't know why it bothered her so much if Ford thought her uptight, but it did. And she'd made up her mind to change his opinion.

Becky closed her mouth while her friend drew a line beneath her lower lashes. As soon as her hand lifted, she asked, "What if he doesn't notice?"

"He's gonna notice. He'd have to be dead not to. Take my word for it. Lips open, honey."

Becky parted her lips. While Roseanne worked her magic on them, Becky envisioned Ford's face when he saw her. Maybe, for once, he'd see her as a woman, not just his business partner. What kind of relationship could he have with this Ronnie woman? Ford had been in Butte Plains for half a year, and she'd yet to make an appearance. If she had a guy as gorgeous and great as Ford, no way would she let him wander off on his own for months. Ford had never given Becky reason to believe his affections were up for grabs, but his actions didn't speak of a commitment to his long-distance relationship. Besides, she had no intention of trying to steal Ford. He'd deliberately insulted her. Today's makeover was payback.

"There. All done." Becky grabbed the hand mirror Roseanne held out to her. "What do you think?"

"Oh, wow." The woman staring back at her couldn't be

her.

"Like it?"

Becky turned her head from side to side, admiring the transformation from all angles. "You're a genius, Roseanne. Where did you learn to do this?"

"Lonely hours spent watching *YouTube* videos."

Becky set the mirror aside. "Business has been that bad?"

"My occupancy rate last year was less than 20 percent. Thank goodness I own the house outright. I'm only paying utilities and the small loan I took out to convert the property into a B&B. As long as I do all the cooking and cleaning myself, I can get by with renting the occasional room."

"Then I won't waste any more of my time feeling guilty about the length of time Scott spent here. I'm sure the extra money helped."

"Sure did." Roseanne got busy stashing everything back into the plastic shoebox she'd used as a travel case for today. "Is he coming back?"

Becky didn't miss the wistful tone of her friend's voice. Even though she complained about Scott's overbearing ways, anyone who knew Roseanne well could see she'd fallen hard for the Yankee and had been devastated when he returned to New York. "Maybe. I'll make sure he stays at The Yellow Rose if he does."

"Thanks." She secured the lid on the box. "Let's get you into your dress and on your way. At least one of us should get what she wants."

~~~

Ford tossed the script for the *KeyP Me Safe Light* show in the wastebasket without reading a single word. They'd tried going the scripted route, and it had been a dismal failure. He had no idea if Becky Jean had tried out the product, but he'd find out soon enough. Ever since their conversation earlier in the week, he'd been thinking about how to play it if it became clear she hadn't tried it. He hadn't tried it either, but he knew
~~~

what the tiny little device could do, and he had plenty of experience with similar items. If necessary, he'd point out the unique features of their pocket vibrator then launch into a monologue about how much fun it had been to use it on B.J.

Becky Jean would be sure to turn varied shades of red, which the viewers would incorrectly interpret as embarrassment. They'd sell thousands of units, and no one would be the wiser except him. He'd be watching his back for the foreseeable future, but the sales would be worth sacrificing his safety.

"Hey, Justin," he said, looking around their tiny studio. "I can see our co-host isn't here yet."

"We've got time. She called about an hour ago to say she'd gone home to change clothes for the show. I sure hope she doesn't have any more suits like the one she had on last week."

"I hear you," Ford said as he adjusted his tie. "It worked out though."

"Sure did. A few more weeks like the last one and I can pay off all my student loans."

"That would be nice." He propped his hip against the display table. "I know what you said when we hired you, about this being an opportunity to get in on the ground floor of something with real potential. And honestly? I thought you were nuts."

"If we'd gone on the air last week the way B.— Ms. Parker wanted, we would have been sunk. The woman has vision, but she can't act."

Ford chuckled at the accurate description. "This whole thing was her idea, so yeah, she has vision. I think once she sees the public doesn't want robots selling them sex toys, she'll be onboard with this fly-by-the-seat-of-our-pants style."

"Are you saying you threw out this week's script, too?"

"Yep."

"Thank you, God."

"You're welcome, but just Ford will do." He kept a straight face until Justin caught the joke and burst into laughter. They were both brushing tears from their eyes when the door opened and Becky Jean stepped inside.

No. Not Becky Jean. *B.J. Parker* walked through the door.

Her auburn hair hung in loose curls around her shoulders—the complete opposite of the tight bun she'd worn earlier. Her makeup was heavier than he'd seen her wear, but flawlessly done. Her eyes sparkled, and the shade of red on her lips matched the dress hugging each and every one of her generous curves. His rational mind knew the garment would pass the HR test for work-appropriate clothing, but damn, it had to be the most unconsciously sexy thing he'd ever seen. The clinging red number screamed look but don't touch in a way that made his fingers itch to peel it off her.

Justin's low, appreciative whistle snapped Ford out of his lustful haze.

"Sorry I'm late." She tossed her purse on one of the conference room chairs lining the walls out of camera range. "My hair appointment ran late."

"Damn, B.J.— I mean, Ms. Parker. You look—"

"Perfect," Ford interrupted before the younger man said what both of them were thinking. "You aren't late. We were just talking about the videotaping equipment you ordered."

Justin gave him a puzzled look but took up the conversation. "In addition to taping during the day, we'll be able to do several weeks' worth of shows in a short period of time. As it stands, we only get one shot at doing it right, but once we start advance taping, we can edit out blunders."

Ford joined Becky Jean on their designated spots.

"Jacket on or jacket off?" she asked.

Hell, he hadn't even noticed the dress had a matching jacket. She dropped the short blazer off her shoulders to reveal the sleeveless dress beneath. His brain leapt into action, conjuring up images of all the ways he could assist her in removing the cover-up. "On. Leave it on." *For now.*

"If you say so. I like the dress either way." She shrugged the fabric over her shoulders then pulled her hair free from her collar and smiled at Justin. "I don't think I'll be as nervous when we can edit out mistakes. If I'd known how popular the show would be, I would have purchased the taping equipment in the beginning."

"You've got nothing to worry about, Ms. Parker. A few mistakes make you human, and people relate to flaws."

She laughed. "Well, they must, because we made plenty of mistakes last week. If we stick to the script tonight, it should go better."

"About the script—"

"Did you try the product, Becky Jean?" She didn't need to know he'd decided to ditch another carefully worded script in favor of pushing her buttons on live television. Nothing good could come of it, but good things did happen when she responded to him without artifice. Last week's sales were proof enough.

"No, I did not," she said. "I've used flashlights and key rings before."

He raised an eyebrow at the one function of their product she'd left out. "Have you ever used a vibrator?"

Color bloomed on her cheeks. "I have a massager. Does that count?"

He had no business imagining the things popping into his head. "I suppose it does." *Lord, she's going to be the death of me.* He glanced at the clock—thirty seconds until air-time.

"On your spots," Justin said. "Ford, a little closer to Ms. Parker."

Ford moved closer. She always smelled good, but maybe because she'd been to the salon to get her hair done her scent seemed more tantalizing than ever. Every breath he took made him more aware of the Siren standing next to him. And like every wise sailor, he knew he needed to steer clear.

Justin held up five fingers. "On in five. Four. Three. Two. One." He pointed his index finger at them.

"Good evening, folks. I'm K. Ford Adams, and this is my partner, B.J. Parker. Thanks for tuning in tonight." Ignoring the exasperated vibes coming from his partner, he thanked everyone who placed orders the previous week then mentioned the availability of the *Safeguard Backdoor Locking*

System for those who hadn't yet ordered. After repeating the 800 number, he turned to Becky Jean.

She jumped in on cue. "Tonight, we'd like to introduce you to one of our newest products, the *KeyP Me Safe Light.*"

Ford followed her lead, moving to the display table. He took up the dialogue, describing the tiny vibrator in his own words while B.J. held one of the miniature marvels up for the camera to capture. So far, she'd gone along with his non-scripted version of the show—mostly because she had no choice on live television. Lifting the small device from her palm, he prayed she'd go along with his next idea.

"Ladies and gentlemen, last week we promised we wouldn't show you a product we couldn't personally recommend. And since I have it on good authority B.J. has not tried out the *KeyP Me Safe Light,* I feel obligated to show you, and her, the benefits of this little jewel."

"Oh no!" Becky Jean placed her hand on Ford's chest to hold him at bay. She shook her head. "No. No. No. No. No."

"Just a little demonstration for our audience, B.J." He smiled at the camera then back at her before moving to stand behind her. Placing his hands on her shoulders to keep her from running, he addressed the viewers. "In case you don't know, B.J. is the Marketing Director here at Adams Manufacturing. She works hard at her job, and I often see her at her desk, late in the day, rolling her head, trying to loosen the tight muscles in her neck. Sound familiar to anyone out there? I thought so," he said amiably, hoping to draw the audience, and Becky Jean, in. He'd only guessed she rolled her head to reduce stress, but from the way she turned to glare at him, he'd nailed her behavior.

"Though there are many uses for the *KeyP Me Safe Light,* this is one of my favorites." He held his hand up to show the key ring around his middle finger and the mini-flashlight/vibrator lying along the length of the digit. With a flick of his thumb against the switch embedded in the end, the device hummed to life.

"B.J. seems a little tense right now. Let's see if we can fix you up." Before she could get a protest past her lips, he brushed her soft-as-silk hair over one shoulder and pressed the humming cylinder to her racing pulse. She moaned as he worked the vibrator up and down her slender neck. No words were necessary. The way her body responded to the sensual massage said it all.

Ford crooned soft words in her ear, imagining what it would be like to have her beneath him, to feel her body respond to his in bed. He shouldn't have to share her responses with anyone, let alone the entire world. If this episode proved anything like the first one, millions of people would be witness to Becky Jean's surrender.

No woman had ever turned to putty in his hands the way she did. Knowing they were not alone, he still couldn't bring himself to stop. Slipping his hand lower, his lips followed the path he'd blazed. His hand trailed down the slope of her neck to her shoulder where he pinched her jacket between his thumb and index finger, slowly easing it off her shoulder.

He managed to repeat the process on the other side, but when he eased back to see what he'd done, the sight of her bare upper arms trapped in the confines of her jacket nearly sent him to his knees. Giving himself a mental shake, he removed the jacket. Just her jacket. Nothing more. But there was something about the demure neckline of her sleeveless dress, it made removing the outer garment seem like a sensual act.

He'd been inside his share of clubs where the dancers had no problem removing what little clothing they wore while moving provocatively. None of those shows had ever affected him as much as seeing Becky Jean's bare arms.

Thanking the heavens the viewing audience couldn't see him below the waist, he smoothed the vibrator along the length of her right arm, massaging and caressing every inch of skin. When he reached her hand, he stroked each finger before pressing the digits together. As he dragged the toy from fingertip to palm, her fingers closed over his like tulip petals folding in for the night.

Becky couldn't take her eyes off Ford's hands. One of hers lay in his open palm while he did all manner of wicked things to it with the vibrator attached to the middle finger of his other hand. She should be taking Ford to task for ignoring the script again, but from the moment he'd swept her hair off her neck, she'd forgotten why she should be pissed at him. When he touched his lips to her neck, she'd turned into a puddle of goo and lost the ability to think at all.

Yes, the vibrator hummed over her skin, but she couldn't blame it for her mental shutdown. No, she blamed it entirely on Ford. Sure, the tiny trembles made her skin tingle, but they were overshadowed by the feel of his hand trailing along behind, leaving fire in its wake.

"B.J.?"

She tore her gaze away from her fingers clamped down on Ford's. Dazed, she studied his face for clues.

"What do you think of the *KeyP Me Safe Light*?"

"Huh?"

He smiled so bright it was like looking into the headlamp of an oncoming train. Something in the back of her mind told her to run, but the message got lost somewhere between her brain and her feet. She stood rooted to the spot, staring up at Ford, their hands intertwined, her heart thumping out an erratic beat. He spoke to someone—not her.

"There you are, folks. If that's not a raving endorsement of the product, I don't know what is! Remember, the number is 1-800- BUT-PLUG. Operators are standing by to take your order."

"And, we're out!" At Justin's triumphant shout, Ford yanked his fingers from Becky's grip, severing their connection. She shook her head and a bead of sweat trickled down her temple. The young tech went around shutting off the hot lights. "Tonight was even better than last week. Man, oh man, we're going to make a fortune if this keeps up."

"I think you may be right." Ford held something out to

her. Becky stared at the lump of red fabric for a moment before reaching for it. "Sorry about dropping your jacket on the floor, but I didn't know what else to do with it. Put the dry-cleaning bill on the production expense report. In fact, I think we should add a clothing allowance to the expenses."

Becky jammed her arms into the sleeves and resettled the jacket on her shoulders. She felt shaky and not at all in charge of her faculties. As the lights dimmed, she shivered in the suddenly cool air.

"Are you all right?" Ford took her by the elbow and led her to the nearest chair. She dropped heavily. "You don't look so good."

"Thanks." She glanced up at him. "I'm fine, just got a little overheated, I think."

"When you're ready, I'll drive you home."

She grabbed her purse and stood. "That's not necessary. I can drive."

"You might be right"—he took the purse from her hands, slung the strap over his shoulder then reached for her elbow again—"but why take chances when I have to go past your place anyway?"

"I suppose." She couldn't think when Ford touched her, couldn't muster up the wherewithal to tell him to mind his own business. "We should check in with the phone bank, make sure they have it covered."

"We hired a dozen people this week and installed enough lines to handle the load, plus an elaborate call-holding system. They don't need us distracting them."

She acknowledged the truth in his statement. They'd spent an exorbitant amount of money on the upgrades as well as converted the old supervisor's office on the production floor to accommodate the new order takers.

CHAPTER FIFTEEN

Ford snuck another glance at his passenger. Becky Jean hadn't said a word since they'd left the factory. He'd hoped some fresh air would do her good, but in the glow of the passing streetlights, she appeared as dazed as he felt. He couldn't leave her alone in her present condition. He'd worry himself sick if he did.

She waited for him to open the car door for her—another sure sign she wasn't herself tonight. For a moment, she reached out to take his offered hand, but snatched hers back before their fingers touched.

Ford stood back, allowing her to stand under her own steam. He followed her to her door where she dug in her purse, eventually producing a key attached to a *KeyP Me Safe Light*. He glanced around, but all he could see in the weak light coming from the porch light were a few clay pots with some sort of flowers bubbling out of them. Her hand shook, but with the aid of the flashlight on her keychain she managed to fit the key in the lock. In case she had ideas about leaving him outside, he trailed close behind her, pausing to remove the key from the lock and shut the door.

As she stepped out of those fuck-me pumps that had been driving him insane for the last hour, he reminded himself he'd brought her home in order to care for her, not to take advantage of her.

When she slipped the jacket off her shoulders and tossed it on a nearby chair, he fisted his hands in his pockets and reminded himself he had no business thinking about how soft her skin had been beneath his fingertips.

And when she turned and faced him, eyes dark with arousal, lips parted in invitation, he forgot everything except how much he wanted to kiss the beautiful woman standing before him.

He closed the distance separating them in two strides. Her scent overwhelmed him. Out of necessity, he'd blocked it out on the set, but they were alone here so he opened himself to her every nuance. Her beauty went beyond the physical. There was a wholesome quality about her that made her radiant in a way he'd never seen before. It both intrigued and scared the hell out of him. He'd never been attracted to wholesome. All the women in his life had been worldly and sophisticated— complicated. They played the relationship game on the same terms he did—without any expectations.

Becky Jean had expectation written all over her face.

He planned to leave Butte Plains as soon as he could find a buyer for his and his mother's share of the factory and negotiate a fair price. Becky Jean deserved someone who would stick around. Someone who would give her the fairy tale.

Before he did something they'd both regret in the morning, he took a step back. Becky Jean followed. He lifted his hands, intending to push her away, but moving with purpose, she wrapped her hands around his head and drew his face down to hers. Her lips were warm and pliant, her kiss more experienced than he would have believed. She nipped his lower lip. He gasped and opened for her.

Damn. Her tongue swept in, dueling with his. His blood

turned to molten lava slaughtering cells in his upstairs brain. Thinking with his downstairs brain, he cupped her ass and dragged her hard against him. She was soft in all the right places, and fuck if he didn't want to take everything she offered. Her fingers tickled the pulse at his throat then went to work on the top button of his shirt. The fastener slid free. Cool air brushed his skin bringing sanity with it.

"Whoa." Backing away took every ounce of decency he possessed. There were at least a million reasons not to peel her out of her dress and sink into her warmth. They were business partners. Never mind she was the hottest thing west of the Mississippi. She didn't strike him as a casual sex type of woman. "We have to stop, Becky Jean." He held his hand up— a stop sign between them.

If he'd actually thrown a bucket of ice water on her head, he couldn't have done a better job of breaking the spell between them. Becky Jean blinked a few times then focused her gorgeous blue eyes on him. Another blink washed away the last traces of arousal, replacing the tender emotion with anger. Cold. Hard. Anger.

Ordinarily, he reveled in pushing her buttons, riling her up to see blue flames in her eyes and a rosy blush on her cheeks, but her anger tonight was different. Sharper. Deeper. If looks could kill, he'd be wearing a toe tag.

"Go, Ford." She pointed at the door. "Get out of my house."

"I'm sorry, Becky Jean, but you know as well as I do—"

"That you're a snake oil salesman? Because you are." She pointed at the door again. "Get out. Now."

"Can't we talk—?"

"About the way you seduced me on camera? About the way you touched me? About the way I—"

The way you felt in my arms? The way your skin feels like satin and your hair feels like silk? The way that dress makes me want to tear if off to see your luscious curves? The way I think about you morning, noon, and night? The way I wish to hell we weren't who we are? "About us?"

"There is no *us*, Ford. There's me, and there's you. For a

minute there, I lost my head. Thought *maybe* I was wrong." The vixen who'd all but attacked him had disappeared, replaced by the shy and all-too innocent woman he'd come to admire.

He'd gone too far during the broadcast, let his desire for her show, and they were both going to suffer for his mistake. "I'm sorry." He inched toward the door. "I'm really sorry."

He knew he should be thanking her for throwing him out of her house. She'd done the right thing. He'd done everything she'd accused him of, and more. As he drove up the hill to his temporary home, he cursed himself for a fool. Not once since Becky walked into their makeshift studio, glammed up to the nines, had he given a single thought to the consequences of acting on his desires. He'd allowed his hormones to overrule his common sense, and Becky had suffered for his stupidity. He owed his partner an apology.

<center>~~~</center>

Oh. My. God. Becky fell face-first on her bed. She'd wanted to prove to him she wasn't some backwoods mouse—that she could be sexy and sophisticated like the women he undoubtedly dated on the East Coast. For once, she'd wanted him to look at her with desire in his eyes. The dress, shoes, and makeup she'd let Roseanne talk her into had done the trick. She'd turned the tables on Ford, saw the way he'd looked at her when she entered their makeshift studio. His eyes nearly popped out of his head, but he'd turned the tables right back on her, reducing her to a puddle of goo in front of God-only-knew how many viewers. And she'd fallen for his seduction. Fallen so hard she'd flung herself at the man, even knowing he couldn't offer her more than a romp in the sack.

"He didn't even offer a quick tumble," she reminded herself. She rolled to her back, refusing to shed a tear over Ford Adams. *Face it. He doesn't want you. You're nothing more than his business partner. Maybe his relationship with Ronnie is more serious than I thought.*

He'd been right to push her away. Girlfriend or not, Ford

135

would eventually leave Butte Plains, and she had nowhere else to go. They'd turned the company around, so it was only a matter of time before he started looking for someone to buy him and his mother out. As strange as his relationship with Ronnie seemed to her, he did have a life to go back to, and she had… nothing.

Her 25 percent of the company grew in value every day. Eventually, it would be worth something—at least enough to keep her going until she found something else to do with herself. Because she couldn't see retaining her portion once Ford sold. Potential buyers would probably want the whole thing anyway, which meant in order for Ford to sell, she would have to, as well.

Was it wrong for her to wish he'd stay? The elder Mr. Adams had known the importance of his business to the town and done everything in his power, except ask his son to come home and help to keep the place open. He'd be proud of what Ford had accomplished in so short an amount of time, but he'd also be rolling in his grave if he knew his progeny's plans to sell. She knew in her heart he'd hoped a year would give his son enough time to realize Butte Plains and Adams Manufacturing were home and decide to stay.

She'd known from the beginning falling for her new partner would be a stupid thing to do, and, after tonight, she also knew she'd ignored her own advice. But for a hot minute when he'd been wrapped around her, bombarding her senses with his lips, his sneaky, seductive words, and the damn vibrator he created, she'd let herself believe he felt something for her, too.

Talk about stupid. She set the gold standard for idiocy.

~~~

Becky ducked into the ladies' room for one last check before her interview. Not a hair appeared out of place, but her tidy hairdo did nothing to quell the butterflies in her stomach. In the weeks following the humiliation of throwing herself at
~~~

Ford and being rejected, she'd dedicated herself to her job, building an entire network on the foundation of their flagship program, the *Adult Shopping Show.* Months of work had gone into converting the original building into a home for the new network. The expanded facilities would allow them to branch out to a full schedule of prime-time and weekend shows, each with a different theme. Talks were underway to feature their competitors' products during the less popular time slots.

Thanks to Ford's creative genius, their product line had expanded exponentially. He complained about not being able to design fast enough to keep up with her marketing plans, but they both knew the opposite was true.

Right this minute, he was doing an interview in one of the new studios with *Forbes* Magazine. A reporter from *Cosmopolitan* waited for her in yet another studio. Afterward, she and her partner were going across town to meet a Realtor about purchasing an abandoned warehouse in order to expand production. They were also looking at a few locations near the Interstate to become a new distribution hub. To say they were busting at the seams would be an understatement.

The previous week they'd hired the same architect who had designed the remodel of the old factory to draw up plans for an extension to the current offices so they could get rid of the portable units brought in to house their newest employees. Her marketing team had increased from one—her—to half-a-dozen-plus underlings. The accounting staff outnumbered every other department except factory workers and the direct sales team.

Becky made a mental note to talk to Ford about his ideas regarding the phone order takers. Outsourcing to India would save them money, but hiring a company out of Dallas to pick up the slack would keep jobs in Texas, if not in Butte Plains. He might not care about creating jobs locally, but she did.

"We're ready for you, Ms. Parker."

Becky gave herself a mental shake and followed the intern down the hall.

Ford leaned against the wall outside the door and listened in on Becky Jean's interview. He'd done at least a dozen in the last few months, but this was her first, and to hear her tell it, her last one. She'd only agreed because the magazine's editor insisted their female readership wanted to hear her success story, not his.

A feminist to the core, he'd let Becky Jean believe she'd badgered him into all manner of equal opportunities for women within their company, but he'd fire every man on the payroll if he could replace them with women as intelligent and driven as his partner. His design set them on the right course, but without Becky steering them along the path, they'd probably be no better off than they were the day of his father's funeral.

The woman deserved her day in the limelight.

"Hey. The receptionist said I'd find you here."

Ford smiled and gave Scott a guy hug. "Did you come to drag me back to New York?"

"No, man. You got a good thing going here, and the new guy is working out okay. He's so good I've actually had some time to work on a few projects on my own."

Even though Ford had made a lot of money designing for other people, while working for others, he'd missed letting his imagination run wild. "I hear you, buddy. I never knew how much I missed the creative process until I got to do it full-time. What kind of stuff have you been working on?"

He knew that smile. Scott had always been a big kid, unable to hide his enthusiasm. "You still have an office?"

"Sure do." He didn't know why he was standing out in the hall anyway. Becky Jean didn't need his help. The woman could take care of herself. He waved his hand, signaling Scott to follow. "Come on."

Ford shrugged out of his suit coat. After hanging it on the back of his chair, he removed his tie and popped the top button on his shirt. Feeling as if he could breathe again, he turned his attention to his guest. "Ronnie didn't come with you?"

Scott shook his head. "Sorry. I tried, man, but she's adamant she isn't going to set foot in this *hick* town. Her words, not mine."

He searched his heart for the disappointment he'd become used to, and found resignation instead. He'd heard the insult before and thought the very same thing a time or two himself, but he'd never heard it from Ronnie. She was too diplomatic for that. The woman was a pro at saying something without saying anything. Her unique ability made her a favorite in her social circle. No party could be complete without Veronica Ramsey.

If she thought Butte Plains a hick town, what must she think of him? He plastered a smile on his face. "Makes me wonder what she sees in me."

"It's always been a mystery to me," Scott said with a laugh. "I always thought she had good taste then she took up with you. Shattered my image of my little sister."

His former roommate knew him better than anyone else on the planet, yet he never said a thing when he'd asked Ronnie out. Ford had taken his friend's silence as approval. "Trust me. Your sister is far from being the saint you led me to believe her to be."

"Hey, I never said she was a saint. Personally, I don't know what you see in her. She can be a brat when she wants to be."

Her holdout on coming to Butte Plains being a perfect example. "Tell me about it." He shuffled a stack of financial reports to the side of his desk. "So, what brings you back to Hicksville?"

His friend beamed. "I have something I want to show you."

"Yeah? You been spending company time designing something on your own?"

"Don't tell the boss, but yes, I have." He dug in his pocket. "See what you think."

Ford turned the prototype over, examining it from every possible angle. "This is incredible." He'd never seen anything so lifelike. "How much is it going to cost me?"

"What makes you think I'm willing to sell?"

He put the object back in its box then rocked back in his chair. "You wouldn't have brought it to me if you didn't want to strike an agreement with Adams Manufacturing."

Scott nodded. "You got me there. Never crossed my mind to take it anywhere else."

Ford tried to contain his excitement. Coming to terms with Scott on this project would put them at the top of the heap in the adult toy market. He couldn't afford to let the opportunity get away from him, but he also knew his friend was shrewd enough to know what he had. He'd come to Adams Manufacturing first out of loyalty and friendship, and if Ford had anything to say about it, he'd still have a loyal friend when the negotiations were done.

"There will be a ton of cost to get it into production. The first hurdle will be figuring out how to mass produce it. Then there's packaging and marketing."

"Not telling me anything I don't know."

"It's worth more than I can offer up front. Adams Manufacturing is expanding fast. Lots of cash is coming in, but lots is going out, too. Would you be interested in a percentage agreement?"

"Only if I can personally oversee every step from creating the molds to designing the packaging."

"From New York?"

"From here. The new guy we hired is doing a great job. So good, I can't believe we didn't hire someone years ago." Scott cleared his throat and fidgeted in his seat. If Ford didn't know better, he'd mistake his college roommate's actions for nerves. "I could stay as long as it takes."

He'd seen the reports from the company he co-owned with the man sitting across from him. The kid they'd hired to take up the slack while Ford revived his family's business was some kind of genius, it seemed. He had yet to meet the guy, but Scott, and the bottom line, didn't lie. But he couldn't imagine why the born-and-bred Yankee would want to spend months in Butte Plains, Texas, when he could easily turn the project over to Ford's team and just sit back and collect his profits—of which there would be a shit-ton of once this product became available to the general public.

"Running away from something? Is what's her name getting too close?" He'd lay odds a woman had something to do with his friend's contract condition.

"You mean Solange?"

"Is she the runway model?"

"Yeah, but this has nothing to do with her. A lot of work went into creating this product, and I want to make sure the consumer gets the best possible version of it."

"And you don't trust me to see to it?"

"You know that isn't true. Look around you. You've got your hands full as it is. I have the time and the expertise to spearhead this project. Can you say the same?"

Scott had him there. "I've got the expertise, but you're right about the time. And the plant is running at capacity. As a matter of fact, Becky Jean and I are supposed to go look at some real estate this afternoon. We're thinking of opening another production facility—among other things. Wanna go with us?"

"You bet. I've got to drop my bags off at The Yellow Rose. Pick me up there?"

CHAPTER SIXTEEN

"Boy, am I glad that's over." Becky Jean sank into the same chair Scott had vacated a half hour earlier. "I don't know how you do it."

"Interviews?" He shrugged. "I can't stand them, but the director of marketing and public relations keeps insisting I do them." He smiled, driving home the barb.

"Okay, okay. I get the message, but you're swimming with the big fish now. People want to know who you are, where you came from. It's good for business."

She had a point, but he didn't like speaking about his personal life to strangers any more than she did. "Speaking of business…." Ford pushed a rectangular box toward her. "What do you think of this?"

"Another one of your designs?" Becky reached for the generic container. His groin tightened as a blush crept up her neck to her cheeks—a response he could have predicted. After all this time in the adult toy business, the products they sold still flustered her.

He reined in his libido. "Nope. Scott created it. He's

142

willing to enter into a partnership agreement with us to produce and market it." He leaned forward. "Go ahead. Pick it up. See what you think."

Becky lifted the lifelike toy from its resting place. Seeing her hands on the replica male appendage caused his real one to ache. God, what he wouldn't do to feel her fingers wrapped around his cock. It had been a hell of a long time since a woman had touched him.

"Silicone?"

He forced his attention to the spec sheets Scott had emailed him. "According to the specs, the inner core is a simple rubber compound. The outer layer, or skin, if you will, can be either latex or silicone. The prototype is latex."

"Some people are allergic to latex." Holding the base in one hand, she wrapped her other hand around the shaft and tugged. The outer layer slid over the core, rising up to cover the head then retreating. He swallowed hard, imagining her fingers wrapped around his flesh, moving up and down his shaft. "Feels very lifelike."

Fuck. He did not want to think about how she came to have that knowledge.

"True." He almost wept with relief as she placed the prototype back in the box. "I'm thinking silicone is the way to go."

"How much does he want?"

Her color had returned to normal since they'd moved on to discussing money. Everything would be great if his dick would do the same. "I told him we would discuss it this afternoon. I invited him to go warehouse shopping with us."

She stood and turned. His gaze landed on her perfect ass. It seemed like forever since he'd helped her remove the prototype of the *Safeguard Backdoor Locking System*, yet the images of her sweetly rounded globes remained fixed in his brain, popping up at inappropriate times—like right then. He remained seated as she moved to the door.

"Give me a minute and I'll be ready to go."

He was ready to go right then, but not in the way she

meant. He needed a minute to wrestle his body under control enough to be seen in public. "Take your time."

~~~

Becky locked the bathroom stall door. Wrapping her arms around her middle, her fists clenched tight, she dropped her forehead to the cool metal. *Holy smoke, what the hell?*

It's business. It's not personal. It's a product. *Something to sell. It's what marketing people do.*

No matter how she spun it in her head, she couldn't shake the images her mind created when she'd held the remarkably lifelike dildo in her hands. Granted, her experience with the real thing amounted to one, but if memory served her, Scott's creation was a near-perfect replica of a generously sized penis. Right down to the satin-smooth skin and ridged muscle underneath. It just lacked the ability to ejaculate.

"No. No. NO! Don't go there."

"Ms. Parker? Are you okay?"

Stifling a groan, Becky lifted her head. "I'm fine, Carolyn, but thanks for asking." Straightening the jacket on her red suit-dress, she stepped out and approached the wash basins. "Can you tell Mr. Adams I'll be right out?"

"Sure thing." The young receptionist turned to go then stuck her head back in. "Mr. Ramsey is back."

She pumped soap onto her palm and stuck her hands under the automatic faucet. "So I heard." The crush Carolyn had for the handsome Yankee apparently hadn't abated in the months since she'd last seen him.

"He sure dresses up the place, don't you think?" Before she could answer, the door swung shut behind the infatuated girl.

"If you say so," Becky mumbled, waving her hand in front of the sensor on the paper towel dispenser. Poor Carolyn didn't stand a chance, she feared. She couldn't thank Ford's college friend enough for bringing them the revolutionary new product, but he could have sent the item by courier instead of
~~~

hand delivering it. She suspected the man had his reasons for coming back to Butte Plains, and they had everything to do with her friend Roseanne. The owner of The Yellow Rose B&B refused to talk about the Yankee, which said a lot about the two of them. She'd seen the way they looked at each other when they thought no one would notice. There was something going on between them—she just didn't have a clue what.

Carolyn's misplaced infatuation gave Becky something else to think about besides her growing interest in her business partner.

"Good luck," she said to her reflection. "You're going to need it."

She took a deep breath and opened the door.

~~~

"Sorry to keep you waiting," Scott said, scooting into the backseat of the SUV Ford insisted the company purchase so he could turn in his rental. "I had a few issues to discuss with the innkeeper."

"I'm sure Roseanne will bend over backwards to make your stay as pleasant as possible," Becky said.

"I'm sure she will." He smirked.

Becky turned in her seat to glare at him. "You know, she asked if you were coming back. I got the impression she might be looking forward to your return, but I'm rethinking that."

Scott smiled. "It's good to know she missed me." When Becky opened her mouth to let him have it, he held a hand up to stop her. "Simmer down. Ms. Meadows and I understand each other perfectly. I'm demanding as hell, but I also pay very well. No doubt my fat pocketbook is the reason she wanted me to return."

"You wouldn't be her first demanding customer." She faced forward. "If you're going to be difficult, it's only fair you pay accordingly."

"Believe me, she earns every penny."

Ford stopped at an intersection and looked over his
~~~

shoulder at his friend. Was that disapproval or something else? Before she could question the two of them, Ford accelerated through the intersection. "Where to first?" he asked.

"The first stop is over on Muleshoe. The Realtor said he'd meet us there."

"Wasn't that place a leather goods factory at one time?" Ford asked.

Focusing on their mission, Becky nodded. "I believe so. Mr. Ferguson said he thinks most of the old machinery is still inside, which could be a problem for us."

"Sounds like a great opportunity," Scott said from the backseat.

"To do what?" Becky scanned the printout of the listing. "What on earth would we need for a leather factory?"

"You're already making sex toys. Why not create a line of leather goods for the people using your toys?"

"He has a point, Becky Jean. We could also make our own line of whips, floggers, restraints—you name it." He glanced over his shoulder again with a smile for his friend. "Nice thinkin', buddy."

Becky groaned. "Great. That's just what we need, to take on another project when we can barely handle the ones we're juggling now."

"I didn't say we were going to buy the place. We've got to see it first. If the equipment is there, we'd have to see if we could find some of the former employees, see what would be involved in getting the place up and running again. It would mean more jobs for more people."

Damn. He knew she couldn't resist an opportunity to add more jobs to the local economy. They passed a diner that had reopened last month. From the looks of the vehicles parked outside, business couldn't be better. "McCrae's is open again."

Ford hummed his agreement. "I heard Mrs. Hanson decided to hire a manager so she could retire." A few months ago, they'd instituted lunch time staff meetings on Wednesday's. Ordering stuffed croissants from the local bakery insured attendance more often than not. Knowing the bakery would remain open meant he wouldn't have to come up with something else to lure their employees to the meeting.

"She told me she wanted to spend more time with Bobby's kids since he and Chrissy moved back home."

"He's a top-notch electrician. Did a good job on the wiring for the remodel of the old building."

"He said his father-in-law is so grateful to have his daughter and grandkids back, he's letting Bobby run his new business out of the old Matthew's Electric building free of charge."

"I'm happy for Bobby, but I kind of hoped we could rent or buy his building ourselves. It would be perfect for our new production facility."

"This place sure has changed since the last time I saw it," Scott said as they passed a truck loaded with building supplies unloading in front of another eatery that had closed years ago. "Have you seen all the stuff opening up along the freeway? Amazing."

"Business is booming in Butte Plains." Becky couldn't keep the smile off her face.

"It's good to see," Scott said.

"Did you notice the new hotel going in? Should be done in a few more weeks. Next time you come down, you won't have to stay at the B&B if you don't want to."

"Yeah, I saw their sign. As long as The Yellow Rose has a room for me, I think I'd prefer to stay there. The level of service is excellent. Can't get that at a chain."

"No, you can't," Ford agreed.

Their agent, Sam Ferguson, waited for them when they pulled into the overgrown parking lot of what once had been Butte Leather Goods. Becky sighed. If the parking area reflected the interior, this place needed more than a cosmetic facelift.

An hour later, she climbed back in the passenger seat. As soon as Ford started the engine, she cranked the air conditioner to full blast and adjusted every vent she could reach to blow on her.

"Hey, greedy much?" Ford claimed the center vent closest to his side for himself.

"How do you people stand this heat all summer long?" Scott complained from the backseat.

"You get used to it," Becky said.

"Fuck," he said before he bent his face over the vent blowing air from the center console into the backseat.

"What did you think?" Ford pulled out of the lot right behind the Realtor's land yacht.

As soon as Sam had opened the big bay doors, letting the bright summer light shine where it hadn't in nearly a decade, the two grown men flanking her had become little boys on Christmas morning. She'd seen the awe etched on their faces and known the only discussion would be over how soon they could sign the papers. Nevertheless, she had to try. "It's a disaster, Ford. The place has more rodents in it than machinery, and it has a *ton* of machinery."

"More like ten tons."

Becky shot Scott a death look then turned to Ford. "I get it, I really do. It's a challenge, but it will still be here in a year or two."

Ford shifted his gaze to the rearview mirror. "Maybe if we had a partner. Someone to share the start-up expense and do most of the work? Say… in return for a bigger share of the profits on the new toy?"

"What? Are you insane?" Becky punched Ford's arm.

"Ouch! Why'd you hit me?"

"How much of an investment are you thinking?" Scott asked.

"We put up 70 percent. You put up 30 percent, and we kick you another 2 percent of the profits on the toy in exchange for you running the place. We split the profits the same way, 70/30.

Becky's head spun as the numbers they were talking grew to staggering proportions. They'd gone from zero credit at the bank to an almost-open-ended credit line, but adding a leather factory to their expansion list would test their limit.

"Make it 5 percent on the new toy and you have a deal."

"Five it is." Ford smacked the steering wheel with the heel of his hand in celebration.

"Oh. My. God. You are beyond insane." She glared at Ford's smugly elated face.

"Maybe," Ford said, "but you love me anyway."

Becky turned to gaze out the side window—anything to keep Ford from seeing the truth in her eyes. He'd been joking, but love was no joke. If she allowed herself to think about it, she knew she'd find herself well on her way to being hopelessly in love with the man—so she refused to think about it.

A few minutes later, they parked next to Mr. Ferguson in front of what had once been a vegetable-packing plant. Becky took one last breath of chilled air before sliding her feet to the sweltering, cracked asphalt and followed the men inside. At least someone had kept the place clean and critter-free.

Ford and their new partner in the leather business couldn't have cared less about the warehouse, but it was exactly what Adams Manufacturing needed in regards to size and location. "The price is above market value," she said. "We'll take it for 20 percent less than the asking price if the seller covers closing costs." She cocked an eyebrow at the Realtor who moonlighted as the Mayor of Butte Plains. "And I assume all applicable permits and zoning issues will be forthcoming from the city?"

"Yes, ma'am. I'll see to it." She shook hands with the older man. "The Buford family has been sitting on this for at least ten years. I think they'll jump at the offer."

She dug a business card out of her purse. "Call me as soon as you hear back from them. We'd like to expedite the closing. We've already ordered machinery. We'll need to get our people in here as soon as possible to get started on the infrastructure."

"Not a problem, B.J.— I mean, Ms. Parker."

Ignoring his embarrassing slip, Becky led the way out, waiting by the car door while the men secured the warehouse door. It had been a hell of a day, and it wasn't over yet. She still had to test the toy she and Ford would be endorsing on the show they planned to tape the next day.

She'd managed to effectively test the other toys they'd featured in the last few months. As a single woman, she'd had a passing acquaintance with dildos and vibrators, so similar toys were simple enough for her to test. After the second week when Ford had broken her down on television with a simple, tiny vibrator, she'd learned her lesson and wouldn't admit to testing. If she hadn't tried it, they didn't hawk it on the show. Having her own opinion of the merits of the devices they sold gave her a measure of control since Ford refused to work with a script.

Despite her promise to herself to never ask for Ford's help again, she found herself in a predicament of her own making. She'd thought she had plenty of time to work up the courage to test one of their newer products, but they were scheduled to tape the segment tomorrow, and she'd yet to get up the nerve to test the product. She tensed just thinking about attaching the tiny clamps to her nipples. She'd done her research, even tested them on her pinky finger. She simply couldn't see herself being able to attach them to a more sensitive area. She needed help, and besides Roseanne, who'd claimed to be unavailable tonight, the only person she trusted to help her was the one person she had no business asking.

He'd been the perfect gentleman about the incident with the butt-plug prototype, and she'd appreciated his restraint at the time. Then he'd rejected her after she practically threw herself at him after their second live broadcast. Message received. He didn't want her. Whether his rejection had to do with her or the mysterious and conspicuously absent Ronnie, she didn't know.

Still, she needed his help, so she'd set her feelings for the man aside, suck up her courage, and ask for his assistance with the clamps. She wouldn't throw herself at him again, but if one thing led to another, she wouldn't say no. If that made her a bad person, then so be it.

They dropped Scott off at The Yellow Rose with a promise to discuss their new joint venture the following day. They were nearly back to the office before Becky got up the nerve to say what she'd been rehearsing in her head for the past few days.

"I need you to come to my place tonight. Use the trail from the top of the butte down to my street. I'll let you in the back door."

He'd parked in his reserved spot right next to her car but kept the engine running as he turned to her. "You want me to sneak to your house tonight?"

"Yes." She nodded once. "We've given the town enough to talk about. They don't need to see you on my doorstep after hours."

"And, why, exactly am I going to be on your back doorstep this evening?"

"I need... help. With one of the products we're showcasing tomorrow."

He frowned, and she could practically see him mentally going through tomorrow's taping list. A wide smile split his face. "The nipple clamps."

She nodded again. "I've never.... I don't know.... Hell, Ford, I'm afraid if I get them on, I won't be able to get them off. When I think about it, I imagine myself rolling on the floor in agony and my hands shaking so hard I can't remove the damn things." Nothing but the truth there. The idea of testing the clamps by herself scared her spitless.

"You want me to help?"

"Don't look so damn happy about it. You're the reason I have to test them in the first place, so it's only fair you have to give up your evening to help me." More truth. If he hadn't insisted she endorse every product, she wouldn't be in this mess.

"Why not ask one of your girlfriends? I bet Roseanne would help."

Roseanne had claimed she had other plans for the evening—and she'd made the claim before the nipple clamps were even mentioned. "She's busy tonight."

"Lucky for you, I'm available to assist you." He cut the engine and opened his door. "I'll be there with bells on. Oh, wait! You'll be the one wearing the bells."

The heat flooding her system had nothing to do with the summer sun beating down on her body as she followed Ford to the front door. Images swam through her brain like mirages—enticing yet untouchable. Tonight, they'd be real. Her breasts grew heavy as she imagined Ford's hands on them, his fingers flicking the tiny bells dangling from her nipples. The pain would be bearable because the expression on her partner's face would mirror the pure lust inside her. At least she hoped so.

Ford opened the front door for her. The new chime they'd had installed to announce visitors sounded like a gong to Becky's ears.

"Bells on," Ford said, with a smile.

Becky made an indecent hand gesture only he could see. His laughter followed her down the hall to her office. It was going to be a long afternoon.

His casual comment earlier in the day echoed in her brain. *You love me anyway.*

Yeah, she did. With every passing day, she fell a little bit more in love with her business partner. Intellectually, she knew better, but her heart refused to listen to her brain, and she'd given up trying to make it. Tonight, she'd follow her heart, and if it led her down a road of broken dreams, then she'd patch together what she could and move on. Life was too short to live with regrets.

CHAPTER SEVENTEEN

In an effort to burn off nervous energy, Ford jogged to the base of the butte then back up again—twice—before continuing along the path running behind Becky Jean's house. If running in the late-summer heat didn't kill him, the wait to get his hands on her would. Walking out on her the night she'd kissed him had been the right thing to do, or so he'd believed then, but as time wore on, he'd come to view the move as one of the biggest mistakes of his life.

He didn't know exactly when he'd stopped thinking about Ronnie, but it had happened. In the time he'd been away from her, the distance between them had become more than just miles. Whoever had said absence makes the heart grow fonder clearly didn't know what they were talking about. They rarely spoke these days, and when they did talk, the conversation lacked dimension. She hadn't been sitting at home alone, pining for his return. Her social calendar was as busy, if not busier than ever, and her interest in his day-to-day life had shrunk to zero.

With every passing day, Ford became more certain he

wanted to stay in Butte Plains.

Ever since the night of their second live show, he'd wanted another chance with Becky Jean. He'd gone too far on set, driven her home, and made the monumental mistake of kissing her then walking out when she responded with more ardor than he'd expected. Maybe if he'd apologized the next day…. But he'd never found the words. What could he have said, anyway? *I wanted to fuck you six ways to Sunday but was afraid you'd want to marry me?"*

Just what every woman wanted to hear.

He'd known then she had feelings for him. Becky Jean didn't invite a man to her bed if she didn't feel something for him.

He'd thought at the time it was nothing more than lust on his part, but time had shown him the error of his ways. He'd never met a more amazing woman. She could do anything she set her mind to, and do it well. If he ever made it to her bed, he'd be the luckiest son of a bitch on the planet.

His lungs heaved as he came to a stop on Becky Jean's back porch. He took a moment to remind himself to play it cool, no matter how hot his blood ran for her. Sure, she'd responded to him like crazy on set, but as soon as the on-air light dimmed, so did she. He'd never taken advantage of a woman before, and he wouldn't start with Becky Jean. But… if she gave any indication tonight was about anything other than business, then all bets were off. He'd learned his lesson about pushing her away, and he wouldn't make the mistake again.

She answered the door wearing the shortest shorts he'd ever seen and a sleeveless blouse with buttons down the front. Her auburn hair fell in a waterfall of curls from a band on the crown of her head. She looked fresh and sweet and sexy as hell in a girl-next-door way that made his lips dry and his legs weak.

Shit. I'm in so much trouble.

"Get in here." She grabbed his arm and yanked him inside. "Did anyone see you?"

"What?" He could hardly breathe much less comprehend

her meaning. Being this close to her, knowing she'd invited him there to get closer, messed with both his brains. Seeing her in her innocently sexy outfit awakened every male cell in his body, but it was her touch that destroyed him.

He closed his eyes and pinched the bridge of his nose while he puzzled out what she'd said. "I don't give a rat's ass if anyone saw me."

"Well, I do. You know how people in this town talk."

"Let them talk," he said, advancing on her. It seemed like he'd been waiting forever for this opportunity, and somewhere between reasoning with himself on her back porch and feeling her hand on his arm, he'd come to a conclusion. He'd waited long enough. He had to find out if the chemistry between them was as strong as he thought. Memories of the kiss they'd shared all back at the beginning of summer haunted his dreams.

He'd take full responsibility for the lost time, but he couldn't clamp her nipples and not touch her in other ways. Fuck, if he didn't prepare her properly, she'd never be able to take the pain anyway. Scott had always been more into that sort of thing than Ford, but he knew his way around the toys. Knew there could be nothing pleasurable or erotic about them if the person wearing them wasn't aroused.

For the first time since their fateful night, he let his desire for her show in his eyes.

Becky Jean took a step back. He took a step forward. His blood pounded past his ears on its way south as the expression on his prey's face changed from worried outrage to something infinitely more enticing—lust. She could play it cool all she wanted, but her body betrayed her. Her gorgeous blue eyes darkened to pools of desire, inviting him to swim in their depths.

"Ford."

"You knew what would happen when you asked me to come here tonight." He'd had his moments of doubt, but no longer. She'd thrown the pass with every intention of him catching it.

"We shouldn't do this."

"Maybe not," he conceded, closing the distance between them slowly, giving her ample time to change her mind. She stood statue still until he came close enough to catch her scent in his nostrils. Her signature fresh, clean scent and another more earthy one hit him square in the libido—arousal. "But we're going to do it anyway, aren't we?"

Her gaze met his. Her pink tongue darted out to wet her lips. "Yes," she whispered.

He wedged one foot in between hers then slid an arm around her waist and pulled her softness within an inch of his hard body. Leaning in, he brushed his lips over the shell of her ear. "Want to know what I'm going to do to you?"

She shivered in his arms. "Wha-what are you going to do?"

God, he loved the breathless quality of her voice. Flexing his arm, he tugged her closer. "I'm going to taste you. All over. I'm going to kiss every inch of you, starting right here." He covered her lips with his, stealing her gasp before plunging his tongue in to capture her groan.

She tasted like chocolate and fine wine, sugar and spice. And everything nice he'd ever dreamed of.

He traced her curves with one hand while the other remained on the small of her back, anchoring her to him. When she arched, pressing her breast into his palm, it was all he could do to keep from tossing her over his shoulder and hauling her to the nearest flat surface. She made him caveman crazy with need.

Breaking the kiss, he searched her face for any sign he'd misunderstood her actions. She gazed up at him, eyes dark with passion, her lips swollen and parted. Every labored breath pressed her hard nipple into the flesh of his palm.

"I've wanted you for so long," he whispered against her lips. "I can't wait to taste you." He nibbled along her jaw until he found the throbbing pulse in her neck. Her head fell back, allowing him better access.

Pressing his mouth to the spot, he inhaled deep. Out of self-preservation, he'd taken to holding his breath around her.

Her scent drove him insane. Hell, it drove him up the wall and clawed at his gut every damn day.

Her nails dug into his shoulders. "The clamps."

"We'll get to them, I promise."

Reluctantly, he released her breast and worked on the buttons standing between him and her body. He had to see her, touch her. Now.

"I want to make you as crazy as you make me. I want to hear you beg me to let you come then I want to sink into your heat over and over again until neither one of us can remember who we were before."

She groaned, and he took the sound as permission to continue.

He slid the last button on her blouse free then went to work on her shorts. As soon as the zipper gave way, she wiggled her hips, sending the fabric to the floor. He leaned back to look at her.

Every man had their own personal definition of beauty, had an image in their mind of what it should look like. Gazing at the perfection before him, he realized how inadequate his imagination had been. It wasn't just the two perfectly formed globes encased in ivory lace or the indentation of her waist or the way her hips flared out to create the ideal place for his hands. It wasn't even the soft mound hidden beneath a scrap of fabric. It was all of her—the entire package—the way she championed others, the way she rose to every challenge, the way she used her incredible intellect to make the most of a situation. He'd learned from others how she'd sacrificed her ambitions for her family when her father became sick. Once she had the chance to put her education to use, she used it to help others. Adams Manufacturing had grown like a monster octopus with a dozen legs—not because of greed, but because she wanted to create more jobs for the people in her community. She had single-handedly rebuilt Butte Plains.

"You're beautiful." He'd said the words to women before, but he'd never meant them more. "So damn beautiful."

She ducked her head as if the compliment embarrassed

her. He put his index finger beneath her chin, compelling her to look at him. "Those are just words, Becky. Let me *show* you how beautiful you are."

Her body trembled under his hands, and, for a heartbeat, he thought she'd changed her mind, and this would be all he'd ever have of her. Then her lips curved upward in a quivering smile, and his heart twisted itself up in knots. Afraid to move, he held still while she gathered the hem of his T-shirt and tugged. "Yes to all of it, but I want to see you, too. I've waited too long."

Christ almighty! "Not so fast." He wrapped his fingers around her wrists, stopping her from undressing him. He wanted to feel her skin against his more than he wanted his next breath, wanted to feel her mouth on him, but he also wanted to take his time. She deserved more than the fast fuck on the kitchen counter his dick wanted. "I want this to be good for you, and the only way I can is for you to let me take charge. I'm not a Dom… I don't always have to have my way, but I'm so close to the edge, if you touch me, it's going to be over before it begins."

He could practically see the wheels spinning in her head as she sized up the situation. If she said no, he'd do all he could to see to her pleasure before his, but he didn't like the odds he'd leave them both wishing they'd never gotten naked together. He was about to plead his case again, when she sighed and he knew he had her.

"What do you want me to do?" she asked.

"Nothing. Just feel." He nodded toward the shipping box bearing the Adams Manufacturing logo sitting on her counter. The shows scheduled to tape this week were all about their new line of bondage play gear. He could hope…. "What have you got in there?"

She glanced at the box. Her mouth opened, but no words came out. He almost smiled, but thought better of it. He reached for the box. "Let's take this to the bedroom, shall we?"

She crossed her arms across her middle. "Ford." His name sounded like a warning on her lips.

He tucked the box under his arm and lied through his teeth. "Product research, Becky Jean. That's all."

"You won't do anything I don't want to do?"

"Swear." If he'd learned anything about his business partner in the last few months, it was she wasn't a prude. Shy. Private. But she'd try just about anything once. He'd be surprised if she tried the nipple clamps again after tonight, but who knew?

"Okay then, but I want a safeword."

There was the Becky Jean he knew, practical to the bone. He nodded, anything to get her moving. The sight of her nipples straining against the lace of her bra drove him insane with need. "Choose."

"Pickle. That should do it."

"Pickle it is." She wouldn't need her safeword, but if having a way out gave her comfort, he would go along. "Let's go."

He followed her up the stairs and down the short hallway he remembered from the last time he'd been in her house. Memories of the plug he'd created seated between her sweet ass cheeks had never been far from his mind since the night she'd called him to help her remove it. God, what a night. Dragged from dinner with his mother and aunt by Becky Jean's frantic call, he'd been out of his mind with worry until he got to her house and found out she'd panicked because she couldn't get the key in to release the locking mechanism on the plug. He'd been both amused and proud —of her for trying the thing, and of himself for creating the toy. As monumental as the test had been for the company, the memory of touching her skin eclipsed everything else in his mind. He'd lost sleep thinking about touching her ass again—hell, touching *any* part of her.

After a quick glance at the contents of the box he'd carried upstairs, he set it on her dresser and turned to find Becky Jean standing halfway between him and the antique four-poster bed occupying the center of the room—her arms at her sides as if she dared him to look his fill. He took the challenge, cataloguing every inch of her from her full lips to her toes curled into the braided rug. Fuck, he'd never seen a more beautiful woman. He had to believe she remained single because of the dearth of eligible men in Butte Plains, because who in their right mind wouldn't want her in his bed every night? She belonged to him tonight, a circumstance he planned to take full advantage of.

"Take off the bra." He held his breath while she reached behind her to undo the back clasp. Held it while she extricated her arms from the straps. Held it while the lace garment fell away from her front to reveal the most perfect breasts he'd ever seen. When his lungs began to burn, he exhaled in a rush. "God almighty, Becks. Look at you."

"What?" Her brows drew together, and she looked down at her chest then back up at him. "Ford?"

He couldn't claim to be a virgin, had seen more than his share of breasts, but he'd never, never been this undone. She would be the death of him. He forced his gaze to her eyes. "They're perfect, Becks."

"They're boobs, Ford. Everyone has them."

"Not like those." He couldn't wait to get his hands and lips on them.

"I'm dying here. Are you just going to look, or are you going to put the clamps on?"

The clamps. Mention of the reason he'd been granted this opportunity in the first place brought him out of his trance. "We'll get to those." He motioned with his hand. "Panties. Off." *Me. Caveman. You. Obey.* He was losing it. Fast.

She hooked her thumbs in the waistband, bent, and pushed the tiny scrap of fabric past her hips. As she straightened, she tossed the garment off to the side. He didn't know where—didn't care.

Becky Jean was all woman, from her generous breasts to the flare of her hips to the thatch of red hair at the juncture of her thighs. Blood he desperately needed to deliver oxygen to his brain diverted to his groin, making him glad he'd changed out of his jeans before coming to her house. The jock strap he'd worn had lost the battle with his dick, but he could live with the discomfort.

His heart thundered, trying to keep up with the demand from his libido while ignoring the one organ he needed to remain functioning. He would not fuck up this opportunity by going caveman on her. Which meant he had to rein in his impulses. *Breathe. Come on, Adams, man up.*

He licked his dry lips with his even-drier tongue. He needed a drink, and he knew just where to get one. "On the bed," he said. "We need to try these cuffs out." He spun around to dig in the box for the restraints he'd seen earlier and prayed Becky Jean would do as he said without question. One brush of her hand and he'd explode. In order to do anything for her, he'd need to insure she couldn't touch him.

When he turned back around, he sent up a silent thank you to the gods for looking out for him. Becky Jean lay spread-eagle in the center of the bed—waiting for him to secure her wrists and ankles to the bedposts. He'd never seen a more inviting scene. He tore his gaze away from her torso. *Focus.* With numb fingers, he unbuckled one of the smaller cuffs then fastened it around her right wrist. "Too tight?" he asked, using his index finger to test the fit. These were the best they offered at the moment, a light, durable nylon fabric lined with flannel, it sported a single buckle fastener. He owned heavier wristwatches.

"No," she said, examining the product with her other hand. "I've been wanting to try these on ever since we started carrying them. It's pretty comfortable, actually."

"You'll tell me if anything changes, won't you?"

"Count on it." She lifted her arm over her head, and he fastened the cuff to the short nylon strap he'd looped around the bedpost.

As he worked his way around the bed, fastening her ankles, he tried to focus on the task at hand instead of the treat awaiting him and not the feel of her skin beneath his fingers or the delicate floral scent he'd come to associate with her. And he sure as hell tried to block out the musky tones of her arousal that awakened the primal male in him.

When he'd secured her left wrist and confirmed she experienced no discomfort from the restraints, he finally allowed himself the luxury of looking at her.

"Fuck, Becks."

She wiggled her ass, pulled and tugged at the four-point restraints, testing her limits and obliterating his. He'd never wanted a woman the way he wanted this one.

He pulled his shirt over his head and tossed it across the room. "You're fucking beautiful."

He put one knee on the edge of the mattress. His gaze met hers.

"Ford." She strained toward him. Everything he had hoped to see on her face was there—desire, need. "Please."

Her softly spoken plea grounded him. He had her right where he wanted her, open and trusting. He wouldn't let her down. "I've got you, Becks." He stroked a strand of hair from her cheek, allowed his thumb to linger on her lower lip. "I'm going to make you feel good, I promise."

She closed her eyes and moaned, rocking her hips up—an invitation he had every intention of accepting. But first, he wanted to know everything about her.

CHAPTER EIGHTEEN

Becky's body dipped and rolled with the motion of the mattress as Ford climbed over her, situating himself between her legs. He still had too many clothes on, which seemed completely unfair and, yet, erotic as hell. Bound to the bed, she felt powerless, until he stretched over her and ground his erection against her throbbing mound, and she understood the power she held over him.

"This is what you do to me, Becks. You're so fucking beautiful, inside and out." He flexed his hips, letting her feel the hard steel of his erection beneath his shorts.

Becky shifted, seeking the contact she needed, but groaned when the restraints prevented her from doing so.

"Relax, baby." Ford pressed her into the mattress with his body flush on hers. His hands traveled along her arms until he twined his fingers with hers. His mouth hovered over hers. "I'm going to see to your every need. I promise."

"Ford," she sighed as he peppered her face with tiny kisses that made her toes tingle.

"Becks. My Becks. Say you'll let me love you." He nibbled

at her earlobe.

"Yes, God, yes," she moaned.

At her acquiescence, he crushed her lips with his. She tensed for a second then his tongue demanded entrance, and she opened for him. Slowly, he melted every bone in her body, seduced her with mouth and tongue until his breath became hers and hers, his.

When he broke the kiss, she strained to follow then sagged against the mattress as he forged a path of wet kisses down her neck… then lower.

"Oh God, Ford," she cried as he tongued one nipple then the other. She arched her back, begging him to take more. He obliged, taking a tight bud into his mouth and sucking hard. A bolt of white-hot heat shot straight to her core. She moaned, and if not for the weight of his body and the restraints binding her, she would have rocketed into orbit.

He pulled her breast taut, grazed his teeth over the aching tip then released her with a *pop*. He let out a delighted chuckle, but before she could verbally brain him for his childish behavior, he bent and took her other breast into his mouth. Becky sucked in a tight breath and held it as he gave this nipple the same lavish treatment he'd bestowed on the other. Her lungs burned by the time he let go and chuckled again at the audible release.

"Fuck, Becks. I could do this all night, but we've got toys to test, don't we?"

Huh? Becky struggled to keep up with his train of thought. He leaned over, reaching for something on the bedside table. The ringing of tiny bells jump-started her brain a mere second before he sat back on his knees. The sight of the nipple clamps in his hands sent a cold chill racing across her skin, which only made her nipples tighter.

"I've only used these things once before," he said, testing the tweezer-like jaws on the tip of his finger. His gaze met hers, the heat immediately chasing away her fear. "These are for beginners."

He took her left breast in hand, squeezing and plumping

it. He flicked his thumb over the hardened bud, making her squirm. "They're still going to hurt like hell, Becks, but I promise to make this good for you. Do you trust me?"

She'd never seen the correlation between pleasure and pain. Didn't understand the concept, but she had Ford Adams promising to make her feel good. How could she pass up the opportunity? She nodded. "Do it."

He bent and took her nipple into his mouth again, sucking until she writhed beneath him. Before she could comprehend his intent, he released her, pinched the tip between his thumb and forefinger, stretching her skin. Mid-gasp, the clamp bit into her skin, stealing her breath. Her fingernails dug into her palms, and she burrowed into the mattress, tried to dig a hole with her shoulder blades to escape the excruciating pain. She bit her lip muffling her screams. Tears slid down her cheeks.

Somewhere amidst the pain she recognized Ford's voice. "Breathe, Becks. Breathe." And his hands, stroking her from rib cage to mound, his thumb brushing her clit over and over again. "You're doing good, Becks. So good. Use your safe word if you need to, baby."

His hand kneaded her other breast—preparing it for the same torture, yet she couldn't force the word past her lips to stop him.

His lips closed over her nipple. She whimpered. Her pussy clenched with need. He moved swift and sure, as if he'd done this a thousand times—and maybe he had. She didn't want to think about him making some other woman crazy enough with need to let him do this to her.

Before she could analyze what she recognized as jealousy, he tugged on her nipple. She cried out, arching her back then digging her shoulder blades into the down comforter in an effort to escape. The pain stole her breath and blanked her mind. Her safeword floated to her lips, dying there as Ford stroked her again. Directing the pain, focusing it to a tiny point.

"So good, babe. Fucking beautiful. Ride it, baby. Gonna make you come. I promise."

Her breasts were on fire, yet the real pain seemed to be

between her legs. *Please. Please.* She raised her hips, begging for relief, for release. She never knew need could hurt so much. "Please." She formed the word with her dry lips, but had no idea if sound had accompanied it.

A brush of warm air on her pussy warned of his intent. The first swipe of his tongue along her slit had her straining to get away. Too much. Too painful. Too wonderful.

Then his hands were under her ass, lifting her. He fastened his mouth to her pussy, and she lost it. The orgasm tore her apart, smashed her to bits, and through it all, he rode her pussy, licking, sucking, biting, until she collapsed into a wrecked and sniveling mess.

"Baby. Look at me." Ford's hand on her cheek, wiping away the snot and tears broke through to her. She managed a weak smile for the beautiful blur above her. "Good girl. You're doing fine, Becks."

Her lip trembled as she fought back another round of tears.

"Happy tears?" he asked.

She managed to nod.

"Ready for another O?"

Is he crazy? She'd never been a multiple-orgasm person anyway, and after the one she'd just had? He could try, but success seemed impossible. She shook her head. Ford laughed and stroked her face again.

"Hang on, babe." As he adjusted her hips, sliding them up onto his thighs, three things registered in her endorphin-drugged brain. He'd released her ankles, he had removed his clothes, and stretched one of their new road hazard red *Safe Sheaths* over his cock. How long had she been out of it?

Something big and hard pressed against her entrance. "Perfect," he said. "I'm sorry, Becks. They say they hurt worse coming off than they do going on."

She struggled to make sense of his words, had only begun to decipher the code imbedded in them when he reached for the clamps. At his touch, pain ricocheted through her then the insistent pressure on her nipples disappeared. Her brain registered relief for a nanosecond before blood rushed into deprived tissues, the blinding pain levitating her off the bed. In the same instant, Ford entered her. The stretch and burn of his possession, magnified by the sensation in her nipples, pushed her over the edge into another orgasm, taking what remained of her, flinging it out to the universe.

She cried out and gripped the nylon bands around the bedposts, anchoring the top half of her body while Ford held her thighs in his strong arms, holding her open for his thrusts. As she came down from the highest high ever, she opened her eyes. She'd never seen anything as beautiful as Ford with his head thrown back, his jaw clenched in ecstasy. The muscles in his arms and chest, coated in a sheen of sweat, flexed as he pounded in to her, seeking his own release. His big cock stretched her tight, but her body adapted, took every inch of him, so when he became impossibly bigger, she noticed. Seconds later, he ground his hips against her like he was trying to dig a tunnel to her heart. A curse exploded from his lips at the same moment his shaft pulsed inside her. She welcomed his weight as he collapsed on top of her like a broken construction crane.

"Fuck, Becks. I think you killed me."

~~~

The first rays of sunlight peeked through the blinds when Becky slipped out from under the heavy arm pinning her to the mattress. Ford slept the same way he lived his life—with everything he had. She lay on her side, taking in his relaxed form. She'd spent most of the night learning every detail of his body, down to the small scar on his shin, the result of a bicycle accident when he'd been ten, he'd said. He'd returned the favor, slowly cruising up and down her body, more than once. Her nipples were still sore from the clamps, and probably would be for a while. The pain had been unbearable until he'd distracted her in the most amazing way possible. Her nipples were uber-sensitive and every touch to them telegraphed need
~~~

to a spot between her legs. She smiled, knowing she'd carry the reminder of their night together with her for some time.

Ford snored, then rolled to his back. The strip of handmade Irish lace edging on the top sheet pulled up to his abdomen emphasized his raw masculinity in a way she decided he wouldn't appreciate, but she sure did.

Before she gave into the temptation to wake him and beg for a repeat of last night, she slipped out of bed. Wrapped in her old terrycloth robe, she took care of her morning needs then headed to the kitchen.

Her shirt and shorts lying on the kitchen floor brought a blush to her cheeks. God, she could still feel the solid weight of him pressing her into the mattress. He'd ignited a fire inside her that had both consumed and transformed her. He'd set the bar so high no other lover would ever come close to matching him. Maybe once the memory of his touch had dimmed she might be interested in another, but she couldn't see far enough into the future. Maybe then she'd look for someone she could spend her life with. Someone who shared her love of home and family, someone who wanted to put down roots. Someone who would love her as much as she loved… Ford.

A sharp pain in the region of her heart made her gasp. She clutched the edge of the counter to steady herself. *Shit.* She'd gone and fallen in love with the man. There was no maybe about it, and ignoring her feelings wouldn't make them go away.

How could you? He's not your forever man. She'd known the truth from the start, but when he'd accused her of knowing what would happen when she invited him over to help her with the clamps, she couldn't deny it. Somewhere in the back of her mind, she'd known, or at least hoped.

The clothes she'd been wearing when he arrived were right where she'd left them on the kitchen floor—a sure sign she'd lost her mind. She picked them up and folded them into a neat stack on the corner of the counter.

Destined to get her stupid heart broken, she had no one to blame but herself.

As she started the coffee, she considered her options, quickly deciding she had none. She mentally steeled herself for what she had to do.

She needed to get Ford out of her house, and fast. If he didn't want to take the trail back to his house, she'd have to find a way to sneak him out to her car for the ride up the hill. The rumors about her and Ford's father were without foundation and had evaporated as untruths tended to do, but if someone saw Ford leaving her house in the wee hours of the morning, the news would burn up the Butte Plains grapevine before the diner switched the breakfast menus for the lunch specials. Not only would her mother be embarrassed, she'd get ideas in her head about rose-covered arbors and wedding vows. Last night had one-night stand written all over it.

"So, this is where you are."

At the sound of his gravely, morning voice, Becky turned from mindlessly staring at the stream of black liquid trickling from the coffee maker. Ford stood in the doorway with her grandmother's lace-trimmed sheet wrapped low on his hips. She had an insane urge to run her palms over the scruff darkening his jaw. Lord, if their customers could see him this morning…. "Huh?" *Smooth. Get a grip.*

"I woke up to an empty bed." He crossed to the coffee pot, opened a couple of cabinets until he found a mug. The brewer conveniently chose that moment to spew the last drop into the carafe. He filled a cup for her, then one for himself. He leaned against the counter and eyed her over the rim of the cup. "You aren't regretting last night, are you?"

How the hell did he expect her to think with so much of his skin showing? "Uh. No." She shook her head in answer to his question and in an effort to jolt her brain into functioning. "Not at all. I was just thinking."

He took a sip of his coffee, smiling as he lowered the mug. "About?"

She shrugged. "About how to get you out of here without anyone seeing you leave."

"I see." He set the cup on the counter and started opening

cabinets again. His back proved as magnificent as his front. The play of muscles as he went from one cupboard to the next made her mouth water and her fingers itch to touch. "Do you have anything to eat? Cereal or something?"

He looked over his shoulder. She pointed to the left.

"Pantry. I should have milk in the fridge, but I'd give it the sniff test first." She couldn't remember the last time she'd been to the grocery store.

Her guest slapped two bowls of dry cereal on the table, sniffed the milk before pouring. He unceremoniously tossed her a spoon before digging into his breakfast as if he'd been denied food for a week. Skeptical of the expiration dates on both ingredients, Becky toyed with hers until her companion came up for air.

"'s good," he said, nodding at her bowl. "You should eat."

She stirred the soggy flakes. "I'm not much of a breakfast person." *But I could eat you.* She forced the wayward thought away before she gave into temptation and the thought a reality.

He glanced at her. "It's the most important meal of the day." He took another bite then shook more dry flakes into his bowl. "Besides, you're going to need your strength."

"For?"

He waggled his eyebrows. His wicked smile told her exactly what he had in mind.

"No." She held up a staying hand. As much as she wanted to strip her grandmother's sheet off his body and take him up on the offer of more mattress calisthenics, she couldn't think of a worse idea. Her heart would never survive another round with him. Plus, they had a business to run. "We've got to be in early today, remember?"

His expressive brows knitted in confusion as he puzzled out her comment. "Oh, yeah. We're signing papers on the new property today."

"And taping three shows."

"That, too."

Ford scooped the last flakes out of his bowl, downed them then rose to take the dish to the sink. "I'd rather stay in bed with you. I enjoyed last night."

"About last night… I sort of forced myself on you. I'm sorry."

"You didn't force anything on me. If anyone's to blame, it's me." He leaned on the counter, his ankles and arms crossed. He could be intimidating, even wearing nothing but a sheet. "You needed help testing one of our products. Actually, we managed to test several of them, if memory serves. I'm always available to help with testing, research, or whatever you need." The matter-of-fact way he offered his services reminded her last night had been nothing more than sex for her partner.

She squared her shoulders, causing her bathrobe to drag across her sore nipples. Stifling a gasp, she dug deep for the strength to resist his offer. "I'll keep your generous offer in mind. In the meantime, you should leave before the neighbors see you."

Ford held his ground for the longest then casually straightened. "We aren't through, Becky Jean." He headed toward the bedroom.

She needed to be careful and not read too much into his words. Last night had been fun, but Ford didn't belong to her, no matter how much she wished differently. They'd made a mistake, taking their relationship outside the realm of strictly business, and no amount of chalking it up to product research would make it right. A shiver danced along her spine. Morning-after regrets were a bitch.

~~~

Out of breath from his mad dash home, Ford slammed the back door of the gatehouse. He snatched a water bottle from the fridge, downed it in one long pull then braced his hands on the counter, willing the cold liquid to douse the fire burning in his gut.

He'd come within an inch of dragging Becky Jean back to bed and keeping her there for the rest of the day. He'd had a lot of sex, but last night had been off-the-charts hot, the best
~~~

ever.

He could still hear those little gasps she made every time he filled her. And he'd never forget the breathless way she said his name when she came. Hell, no woman had ever given him as much as she had, not even Ronnie. Especially not Ronnie.

Shit. Ronnie. Their relationship had been dead for months, but they'd never acknowledged as much. Hell, how could they when they rarely spoke? He made a mental note to talk to her soon, make it clear they were through.

Popping a pod into the coffee maker, he rinsed the mug he'd used the previous morning and placed it under the spout in time to catch the first drip. While the beverage brewed, he recalled every minute in Becky Jean's kitchen.

He'd been distracted by the thin V of skin showing between the lapels of her robe she'd put on when she got out of bed. The sight of her mussed hair had taken him back to the night before when her hair had spilled across the white pillow case and tangled with the lace edging.

He blew on the steaming cup of coffee then took a sip while he fished a protein bar out of the open box on the counter. He couldn't imagine not holding Becky Jean again, not sinking into her welcoming heat, losing himself in her incredible blue eyes. She was the most caring, genuine person he knew, and she deserved better than him.

He arrived at the plant to find Becky Jean already hard at work, looking sexy as hell in another of those suits capable of inciting a riot. "Good morning, Mr. Adams," she said. "Taping begins at ten this morning in the new studio. I've put a new proposal on your desk. I'd appreciate a response no later than the close of business today."

Damn. Seeing her in her prim-and-proper business-woman mode turned him on. Memories of just how un-businesslike she had been in bed the night before were gasoline on a bonfire he had no chance of putting out. He'd have to be careful, or he'd be consumed by the conflagration. He returned her polite smile with one of his own. If she wanted to pretend she hadn't begged him to do wicked things to her last night, he'd let her. For now. "Good morning to you, too, Ms. Parker. I'll read over your proposal, but I'm certain whatever you have in mind is in the best interest of Adams Manufacturing." He stepped into the hall then leaned back into her doorway. "See you at the taping."

The proposal met his every expectation. While increasing payroll, adding more shows featuring products from other manufacturers would add to their bottom line without stretching their capital reserves the way the new facilities they'd committed to would. Becky Jean had been wasting her time as an office manager. The woman had a head for business like no other he'd ever seen—which turned him on like crazy. The way she said *spreadsheet* got a physical reaction from him every damn time.

CHAPTER NINETEEN

Becky waved Amy away. "That's fine," she said, examining her hair and makeup in the mirror. She could do her own makeup, but they could afford to hire someone to come in on taping day, and the extra money her former classmate earned allowed her to hire a part-time person in her salon. "I think I'm done. Why don't you see if Ford needs anything?"

Amy met her gaze in the mirror. With an understanding look, she patted her on the shoulder. "I don't know how you do it."

"Do what?"

"Go on television with Ford week after week to sell sex toys and not jump his bones. It must take nerves of steel."

Becky turned and made a beeline for the rack of dresses the owner of the new downtown boutique had sent over for her. Three hung facing out for today's tapings. "Ford and I are business partners." She fingered the multi-colored silk she planned to wear during the nipple-clamp show. When she'd tried it on, the fabric had skimmed her curves in a gentle caress reminding her of the way Ford had touched her face, soothing away the pain and stealing another piece of her heart.

"I'm just sayin', you two are H.O.T. on screen together. It's no surprise your toys are selling like hotcakes."

"Sex sells." Becky fell back on her standard answer.

"Remember, the blue dress first then the pink block print. The watercolor silk is last," she said. "No one would blame you if you hooked up with him. You know that, don't you?"

No. She didn't know any such thing. She'd been on the wrong side of the grapevine before, and she didn't want to be there again. "This is business," she repeated. Maybe if she said it enough times, she'd begin to believe it herself.

"Whatever you say, girlfriend." She opened the dressing room door. "I'll check on Ford, then take a break. Text me when you're done with the first show. The pink is going to require a few changes in your makeup to keep you from looking like a clown."

Becky waited until she heard the door close behind her friend before she allowed her knees to buckle. Business her ass. She was ass-over-teacups in love with Ford Adams and up to her ass in trouble. If the chemistry between them before convinced people to buy their products, what would happen now? In the past, she'd only imagined Ford helping her test the products she endorsed on each show. Last night, they had tested all three of today's featured products—together, and thoroughly. Putting her experience into words, sharing it with the viewing audience? She shook her head. She couldn't pull it off. Everyone would know she'd slept with the man.

She yanked the blue dress off its hanger. A sedate sheath, it combined business appropriate with understated sex appeal. From the assortment of costume jewelry, courtesy of yet another shop recently opened in town, Becky chose a string of chunky pearls and a matching bracelet. To complete the look, she slipped on a pair of nude-tone heels provided by the new shoe store. All would be listed in the closing credits in return for their generous donation. Afterward, everything she wore would be sent to a charity in the county seat set up to help abused women escape their circumstances and find jobs to support their families. Adams Manufacturing had hired several from the program and hoped to hire more.

No matter what she had going on in her personal life, the business she and Ford were building was making a difference. Butte Plains had grown. Closed-up shops were reopening as new enterprises. People were moving in, not out, for a change. Ford hadn't mentioned selling or moving in months, but had he noticed the changes in his hometown? He seemed to spend all his time in his office or at home. Even when his friend Scott visited, they rarely hung out together.

A knock sounded on her door. Becky took one last look in the mirror then turned to answer. Ford leaned against the doorjamb, looking like he'd stepped off the pages of *GQ*. His smile was as wicked as ever, but a new, darker flame burned in his eyes as he raked his gaze over her from head to toe. "Lordy, you could make a flour sack look sexy, Becky Jean."

She couldn't help but laugh at his exaggerated southern accent and pseudo compliment. She stepped out, shutting the door behind her. "I'll take your hillbilly remark as a compliment and ignore the fact you just called a very expensive dress a flour sack."

"I did no such thing," he protested, following her down the hall to their new studio. "The dress is gorgeous, but no one could wear it the way you do."

She stopped in front of the studio door and turned. She put her hand up to keep him from bowling her over and it landed on his chest. Before she could move it, he trapped it with one of his own. "Last night was special, Becks."

She tugged on her hand, but he wouldn't let go. "I'm not saying different, but we can't do it again. We shouldn't have done it in the first place."

"Maybe not," he conceded. "But we can't undo what's done, and I don't want to pretend it didn't happen."

"Don't pretend, Ford. Forget. It's what I'm going to do."

She pushed down on the door handle, leaned hard against her shoulder, and the heavy, soundproof door moved inward. With a fake smile plastered to her face, she greeted their recently hired crew.

Well, shit. Ford let the door swing closed in front of him. He'd hoped Becky Jean would have had a change of heart since she'd heaved him out her back door without so much as a good-bye kiss, but clearly, she hadn't. She seemed determined to act as if nothing had changed between them, when he knew different. Everything had changed.

He straightened his tie and shot his cuffs. She thought she could shut him out? The woman had another think coming.

"Let's get this show on the road," he said, entering seconds behind his co-host who began to rearrange the products on the display. Justin gave him a thumbs-up as Ford took his place on set. The young man had risen to the challenge of expanding from one live show to taping multiple shows in one day. He played an integral part in their rapidly growing television network, too. They'd be lost without him as neither he nor Becky Jean knew much about the broadcasting world.

"Ready when you are." Justin looked up from his clipboard. "I'd like to get done early today, if we can, so let's try to do these in one take, if we can."

"Not a problem." By ditching the live broadcasts, they'd gained the ability to edit the shows, which could be a good thing, but not when it came to Becky Jean's candid responses to the things he said and did to provoke her on set. The less retakes today meant less opportunities for her to edit out what he knew would sell the product. "It'll be like the good 'ole days when we were live."

Becky Jean glared at him as she took her spot beside him. "Don't you dare," she hissed at him.

Ford arched one eyebrow and grinned at her warning. Today's shows were going to be the best yet. Now that he knew her body intimately, he had every intention of using his knowledge to arouse and fluster her to the point everyone watching would want what she was getting. Which meant sales would go through the roof.

Justin held his hand up, fingers spread to tick off the seconds. "We're rolling in five, four, three, two, one."

"Good evening, folks. I'm K. Ford Adams and this is B.J. Parker."

Becky smoothed the multi-colored silk over her hips, refusing to look in the mirror again. Why hadn't Amy returned with the nipple cover-up patches she'd sent her for? No one would see Becky's soaked panties, but *everyone* would notice her headlights were on.

She absolutely hated her inability to control her physical responses to Ford's touch, and Lord, did he know just how and where to touch her. Thanks to the night they'd spent together, he knew every erogenous zone on her body, and he'd proved in the first two shows he wasn't above using his knowledge to embarrass her. Justin had even stopped taping in the middle of the second show to adjust the lighting to account for the color in her cheeks. She doubted there were enough filters in the world to counteract the shade of red she would turn when she had to endorse the nipple clamps Ford had used on her.

Damn, they'd hurt, but he'd distracted her through the worst of it then used the pain to give her the hardest orgasm of her life.

She'd run the experience over and over in her mind, searching for the words to convince their viewers to give the tiny little torture devices a try, and come up empty.

Ford won't have any problem coming up with the words. He never did. Fans of the show ate up his sexy-as-hell confidence. The more he made her stammer and sputter, the more products they sold. Parts of their shows were viral sensations, shared over and over again on social media with comments about his hotness and how lucky she was to be his co-host.

Someone tapped on her dressing room door. "We're ready for you, Ms. Parker." She recognized the voice of the young woman they'd recently hired to assist Justin.

"I'll be right out, Kiley." Becky forced herself to take one last look in the mirror. She made a mental note to order a lifetime supply of the little nipple concealing patches as soon as possible, but for the time being she'd have to pretend her nipples weren't standing up like traffic cones.

All eyes turned on her the second she walked through the door to the set. Holding her head high, she took her place beside Ford then nodded to Justin. "Ready as I'll ever be," she said.

"Good evening, I'm K. Ford Adams, and this is B.J. Parker." Ford launched into the familiar intro on the director's signal. "Last time we introduced you to the *Safety First Restraint System*, designed to allow you complete access to your partner's body while keeping them safe and secure. As you've heard us say on every show, our products are meant for you to enjoy in the context of a SSC relationship—Safe, Sane, and Consensual.

"Still, you have to be a little bit crazy to want to try the items we have for you tonight, isn't that right, B.J.?"

The way his voice dropped when he called her by her on-air nickname reminded her of the way he said her name when he had his hands on her, stroking her to climax. Her cheeks heated and her sex throbbed. "Yes, you do, Ford, but if used responsibly, *the Safe and Snug Nipple Clamps* will provide you with an experience like no other."

Ford splayed his hand on the small of her back, guiding her to stand behind the display table. "You sound as if you speak from experience, B.J. Tell me, have you tried the *Safe and Snug Nipple Clamps?*"

She could do this. She swept her hand over the display, praying the cameras would follow the movement and zoom in on the product while she spoke instead of her flaming face. "Yes, Ford, I have tried them."

He picked up a set identical to the ones he'd used on her the night before and held them in his palm for a close-up. They looked tiny in his hands, but when they'd bit into her nipples, she'd thought a merciless giant had a hold of her. Realizing her real thoughts were *not* a selling point, at least not to her, she decided to keep her mouth shut. Let him sell the damn things.

"They look so delicate," he said, flicking the tiny bells hanging from them. "I'm sure the viewers would like to know more." Ford replaced one of the clamps on its display card then held the other between his thumb and forefinger, squeezing to make the jaws open much like he'd done before placing the first clamp on her breast the night before.

Becky's heart raced, and her knees trembled in tandem with her lower lip. Remembering the searing pain she'd experienced, she barely contained the squeak forming in her throat. "I imagine these would hurt like the devil," he said, his voice dropping lower and taking on a darkly sensual tone that had her clenching her thighs together. She tore her gaze away from his hand, then wished she hadn't. The carnal hunger she saw in his eyes robbed her of speech.

"I didn't know you were into pain, B.J."

"What?" She gave him a questioning look and shook her head. "No. I'm not."

He pinched the tip of his little finger with the clamp, grimacing under the pain. "Ouch! You put these on your nipples?" He removed the toy and gave his hand a dramatic shake.

"Well… I didn't… I mean—"

"Ahh, I understand. You didn't do it yourself, someone helped you." His wicked grin told everyone what they'd done.

Embarrassment ratcheted her body temperature up to flaming. No light filter in the world could compensate for the color in her cheeks.

"Yes," she said, fixated again on the clamp he snapped open and closed.

"I suppose it would make a difference, having someone there to take your mind off the hurt." He clamped his little finger then traced the digit down the length of her arm, leaving a wake of gooseflesh behind. "Did he take your mind off your nipples, B.J.?"

"Yes."

"And did the pain go away?"

She shook her head. "No."

"No?" he asked, feigning surprise at her answer. He'd been there, knew the pain had never gone away, just changed.

"It didn't go away… just became different… less pain and more an ache I felt everywhere."

"Everywhere?" No one with hearing would mistake his one word question, not with the way his gaze dipped low.

She wanted him more than she wanted her next breath. Her nipples were hard as diamonds and probably casting their own shadows under the harsh studio lighting. She grasped his wrist before he could draw another line down her arm with his torturous toy. It was time to turn the tables on K. Ford Adams before he reduced her to a puddle of hormonal goo in front of the world. She brought his hand up between them and removed the clamp. She licked her dry lips first—a warning— then flicked her tongue over his aching pinky—a reminder, she hoped, of the way he'd prepared her nipples before clamping them. "Yes, *everywhere*, Ford. I wish I could explain the feeling better, but any woman who's been distracted by her lover will understand the concept of heightened awareness. You feel as if you're walking a high wire—all your senses are engaged. You're tuned in to every cell in your body. Tense with expectation."

She dropped the clamp to the display table and selected a larger version. She licked his finger one more time then, gaze locked on his, affixed the clamp to it. His nostrils flared and his eyes grew dark. As subtly as possible, she shifted so her stomach brushed his erection below the display table.

"Then you're taken out of your world into another one where there is only you and your lover and the exquisite pain of need." She held his hand between both of hers, stroking her thumb over his palm while she spoke. "You know the feeling, don't you, Ford?"

She knew the look on his face. She'd seen it last night, right before he came. Since she couldn't very well have him coming on set, she lowered her eyes, breaking the invisible connection between them. She turned to the camera. "Any words I could use to describe the sensation of wearing the clamps would pale in comparison to the actual experience. I will say this, wearing them is only half the fun. The other half happens when you take them off." As the words left her mouth, she removed the clamp on Ford's finger. He let out a yelp and tried to yank his hand from her grasp. She held on, massaging his pinky and palm while he dealt with the pain of blood rushing back into the tip of his finger.

She faced the camera with a smile. "The *Safe and Snug Nipple Clamps* are best used with *Safety First Restraint System.* Remember, Safe, Sane, and Consensual."

She smiled until Justin yelled, "Cut," then she dropped Ford's hand and stormed off set.

PART THREE

It is a truth universally acknowledged, that a man in possession of a good fortune, must be in want of a wife.
Jane Austen

CHAPTER TWENTY

"She's killing me." Ford hunched over his scotch on the rocks. His best friend since college, Scott, occupied the barstool next to him.

"We aren't talking about my sister, are we? 'Cause if we are, I'm out of here."

Ford shook his head. "No. Ronnie and I are done." Though he hadn't spoken with her as he'd planned, he believed their relationship had died a natural death. Her lack of pleading with him to come back to take her to any of her society functions proved she'd moved on. "Haven't talked in weeks."

"Can't say I'm sorry or surprised. Never did think you two were suited." Scott finished off his drink and signaled the bartender for a refill.

"Really? Why didn't you say something?" Once, he'd thought he and Ronnie were very well suited. Just went to prove what he knew about relationships. They'd used each other, nothing more.

Scott shrugged then thanked the bartender for the refill she placed in front of him. The woman looked barely legal to work behind the bar, and gorgeous in a way only Texas women could be with her ample cleavage showing, a mane of chestnut hair made for wrapping around a man's fist. Her smile said she'd give you a ride if you were interested. She didn't interest him, but he admitted to being surprised when Scott ignored her, too. He waved the girl away, indicating he didn't want a refill or anything else she might be offering. He'd forgotten their conversation until Scott spoke. "Your relationship wasn't any of my business. Can't say I liked the idea of you with my sister, but she's a grown woman. If she wanted to make a mistake with you, I couldn't stop her, and likewise, I might add." He downed half his drink in one gulp and signaled for another.

Ford finished his drink and signaled for the check.

"So, if it isn't my sister who's killing you, it must be your partner."

Maybe he'd been too hasty in requesting the check. He pushed the paper back to the bartender. "Another round," he said, wagging a finger at both their glasses. Silence reigned until two new glasses sat in front of them. "What makes you say so?"

Scott snorted. "Seriously? Don't you watch your own show? I keep watching 'cause I don't want to miss the explosion when it finally happens. The chemistry between you two is off the charts."

He knew it was, and if the sales figures were any indication, the viewing public knew it, too. He just wished he knew what to do about it. "Wait until you see the shows we taped for next month." *Especially the last one.* She'd spun the tables on him, had him panting and ready to blow in his pants. He'd asked Justin to let him see the final edit, but the bastard refused. He'd suggested they add more phone lines then mumbled something about being a millionaire as he walked away.

Ford stroked his pinky finger through the condensation on the outside of his glass. An image of Becky Jean's tongue licking the hurt away came to mind. He shifted on his stool, making room for his instant wood. Anything would bring the images to mind these days, and every damn time, the results were the same. There would be an explosion alright. It just wasn't the kind Scott had in mind.

"I can't wait. Watching the two of you is better than watching porn."

Ford had nothing to say to his friend's comment. He'd rather watch Becky Jean than porn any day.

"So, have you slept with her yet?"

He'd never told Scott he was sleeping with Ronnie. The man had correctly assumed it at some point, and they'd never really talked about it until today. If he hadn't felt the need to tell his buddy he'd slept with the man's sister, he sure didn't feel the need to tell him the details about his relationship with Becky Jean. "None of your business."

"I'll take your response as a yes," his friend said. "But I don't see what the problem is, unless it was one and done on her part."

Ford stared at his mostly empty tumbler.

"That's it, isn't it? You were her one-night stand?" Laughing like a loon, Scott slapped the bar. Ford could feel the gazes of everyone in the place on them.

"Shut the fuck up, man. This isn't funny."

"The hell it isn't. Fuck-and-run Ford Adams has been caught! I bet you can't even count the number of one-night stands you've had, but all of them were on your terms. My sister lasted longer than any of them, but I'm sure she dug her claws in and wouldn't let go." He guffawed and shook his head. "Damn. Never thought I'd see the day."

Ford fished his wallet out of his back pocket and stood. "Like your record is any better, buddy. We called you Scooter because you scooted out of their beds before they finished coming." He tossed a few bills on the bar to cover their drinks. "See you around."

Scott couldn't be more wrong. Becky Jean had every right to take what she wanted. He'd never indicated he wanted more, and neither had she. What really twisted his short hairs was he hadn't expected her rejection to hurt as bad as it did. Damn it. He wanted more.

~~~

So far, so good. Becky Jean rocked back in her desk chair. It had been three days since she'd made the monumental mistake of taking Ford to her bedroom, and she hadn't relapsed since. Oh, she'd wanted to, and judging by the leering glances and innuendo coming from her business partner, he did, too.

But they couldn't. She couldn't. *Once had been a mistake. Twice would be insane.*

The company was doing exceedingly well. Yes, they were spending lots of money, but their expenditures were nowhere near the amount coming in. If she figured in the new real estate acquisitions, and what those would add to their bottom line, Ford had to be well on his way to becoming a billionaire. Hell, he might already be one. Which meant, he'd be looking for a way out soon. He'd never made any promises about staying, and since Adams Manufacturing had a solid future, he had to be planning to return to his other life. The one-year stipulated in his father's will would be up soon. When the date arrived, she could kiss her partner good-bye.

Becky leaned forward and flipped the pages on her old-fashioned desk calendar. Had he already talked to potential buyers? Would he do so without telling her?

She'd known the day would come when she'd have to decide whether to sell or not. The last few months had flown by faster than debris in a twister, leaving her disoriented. If one of Ford's buyers wanted her share, too, would she sell? And if she didn't, would they want her to remain in her current position? She couldn't imagine they would. Anyone who owned the majority of a company would want to bring in their own people to make sure things were done according to their
~~~

wishes. Her opinion, backed by her very small minority share, wouldn't mean a thing.

Once again, she found herself in a position where none of the choices were hers. Her future hinged on the decisions of someone else. Deep inside, she realized her father's illness had been beyond his control, but the result was the same. Choices had been taken out of her hands. Then Ken Adams had died, locking her into a situation where she had no choice but to help Ford. She wanted the roller coaster to stop so she could get off. She didn't mind a fun ride, but for once, she'd like to choose the ride for herself.

She glanced over the contract in her hand—the one linking Adams Manufacturing to Scott Ramsey's new leather factory for the next ten years. Scott had made a commitment to live in Butte Plains for the next decade, but Ford, his best friend, had made no such commitment. Maybe she'd misread her partner's intentions. It had been months since he'd mentioned selling out. But yet… the calendar stalked her, the one-year mark creeping closer with every turn of the page.

Becky shuffled the papers on her desk. Poised to launch their shopping network into a twenty-four hour business, HR had been working overtime to narrow down possible spokespersons for the various new programs designed to showcase their competitors' products. She'd promised she and Ford would sort through the prospects today so they could be called in for personal interviews. Gathering the headshots and resumes to discuss with Ford, she stopped in her doorway.

Carolyn's distinct voice floated down the hallway. "Like I said, Mr. Adams is in a meeting. You'll need to make an appointment for another time."

The receptionist never raised her voice to a level to be heard this far away. *What the heck?* It wasn't like Carolyn to be rude.

"If you aren't going to tell him I'm here, I'll find him myself!" The clear, cultured, feminine voice reminded Becky of someone, but she couldn't pinpoint who. She changed direction, intending to add her support to the young woman at the front desk. They didn't pay her enough to put up with pushy people. She'd taken one step when a woman turned the corner, heading straight for her. Tall and sophisticated. Beautiful. No, stunning. Perhaps one of the models being considered for the network shows? Deciding right there to remove the woman from the list of possible hires, Becky used her body to block the hallway.

"You can't go in there," she said.

The woman had a few inches on Becky, even without the spiked heels she had on. She stopped, gave Becky the once-over, and, from the expression on her face, found her lacking in everything from appearance to the way she smelled. "And you're going to stop me? I don't think so." The interloper swept past in an invisible cloud of expensive perfume. "Ford Adams? Where the hell are you?"

Becky sneezed then followed the stranger. Rounding the corner into Ford's office, Becky stopped in her tracks. She blinked once, twice, but the image of her partner lip-locked with the strange woman didn't go away.

Carolyn skidded to a halt behind Becky. "I told her she couldn't disturb Mr. Adams."

Becky turned to the receptionist. "It's okay… I think. It seems Mr. Adams knows this woman."

Ford pushed the newcomer away and wiped his mouth with the back of his hand. "What the hell?"

"You have some nerve, Ford Adams." The woman pulled a rolled up magazine out of her designer handbag and waved it in his face.

"Have you seen the cover of Forbes this month?" She tossed the periodical on Ford's desk. "They're calling you The Backdoor Billionaire!"

Ford smiled and reached for the magazine. "Really? That's awesome!"

"Are. You. Kidding. Me?"

Ford scanned the cover, then held it up for Becky to see. "Becks! Did you see this?"

The woman spun around. The way her eyes drilled into Becky made her want to make a cross with her index fingers to ward off evil spirits. "No. We were supposed to get an advance copy." Maybe they had. She didn't have much time for reading magazines these days.

"Who's this?" Evil Woman demanded, half turning to look over her shoulder at Ford.

He cleared his throat and stepped around the woman. "Becky Jean, Carolyn, this is… Veronica Ramsey, Scott's sister. Ronnie, I take it you've met our receptionist, Carolyn, and this is my partner, Becky Jean Parker."

Ronnie. So, the phantom girlfriend materialized. The one who couldn't be bothered to stand beside Ford at his father's funeral or support him in his struggle to save his family business. Unable to meet Ford's gaze, to see whatever emotion might be there, she focused on Ronnie's face and, with clenched fists, held on as the roller coaster nose-dived, leaving her stomach behind.

"Why didn't you just say you were his girlfriend?" Carolyn asked.

Mustering every scrap of professionalism she could find, Becky jumped in. "It's nice to meet you, Ms. Ramsey. We all think a lot of Scott around here." *Can't say the same about you, though. What could Ford possibly see in her?*

"Where *is* my brother?" Veronica stared down her sharp nose at them. She was on a mission. Just what it could be, Becky had no idea. One thing she knew for certain—Ronnie would not fail, and the woman didn't take prisoners.

"I believe he's at the new leather goods factory he purchased. I'm sure Carolyn can give you directions." *Of course, they'd be driving directions, not broomstick directions.*

"No need. I'll give you a ride." Ford reached for his keys in the center desk drawer.

"But, we have to go over these applicants. I promised HR—"

Ronnie's laugh cut Becky off. She turned on Ford. "Are you serious?" *This is what you've been doing down here in*

Butt Plug, Texas, for all these months, deciding which machine operator to hire?"

"Come on, Ronnie." Ford grabbed the witch by her elbow. Becky and Carolyn cleared a wide path to the door. "I'll give you a tour of the town, then we'll hunt up your brother."

As Ford ushered the woman out, Becky heard her say, "Really, Ford? That mouse is your business partner? How have you managed—"

The front door swallowed the rest of the woman's rant, then Becky became deaf to her surroundings. The derisive tone of the woman's voice made her furious. *Mouse?* Who did Ms. Expensive Designer Everything think she was anyway?

"Ms. Parker?"

"Hmm?" Becky forced her attention to the young woman beside her. "What? No worries, Carolyn. You did the best you could."

"Are you going to be okay? I mean, who does she think she is? I guess I just thought you and Mr. Adams—"

"Are business partners. That's all." If she'd ever hoped for more, those dreams had been thoroughly crushed under four-inch stilettos.

"But—"

"But nothing. Mr. Adams had a life he had to temporarily give up to come here. Seems his life has come to take him back."

She hadn't meant to be harsh, but she didn't want to discuss her and Ford's relationship, or lack thereof, with the staff. Besides, as of the moment Scott's sister walked in the door, any relationship other than a professional one between Becky and Ford became impossible. Whatever feelings she had for the man were never hers to have. He belonged to another.

The idea of being the other woman made her sick to her stomach.

Becky waited until Carolyn left before sitting behind her partner's desk. She glanced at his latest drawing and contemplated how her life had come to this. Instead of inventory sorted into domestic and agricultural, she thought in terms of insertables, vibrating, stationary, and portable. She dropped the head shots she'd hoped to discuss with Ford in the center of his desk. This time last year, she'd worried about hiring the right sort of person to operate dangerous machinery, and today? The HR department that hadn't existed a year ago expected her to decide which drop-dead gorgeous models would represent the company on television.

"This is insane." She advanced Ford's calendar two months to today's date then thought better of it and returned the pages to their original position. Did he even realize it had almost been a year since his father passed? All the reminder he needed had just walked in the front door.

She thumbed through the model's photos, selected her six favorites, and moved them to the top, securing them with a paperclip she found in his top drawer. Ford would probably be grateful she'd done the onerous job herself, saving him the trouble of participating in the decision. After all, he had his hands full with the wicked witch of the east.

CHAPTER TWENTY-ONE

After settling Ronnie in the passenger seat of his car, Ford took his time walking around to the driver's side. *What the hell was she thinking, barging in like she owned the place then insulting everyone she came in contact with? Who does she think she is?*

Ford stood beside the door for a moment, willing his anger to dissipate. He'd learned from bitter experience, yelling at her would do no good. The louder he got, the less she listened, and she needed to hear him. But first, she had some explaining to do.

She refused to look at him as he joined her in the car. He cranked the engine, adjusted the air conditioning, and muted the radio before backing out of the parking space reserved for him. In the last few months, his car had spent more time in his company parking slot than it had at the gatehouse he called home. At first, it had been out of desperate necessity. He'd put in long hours trying to coax the company back from the brink of bankruptcy. Once things began to turn around, the hours had been spent dreaming up new products to keep the company moving forward. These days, he spent his time doing what he loved—designing. And he had the time to design because Becky Jean did everything else, and did it well. He wouldn't let anyone come in and insult her the way Ronnie had.

He exited the parking lot and took the longest possible route to Scott's new leather factory. "What are you doing here?"

"I would think my reasons would be obvious."

To some, maybe, but he didn't have a clue. "Maybe to you, but not to me."

"My boyfriend and my brother have forsaken me for this place. I've come to see why, and to take you both home. I'll drag you if I have to."

Ford unclenched his jaw. "First, no one has forsaken you. Scott and I have asked you to visit on numerous occasions. Second, I'm only your boyfriend when you don't want to attend events alone. We had an agreement—no strings, no commitments." He glanced at her. "Don't even try to tell me you've been alone the entire time I've been here."

Before she could respond, he continued, "Third, I can't go back right now. We're expanding at a staggering rate. Becky couldn't possibly handle it all on her own." *Liar.* Becky could handle anything and did on a regular basis. He'd be lost without her, not the other way around.

"That's what employees are for. You hire people to do the jobs you don't want to do, and anything else you do via videoconferencing until you sell. Then it's all someone else's problem."

"Sell?"

He didn't think a block of ice could get any colder, but judging from the frost coming off the woman next to him, it could. "Yes, sell. Remember your original plan? Hang on for the year stipulated in your father's will then sell the factory and come home."

"I don't know what you're up to, but get this straight. I'm not selling."

"Don't be ridiculous." Her laugh chilled him to the bone. "Of course you are. Everyone and everything has a price."

Ford braked hard at a stop sign. He gripped the steering wheel, knuckles white and jaw clenched, as he held onto his patience by the thinnest thread. He didn't believe for a second she missed him. If she had, she would have shown her face in Texas months ago. Coming here had to be an excuse for… something. He just didn't have a clue what.

If he had any doubts his relationship with Ronnie had run its course, she'd erased them today. From the minute she'd walked into his office and kissed him like a drowning victim stealing the air from his lungs, he'd felt nothing beyond anger toward her. He could barely recall the desire that had brought them together the year he and Scott graduated from MIT. She'd attended the commencement ceremony and the party afterward, showering him with the kind of attention he hadn't been able or inclined to turn away. With her love of fashion and everything fashionable, she dazzled, and he'd followed her like a lost explorer followed the North Star. Being outside her orbit for the last few months, he'd found his own way. He liked the direction he was going, even if she didn't.

"No. I'm not." He checked for traffic, and, seeing none, he took a moment to compose himself. "Why are you here, Ronnie? And cut the bullshit about wanting me to come home. If you wanted me to come home, you would have been here a long time ago."

"You don't know anything about me. You never did."

And the inner bitch shows her face. He would have laughed had she not been so predictable. The sooner he found out what she was up to, the better. On the flip side—he knew she wouldn't tell him until she was good and ready.

"Where are you staying while you're here?" he asked, accelerating through the intersection.

"With you, of course."

Oh, hell no!

"This is a small town. It wouldn't be appropriate." He turned on Walnut Street. A large, yellow Victorian stood proud a few blocks down. The old maple in the front yard was majestic in its fall colors. "Scott's at The Yellow Rose. We'll stop in and see if they have a room." If they didn't, he'd kick Scott out, put him up in the gatehouse, and move in with his mother if he had to. He only wanted Becky Jean in his bed, and she probably wouldn't ever speak to him again after today.

"You have to be kidding me. Ford? You are kidding, aren't you?"

Ignoring her whining, he pulled to the curb in front of the only B&B in town. Bright yellow and orange mums lined the recently repaired concrete walkway up to the front porch. It appeared things were looking up for Roseanne. He almost hated to dump Veronica on her. She didn't deserve the punishment. "No, I'm not kidding. Trust me, Ronnie, this is for the best."

Her laugh sounded more like a cackle. Why had he not noticed that before?

"Have you seen the sign at the city limits? Someone changed it from Butte Plains to Butt Plug. It's because of you and your ridiculous sex-toy business, so don't tell me you're worried about propriety. I'm not buying it."

He smiled at the image of the revised welcome sign. *The town's old guard must be beside themselves.*

"Ford Adams! Tell me what's going on! I thought we…. I thought—"

"You thought wrong." Time and distance allowed him to see past Ronnie's outward beauty to the spoiled brat beneath the surface.

She huffed out a breath. "I've waited patiently for you to come home, and I'm sick and tired of it. People understood the reason you had to stay at first, but the company is doing better than ever. There's no reason for you to still be here. Tell me, Ford. Why *are* you still here?"

Unbidden, an image of Becky Jean, her face a mask covering her emotions as Ronnie clung to him, popped into his mind. She'd put up a seemingly impenetrable barrier between them since the night he'd spent in her bed, and, given what she'd seen in his office earlier, he couldn't imagine how he'd get through to her after this.

It's where I want to be. He'd known it for a while, but saying the words out loud would be irrevocable. He'd been happier since coming back to Butte Plains than ever before. He was doing what he loved—with a woman he loved.

His brain skidded to a stop, hung up on the realization he had fallen in love with Becky Jean. He forced air into his lungs and steeled himself for the panic attack sure to follow such an earth-shattering revelation. But instead of panic, a pinpoint of heat sparked in the region of his heart, erupting into a flash fire of warmth and contentment.

No, there was nothing scary about loving Becky Jean—except she probably hated his guts. He'd once heard a person could only hate someone they loved, as both emotions stemmed from passion. And Becky Jean had passion. She'd shown it to him the night he'd spent in her bed. He hadn't imagined the way she'd responded to his touch or the way she'd given herself to him. She felt something for him. Love or hate. Two sides of the same coin.

He could work with that.

"It's where I want to be." His tone brooked no argument. It was high time he set things straight. "You were rude to Carolyn and Becky Jean. Neither one of them deserved to be treated with such callous disregard. You owe them both an apology, and, in the future, I expect you to treat them with the respect they deserve." He didn't wait for her response. Exiting the car, he stalked up the sidewalk, ready to buy the Victorian and evict all the registered guests if it would keep Ronnie out of his home.

~~~

There was no accounting for taste. It was the only explanation for why Ford would be involved with someone like Veronica Ramsey. Ever since the witch had shown up, uninvited, the previous week, Becky's life had been Hell. The half-assed apology the woman had given for the way she'd
~~~

behaved the day she arrived had been as shallow as a hastily dug grave.

"I swear, if she comes in here asking for more financial data one more time, I'm going to go flying monkey crazy on her."

"Were you talking to me?"

Becky jerked her attention away from the stack of purchase orders on her desk and to the man standing in her doorway. Ford looked good enough to eat, leaning against the doorjamb in his faded jeans and a *Don't Mess with Texas* T-shirt.

"Nope."

Ford's gaze swept her office. "Talking to yourself, then. That's not a good sign." Without invitation, he settled into the one guest chair facing her desk. "So, who has you in such a snit you're talking to yourself?"

How could such a brilliant man be so clueless? Veronica had everyone in the place looking over the shoulder for witches on broomsticks. "Nobody." She shuffled papers around on her desk, hoping if she appeared busy enough, her partner would take the hint and leave. When he gave no sign of moving on, she clasped her hands together on the cleared blotter and changed the subject. "How's the new line of male products coming?"

"Good, if I do say so myself." When he talked about his work, he looked like a kid in a toy store. A smile lifted both sides of his mouth, and his eyes twinkled with a light from within. She couldn't be mad at him when he looked at her that way.

Becky nodded. "I talked to Scott this morning. He's sending over a contract for the leather goods you designed. Once the paperwork is all squared away, he estimated three weeks until the first shipment is ready. I think direct sales is the way to go on this one."

"No middleman means more profits." He rubbed his hands together. Like either one of them needed more money. "We should slot out some time on the shopping channel to showcase the new line."

"Already done." She sorted through the folders on her desk, picked one out, and slid it across the desktop. "Here are the schedules for the next two months."

"Only two months?"

Becky looked up at him. "You want more?"

"Why wouldn't I?"

"Oh, I don't know. Maybe because you'll be who knows where by then?"

He tilted his head to one side and narrowed his eyes at her. "What makes you think I won't be here?"

"Ms. Ramsey said—"

"She was here? What, exactly, did she say?"

Ford spent most of his time in his office, drawing on his sketchpad or computer, but he still managed to have a clue about most things happening in the office. Could it be possible he hadn't asked Veronica to help him, and he had no idea what his girlfriend had been up to the past week? "She's been here every day this week, asking to see the financial reports, production schedules...."

His face turned a shade of red she'd never seen before, and he clenched his fists at his side.

"Did she say why she wanted the reports?"

"She said you asked her to get them."

A muscle ticked in his jaw. "Did she say why?"

"No. I assumed you were talking to a potential buyer."

His gaze bore into her. "I'm not selling, Becks. Not today. Not next week or next month. Not ever."

"Oh." Her heart did a flip at the use of the pet name he'd given her, only to plummet to her stomach as she realized what he'd said. "Then...? You...?"

"No. I didn't ask her to get them for me. I knew she had to be up to something, coming here, but I had no idea what. I still don't." He tossed the schedule she'd just handed him on her desk. "Shit. I've got to go."

"Ford!"

He stopped in the doorway and turned.

"What's going on?"

"I don't know, but I'm going to find out."

He couldn't remember being this angry, ever. For the last week, he'd ignored Veronica, and since she hadn't bothered him, he'd assumed he'd made himself clear on the subject of selling and going back to New York. She'd shown up the next day, apologized to Becky Jean and Carolyn, and he hadn't seen her since. He'd assumed she'd decided to spend her time visiting with Scott, but in truth, he had no idea she remained in town. *Should have paid more attention.*

Well, he was paying attention now. He grabbed his car keys out of his desk drawer. Whatever plans she had, he would put a stop them.

CHAPTER TWENTY-TWO

"Where is she?" he demanded.

Scott looked up from his cluttered desk, a blank stare on his face as if he'd just woken from a coma. "Who?"

"Veronica. Where is she?"

His friend shrugged. "No idea. Thought you were keeping her occupied."

Ford slapped the doorframe. "Fuck!"

"Something wrong?"

"Do *you* know what she's up to?"

"Up to?" Scott rocked back in his chair. "No. I've barely seen her since she got here. She hasn't taken a single meal at the B&B. I thought you and her—"

"I told you, we're over. Have been for a while." Ford dropped into the old leather visitors' chair—a remnant left behind by the previous owners. He shook his head. "I knew she was up to something when she showed up all of a sudden, but I had no idea."

"What?"

"I just found out she's been poking around in the plant's financials. Even had the balls to ask for copies of reports. She gave Becky Jean the impression I wanted them, probably to give to a prospective buyer."

"Shit." Scott straightened. "And you knew nothing about this?"

"Not a thing. I've been working my ass off this week, working out the kinks in a new toy I plan to unveil at the trade show next week in Vegas. I've barely come out of my office to eat, much less sleep." He raked his hands over his face. "What the fuck is she up to?"

"I've never pretended to understand Ronnie, so don't ask me."

"I've got to find her, put a stop to this shit."

"Did you try The Yellow Rose?"

"Not yet. I'm going there next." Ford stood. "Thanks, man, for listening. I know she's your sister and all, but I could easily strangle her."

Scott snorted. "No offense taken. She's always looked out for herself first and everyone else last. She's definitely up to something. If she shows up, I'll let you know."

"Thanks."

A stop at The Yellow Rose provided no more information on Ronnie's whereabouts. Roseanne confirmed she hadn't seen much of her new tenant. Like Scott, she'd assumed Ford to be the reason. Leaving instructions to call him the minute Veronica returned, Ford headed back to the plant.

With a little luck, the 3-D printer would have spit out his new creation while he'd been gone. If everything went well, he could have enough samples produced in time to hand out at the trade show.

He stopped at Becky Jean's office long enough to tell her not to give Ronnie any more information, and assure her he remembered the trip the following week. They were taking a few interns from the business program at the county junior college over in Plainview to fetch and carry, and several of the new spokesmodels they'd hired for the network shows. Between them, their booth would be well staffed for the week-long event, which meant he'd have plenty of time to spend with Becky Jean.

Neither one of them had had a day off since they'd become business partners, and he planned to take full advantage of the opportunity to get away for a little while.

Becky Jean's brother, Colin, had called a few weeks ago, asking for Ford's help. Turned out, he planned to be in Las Vegas, too. His new record label had booked him and his band as an opening act for one of the major acts in town, and he wanted Ford to help him surprise Becky Jean who had never seen him play in person.

The concert was just one of the surprises he had for his partner. They both deserved to have a little fun.

Speaking of which…. He examined his new creation. It didn't look much different than others he'd seen. It was what went on the inside that made this model unique.

~~~

Ford vibrated with anticipation as he helped the interns put the finishing touches on their booth in the Las Vegas Convention Center. He'd sent Becky Jean back to the hotel to rest up and get ready for their big night on the town. He'd finally told her about the concert tickets after her brother had called to let him know about the giant billboard in front of their hotel proclaiming him the opening act for the next few days. Colin had been disappointed about not being able to surprise his sister, as had Ford, but the concert paled in comparison to the other surprise he had for his partner.

She would have found the toy. If Becky Jean did as his note instructed, it would be worth every penny of bribe money he'd paid the housekeeping staff to have the gift-wrapped package placed in her room while she'd been out.
~~~

Since the night they'd spent together, she'd been careful to feature toys on the show she could easily test solo. Technically, his new creation fit into the same category but would be a lot more fun with a partner.

"Ford! What are you doing?"

On his knees organizing the boxes stashed beneath one of their tables, the familiar voice startled him.

"Fuck!" he hissed, extricating himself from the dark cavern created by the tablecloth. He bumped his head on the table, uttered another curse, and stood. Scott's sister and a man he didn't recognize faced him. "Ronnie. What are you doing here?"

"I thought I would surprise you."

"Who's this?" He nodded at the man standing an almost-appropriate distance behind her. It could have been the way he looked at Ronnie like he could see through her clothes that made the gap between them seem intimate.

The woman glanced over her shoulder and beckoned her companion forward. "Ford, I'd like you to meet Carter Hargraves. Carter, Ford Adams."

The man extended his hand. Out of habit, Ford did the same while he searched his memory for a reason the man's name sounded familiar.

"Nice to meet you," Carter said. "You're a difficult man to reach."

Things clicked into place. Dozens of messages over the last few weeks from the CEO of their biggest competitor, Toy Haven. Messages he'd ignored. "Not if I have reason to speak to you."

The other man raised one eyebrow and smiled. "Can we go somewhere and talk?"

"No." He didn't want to keep Becky Jean waiting. He scanned the booth one last time to make sure everything was in place for the opening the next morning then turned back to his unwanted visitors. "I don't know what Veronica has told you, but Adams Manufacturing has been in my family for four generations. It's not for sale."

Hargraves glanced at Ronnie who smiled and wrapped herself around the man's arm, snuggling up to him like a dancer to a pole. "Don't believe a word he says, Carter. Everything has a price. Tell him what you're offering. He'll change his mind."

Ford glared at the woman then held up a staying hand before either one could utter another word. "Don't bother." He scooted through the gap between the partition separating their booth from the next one and the table. "Ms. Ramsey is mistaken, Mr. Hargraves. If you'll excuse me, I have plans this evening."

"Don't be ridiculous, Ford. Ford! Come back here!"

Seething, he kept walking until the sound of cars breezing past on the street drowned out Veronica's screeching. No doubt she'd used the financial information she'd conned the staff out of to convince their biggest competitor to make an offer for the company. Why, he didn't have a clue. He'd told her in no uncertain terms he had no plans to sell, made it plain he liked his new situation.

His mind reeled, trying to grasp the woman's reasoning and came up empty. "What part of no does she not understand?" he mumbled as he entered the hotel lobby and headed toward the elevators. He keyed in his floor then shook his head to dislodge the anger and disbelief at Ronnie's actions. He'd deal with the woman later. He had much more pleasant things to deal with tonight.

~~~

At Ford's insistence, Becky had left him to finish setting up their booth so she could get some rest before their big night on the town. Unable to sit still, she stood at the floor-to-ceiling windows of her hotel suite and stared at the electronic billboard dozens of stories below flashing her
~~~

brother's picture every thirty seconds. Yes, she'd timed the intervals. She had known her brother was doing well. He called often enough, but, in the last year, she'd barely come up for air, and had somehow missed his rise to stardom. Well, almost stardom. Soon, he'd be the headliner and some other hopeful would be his opening act.

Tonight would be awesome. First, dinner with Ford, their new business partner, Scott Ramsey, and Becky's best friend, Roseanne Meadows, who had accompanied Scott to Vegas. Her friend still refused to talk about what went on between her and the Yankee, but anyone with eyes could see *something* was going on.

After dinner, the four of them would return to the hotel where they had VIP seats for the concert. Thankfully, she'd had a little warning and had been able to call Amy to help her find a dress for tonight. She'd picked out the black beaded halter-style gown with the slit up the side that both allowed her to move and exposed enough leg to be sexy. Amy had assured her men's heads would turn when she walked by.

Becky squelched a giggle before it made it past her lips. She'd never been to Las Vegas, but she'd heard plenty about the place. Maybe she'd been cooped up in her office for too long, but it felt good to be away—to have a *view* from her window! She loved Butte Plains, but she'd been too busy lately to enjoy her hometown. Even though this was a work trip, she fully intended to squeeze every drop of fun out of it she could—starting tonight.

She spied the gift the moment she stepped into the bedroom. Wrapped in the glossy-white paper and signature red ribbon Adams Manufacturing used to wrap gift purchases for shipment, she knew instantly who it had to be from. *Ford.* She shook her head and placed a fist over her heart to assuage the ache she experienced every time she thought about him. *Lord, what now?* Working with him was pure torture sometimes, but she wouldn't trade those times for anything.

He'd said he wouldn't sell his part of the company, but he hadn't said he would stay in Butte Plains either, so she refused to let her heart beat for what it wanted—a lifetime with the man she loved. Plus, he still had a girlfriend, or whatever. Roseanne said the woman had become a ghost around the B&B, evaporating into thin air. Sneaky. She'd led everyone in the office to believe the documents she requested were for Ford, when she wanted them for her own purposes. No one seemed to know where she went every day. Whatever she was up to, it had to be no good.

Becky forced the evil woman out of her thoughts. Tonight, she resolved to have a good time. No thinking about unpleasant things.

She picked up the box, tested its weight in her palm. Light as air, she had no idea what could be inside. The ribbon came away with a light tug on the end of the bow, and a fingernail under the squares of tape on the bottom and sides loosened the heavy paper wrapping. A plain envelope lay atop the nondescript box. Inside, a note from Ford.

Becky,

I designed this for you. Wear it for me tonight?

Love,

Ford

Love? Her crazy heart skipped a beat at the salutation, even though it probably meant nothing. She set the missive aside and opened the box.

Her hands trembled as she lifted the lace thong. Sewn into the triangle of fabric was what could only be a vibrator. She'd seen similar ones in their competitors' catalogs and knew Ford would eventually get around to designing a better version. Besides being incorporated into an actual garment, this one didn't look special. But she knew her business partner—if he couldn't one-up the competition, he didn't waste his time.

"How is this one different?" she said as she examined it. Immediately, she noticed there were no wires, no controller, not even an on/off switch. Another glance at the box confirmed she hadn't missed any parts. She raised one eyebrow, considering the construction again. The wearer would have no control over whatever magic tricks the toy could do.

Was she brave enough to wear it not knowing when Ford would activate it, or what to expect when he did? Maybe.

Becky placed the device back in its box then headed for the shower to wash the grime of travel and booth setup away. Every drop of soapy water carried another of her worries down the drain, leaving her relaxed and in a better mood than she had been in for ages. Her staff back in Butte Plains were competent and capable of handling whatever came up over the next few days. They'd brought enough people with them to staff their booth at the trade show, and they'd been well trained, which left plenty of time for her to have some fun.

And where better to do it than Las Vegas? Sin City?

After moisturizing every inch of skin she could reach with the expensive lotion both Roseanne and Amy had insisted she needed, she dried her hair, leaving it down so it fell in soft curls over her shoulders. Without a moment's hesitation, she stepped into the lace thong Ford had gifted her with. She wouldn't tell him she had put it on. *Let him guess.* A shiver raced down her spine as she speculated about what she would experience when he chose to activate it. Would it even work? It was hard to imagine something so small with no visible signs of a working mechanism would actually do anything. But, knowing Ford, the tiny device would deliver the goods. Whatever they might be.

The dress fit like a dream, and she had to admit, she didn't look half-bad in it. With every move she made, the heavy beading picked up the light, sending it back into the room in tiny sparks. Ford's latest invention rested undetectable between her legs. *Clever*. She couldn't imagine wearing the others she'd seen for hours—they'd simply be too uncomfortable. But it would be easy to forget about this one.

She'd just pulled her hair behind her left ear and secured it with a rhinestone clasp when a knock sounded on her door.

"Just a second," she called out. She slipped her feet into strappy sandals then grabbed her evening purse off the end of the bed. "Sorry—"

The rest of her apology for keeping him waiting died on her lips the second she laid eyes on Ford. The tingling in her lady parts had nothing to do with the device concealed in her panties and everything to do with the man standing before her. *Holy Jesus.* He looked good no matter what he wore, but this…. "Wow."

"You like it?" he said, brushing invisible lint from the jacket of his tuxedo. "I asked Scott to pack up some of my clothes for me the last time he went back to New York. Never thought I'd need this again, but I'm glad he sent it." His gaze traveled from the sparkly clip in her hair down to the slit in her skirt where it lingered before slowly making its way back to her face. She knew he couldn't possibly tell if she wore his gift, but she held her breath anyway, waiting for him to say something about it.

"Just look at you, Becks. It ought to be a sin to be as beautiful as you are." His heated perusal and the sincerity in his voice brought a flood of heat to her face, and lower.

"The dress isn't too much, is it? Amy insisted it would be appropriate for tonight."

"Remind me to give your stylist a raise when we get back. The dress is fabulous, but it's the person wearing it that makes it stunning."

She blushed at his praise. "Stop it." Much more of his praise and she wouldn't be able to function. The fact he hadn't brought up the subject of his gift made her more aware of it nestled between her legs. If that's the way he wanted to play it, she would play along.

Fighting off a massive case of nerves, she checked her purse one last time. Room key. Lip gloss. A single, folded tissue. I.D. Cell phone. Credit card. Cash for tips or a cab if she needed one. "Are we meeting Scott and Roseanne at the restaurant?"

Satisfied she had everything she might need, she pulled the door closed behind her. Ford offered his arm, and she took it, letting him guide her toward the elevators. His mama had taught him well.

"Yes. Is that okay?"

"Works for me. I'm still surprised Roseanne is here with him. I didn't think she even liked him."

Ford shrugged, ushering her into the elevator car ahead of him. He pushed the appropriate button then resumed his place beside her. "I guess she likes him well enough."

"I suppose so." She couldn't help but worry about her friend. What little she'd said about her long-standing guest led Becky to believe she might not like him all that much.

They stepped out of the elevator on lobby level. Ford spun her around to face him. "If there's one thing I know about Scott, it's the women he's been with have all been with him because they want to be. Keep that in mind tonight. Roseanne has chosen to be where she is."

"Okay." She nodded and pressed her lips together. "I'll try to remember."

His words rattled around in her head as she let him lead her from the hotel into the massive attached indoor mall housing some of the best restaurants in the city as well as expensive boutiques and high-end jewelers in a realistic outdoor setting. The lights had been dimmed, mimicking a jewel-toned sunset she would have found romantic if she hadn't been so focused on figuring out what Ford had meant about Roseanne choosing to be there. Of course she had chosen to be there, or she would have stayed at home.

Ford gave his name to the maître d' who then went to check on something. Ford snapped his fingers in front of her face, and at the same moment a sharp vibration jolted her clit. Becky wrapped her free arm around her middle and just managed to stifle a squeal before it passed her lips. Her gaze snapped to Ford's.

Taking both her hands in his, he drew her forward then leaned down and spoke low into her ear. "You're thinking too hard about the wrong things, Becky Jean. What's between Scott and Roseanne is their business. Focus on what matters to you tonight."

With every word he spoke, the device between her legs vibrated, changing in intensity to match his inflection; ceasing with each pause. She gasped as realization dawned and the damned thing reacted to her voice. *Oh Lord. It's sound activated!*

She drew back and her gaze landed on the small American Flag pin attached to his lapel. She'd thought it homage to their Made in America marketing campaign. Clamping her lips shut, she looked up at him.

"I knew you would wear it."

She whimpered as his words, spoken at a conversational level, translated into a series of vibrations she couldn't ignore.

"Do you like it?"

His voice stroked her clit with each word he spoke. She nodded. His invention was evil and ingenious and Lord, the most erotic thing she could imagine!

He let her left hand go and reached into an inner pocket of his jacket. No vibrations accompanied his next words. "The microphone is in the flag pin, as I see you've figured out. Be a good girl, and I'll let you eat your meal in peace."

She raised one eyebrow. "And if I choose to be bad?"

"It's calibrated to pick up loud noises from any distance, or voices within about eighteen inches. You decide if you want me to activate it or not." He smirked. "It's up to you, darlin'."

"Mr. Adams? Your table is ready."

CHAPTER TWENTY-THREE

Ford tucked her arm in the crook of his, leaving her no choice but to go along. He seated her then took the chair next to hers. How close did the transmitter have to be to operate? If he'd sat across from her, would he have been too far away?

She took the menu offered and listened as her partner ordered wine and appetizers from the waiter who had appeared like magic.

"I'm really looking forward to the concert later," Ford said without taking his eyes off his menu.

The concert. The very *loud* concert. Oh, he was an evil one! "You wouldn't."

"Not during your brother's set. That would just be weird."

Weird pretty much summed up her life these days. She'd once lived a quiet, if not boring life. There had been plenty of ups and downs since Kenneth Adams passed away, but thanks to his son, she hadn't been bored a single day. "And it wouldn't be weird to do this in front of our friends?"

He shook his head. "Nope." He looked up as another waiter placed a loaf of artisan bread on a small cutting board in the center of the table. Ford reached for the carving knife and cut off a chunk, offering it to her. Becky declined. "Trust me. If Scott figured it out, it wouldn't bother him in the least. Since Roseanne is with him, I doubt she'd care either."

A cold chill raced down her spine. She opened her mouth to protest that he couldn't possibly know what her friend would think when Ford stood. She followed his gaze to see the couple in question making their way to the table.

Scott held the chair across from her for Roseanne, sinking any chance she had of having a private word with her friend. As he resumed his seat, Ford smiled and winked at her. She stuck her tongue out at him then sat back as he reached inside his coat.

No. He wouldn't.

"How was your flight?" he asked the newcomers. Becky Jean bit the inside of her cheek to keep from whimpering. She clenched her thighs tight which only served to concentrate the sensation. He kept up a running conversation for several minutes. She thought she might die as the microphone/receiver picked up every word Roseanne spoke and several of Scott's, keeping her on the sharp edge of arousal. How in the world would she make it through the concert?

"We're going to debut a new product at the show this week." He turned his attention her way. "Why don't you tell them about it, Becks?"

She thought about begging, but she let her eyes do the job, silently pleading with him to turn the damn thing off. Masturbating in public went way beyond her limits. He reached into his coat and the tension in her shoulders released. She wouldn't rest easy until she knew for certain he'd turned the infernal thing off.

"Go ahead," he said. She let her thighs and stomach muscles relax. "You can probably describe the operation of the *Your Secret is Safe Personal Vibrator* better than I could."

He'd even named the product! She narrowed her eyes at him then quickly shifted gears as he reached for the switch again. He would pay for this! "Hmm. Let me think." She picked up her wine glass and sipped. Over the rim, she caught Scott's amused expression. Immediately, she shifted her gaze to Roseanne who did a terrible job of containing her mirth. A pit opened up inside her, and her stomach slid all the way to her toes. She turned to her partner. "You told them, didn't you?"

"No. I swear." The smile on his face made her want to crawl under the table. "I think you just did."

Shit.

Roseanne laughed out loud. "Oh, God, Becky! If you could have seen the look on your face!" She leaned over the table and whispered loud, "I thought you were going to come right here in the middle of the restaurant." She sat back up and asked Ford, "When can I get one of those things?"

"Stop by our booth tomorrow and I'll make sure you get one. I had enough made up to give one to each of our best-selling retailers. Since it's been tested and approved, I think we can go into production pretty quickly. What do you think, Becky Jean?"

"I think you played a dastardly trick on me."

He flashed her the smile that had sold millions of sex toys via their home shopping television show and made him a billionaire. "They don't call me *Kinky* Ford Adams for nothing, you know?"

Scott laughed. "I saw that! It was the article in *Forbes* magazine, right?"

"I don't know. Do you remember, Becks?"

"*Barron's* called him kinky. *Forbes* labeled him the Backdoor Billionaire."

"That's right." Scott laughed. "God, who would have thought it?"

"Not me." Lifting his wine glass to his lips, he took a sip. "I just wanted to keep the doors open for the year stipulated in Dad's will and not lose everything we had in the process. Never dreamed things would take off the way they did." He turned his gaze on Becky. "I owe it all to Becky Jean. Without her marketing and vision, we might have survived the year, but we would have bled money the entire time."

She could feel everyone's eyes on her. Ford had said much the same to her on numerous occasions, but this was the first time he'd acknowledged her contribution to others. This time when she squirmed in her seat, it had nothing to do with Ford's infernal new device.

"I just put together a reasonable marketing plan. And anyone in the business knows, if your product is inferior, there's nothing in the world you can say to make people buy it."

"Are you saying our products are superior?"

"You know they are. Thanks to you"—she nodded at Ford then to Scott—"and you, too. The two of you have come up with innovative ideas that have the competition scrambling to keep up."

"So tell me about this new one," Roseanne said. "How does it work?"

Ford withdrew a small, square plastic box from his suit coat. It looked like a battery compartment for a toy, but there were no wires running from it, only an on/off switch on one end. "This is the transmitter and control box." He pointed to the pin on his lapel. "This is a microphone." He went on to explain how they would sell it with various types and styles of microphones to suit everyone's needs.

"And the receiver part?" Roseanne asked Becky.

"Is no bigger than a quarter and is sewn into the fabric. You could wear the panties anywhere, and no one would be the wiser."

"Unless you can't control your responses," her friend added.

~~~

Becky wiped tears from her eyes with one hand and held fast to Ford with the other as he maneuvered them to the stage door following Colin's set. She was so freaking proud of her brother! She'd always known he had talent, but his sister's opinion didn't count. The reaction from the audience tonight had confirmed her assessment, though.

The guard scrutinized their credentials before ushering them backstage where another guard pointed them in the right direction. With the familiarity of their years growing up together, she easily found him talking to a group of men dressed in black T-shirts with STAFF printed on the back in bold lettering.

"Colin!" she cried out. Breaking her connection with Ford, she launched herself in his direction.

"Becky Jean!" A smile broke across his face, and he grabbed her up in a hug, nearly crushing her ribs. "God, am I glad to see you."

"You were awesome!" She sniffed as more tears threatened. Colin set her down but seemed as reluctant to let her go as she was of him. "I'm so proud of you I could bust." She wiped her eyes.

"You look like a million bucks in that dress."

She didn't want to think about what she'd spent on her gown. All their lives they'd had to watch their pennies. "Don't get me started on what it cost," she warned.

"Colin," Ford said, snaking an arm around Becky's waist. He extended his other to shake her brother's hand. "Ford Adams. It's nice to finally meet you. Your sister speaks of you often."
~~~

"Nice to meet you," Colin said. "Thanks for helping me surprise Becky Jean, even if I did have to spoil it at the last minute."

"You should see her out front. Every time we walk past the marquee and your photo shows up, she points and shouts, 'That's my brother,' at the top of her lungs." Ford laughed as he hauled her closer.

Colin smiled. "Who'da thunk it? Right, Sis?"

"I never doubted you would make it."

"You might have been the only one, but I'm grateful for your support. Always have been. You're probably the only person who never tried to discourage me from pursuing my love of music."

Becky's heart was so full she was sure it would explode any minute. Colin had always had talent, but in the past few years, he'd grown into it. Success looked good on him. "Dad would be so proud of you."

Colin's smile dimmed, and his eyes glistened. "I know he would. He thought it was his duty to try to talk me out of going to Nashville, but when he failed to convince me, he backed off. Let me find my own way."

"Mom sends her love. She said you promised to fly her out for your debut at the Opry?"

"I did. I want you to come, too, but I figured you could afford your own plane ticket." He laughed, one eyebrow raised.

"Oh, you!" Becky's cheeks grew warm. "Yes, I can afford mine and many, many others, thanks to Ford. He saved the town, Colin. You wouldn't know it anymore. Businesses are reopening. Most of the vacant houses have been bought up and new ones are being built."

"Sex sells, they say." He winked at her and her face flamed.

"I suppose it does."

"I've got some time tomorrow. Ford sent me a pass to the convention. I thought I could come by around lunch? Maybe we could get a bite together?"

"I'd love to! I have to warn you, our products are… are…."

"I know all about your products, Sis. I'm all grown up, remember?"

"Of course you are. It's just—"

"It's time for us to get back to our seats," Ford said. "Say good-bye to your brother. You can take all the time you want tomorrow to catch up with him."

"Bye, Sis." Colin gave her another bear hug. "Thanks again for coming. Noon okay tomorrow?"

"Perfect," she said.

"Colin."

"Ford," her brother said before he turned to greet a group of female fans who'd been waiting impatiently for him to acknowledge them.

They returned to their seats just as the lights dimmed for the headline act.

"How's Colin?" Roseanne asked.

"He looks great! We're having lunch tomorrow. You should come."

Before her friend could answer, the stage burst to life as the renowned country rock band made their appearance. Becky stood along with everyone else to applaud. The opening chords of their first song rocked the building, but the accompanying vibration between her legs had all her attention.

She'd forgotten all about the tiny device in her panties. Now she couldn't stop thinking about it. She grabbed Ford's arm, turned her face into his sleeve, and held on for dear life as his wicked creation pulsed in time with the music. *Holy smoke!* She'd thought it couldn't be more devastating than it had been when he'd turned it on in the restaurant, but boy had she been wrong.

The song ended, and the crowd settled into their seats. Thankfully, Ford turned the thing off while the lead singer spoke to the crowd, but the instant the band fired off again, so did the vibrator. Their second number was a ballad, and while the first song had translated into intense sensations, this one stimulated in soft waves, wrecking her control. Once again, she buried her face in his sleeve and squeezed his arm until her fingers cramped.

"Ford," she pleaded.

He turned slightly, brushed her hair back from her face and leaned in so he could be heard. "Don't fight it, sweetheart. Let it come."

Of course, the microphone picked up every word he said, adding another layer of torture for her to deal with. She squirmed in her seat, and focused everything she had on not coming. *Oh god. Oh god. Oh god. Ford.*

"Quit fighting it, Becks." He stroked her arm from shoulder to elbow while holding her as close as the theater seats would allow and placing soft kisses on the top of her head. She knew the song—had always loved it. It ended on a long, sustained note that warbled and spanned from one octave to another. There was no way she could ride it without coming. She just prayed everyone around her would be too caught up in the emotional ending on stage to witness her surrender to the inevitable.

Ford nibbled on her earlobe then whispered, "God, I love making you come."

As the last word passed his lips, the lead singer let loose, working the syllables up and down the musical scale. His keening wale of love lost forever wrung emotion from the audience who had grown quiet with expectation. Her clit throbbed in time with the music. Every muscle in her body tensed. *No. No. No.* She fought to hang onto the last threads of her control.

With a final burst from his lungs, the singer hit the last note. The crowd erupted, applauding and cheering at the same instant Becky lost her battle. The orgasm barreled through her like a runaway locomotive. She threw her head back, and before the scream rising from her core could make it past her lips, Ford yanked her into his lap and covered her mouth with his. Her entire body quaked with the force of her release, but Ford's hands were on her, his arms bracketing her, holding all the pieces of her together until they somehow reassembled themselves.

The audience rose to their feet—all except the two of them—as the band segued into another of their fast-paced hit songs. Becky jerked, the vibrations almost painful after her intense orgasm. Ford chuckled. Shifting her slightly, he reached into his jacket pocket. She welcomed the ensuing calm between her legs, but on the other hand, her body craved the stimulation. She clenched her thighs, savoring the last lingering internal spasms.

"Better?" Ford asked.

Unwilling to trust her voice, she nodded against his shoulder. She didn't seem to have a solid bone in her body, but the man holding her seemed to be granite from his chest to his thighs supporting her. The thick ridge of his erection gouged her hip—a reminder he'd given, not taken. He held her through two more songs she barely heard for the warnings clamoring in her head. She wanted so much more from this man, but even though he claimed he wouldn't sell his and his mother's share of the company, he hadn't said anything about staying in Texas. She'd foolishly fallen in love with him. Spending more time in his bed would only make his leaving worse, but if he asked, she wouldn't turn him down.

Holding her in his lap while she came down from what had appeared to be an intense orgasm was Heaven and Hell. He had her right where he wanted her, in his arms, but he couldn't do the things he wanted to do to her, with her, in the middle of a concert. If anyone had noticed her behavior earlier, they'd given no indication—save Roseanne and Scott who'd picked up the cues early on and had the decency to look away.

"Is she okay?" Roseanne mouthed.

"Fine," he silently answered.

Becky Jean's friend smiled her understanding. Ford made some hand gestures he hoped conveyed his intention to get them out of there. Roseanne wiggled her fingers in a good-bye gesture, so he figured the message had been received. Scott caught his gaze, leaned in so his date could speak into his ear. He lifted his head again and nodded.

With his intentions known to their friends, he shifted Becky Jean so she could hear him. "Can you walk?"

She looked up at him, confusion marring her features.

"I want to take you someplace private," he said into her ear.

"Okay," she said with a nod.

"Think you can walk out of here?"

Another nod then she stood. Roseanne tugged on the hem of his coat. He turned, and she handed him Becky Jean's small purse. He smiled his thanks, then with a hand on the small of her back, he followed Becky Jean past the others in their row. Once they'd cleared the theater doors, he took over, guiding her through the casino to the bank of elevators that would take them to their rooms. He paused before pushing the call button. "Unless you'd like a drink?"

She'd worn the vibrator of her own free will, but he'd been the one to force her orgasm. The least he could do would be to offer her the opportunity to slow things down— or heaven forbid—say no. When she shook her head and nodded to the button, his lungs began to work again.

If she'd said no, he would have respected her wishes, but it would have cost him to do it. Nothing short of burying his cock inside her would ease the ache in his groin. She was so damn beautiful, and fuck, he loved to watch her come. He would have nail marks in his arm from where she'd clung to him earlier. Did it make him a bastard to be proud of the marks she'd put on him in the throes of passion? If it did, he'd wear the label.

The doors opened, and, luckily, they were the only ones to enter the car. As soon as the doors closed, he backed her into the corner and switched on the device.

"Do you have any idea what I'm going to do to you?" he asked, letting his invention translate his words into action. He traced the line of her jaw with the knuckle of his index finger then stroked his thumb over her quivering bottom lip. He didn't expect a verbal answer. Instead, he watched her breath hitch and her eyelids flutter shut. He pressed his hips into hers, letting her feel what she did to him.

"I've wanted you since you opened your door this evening looking like a goddess." He paused, adjusted to better feel the vibrations. Satisfied with the new position, he continued. "Your sexy leg sticking out of the slit in the skirt—taunting me." His fingers found her bare thigh. He slipped his hand beneath the heavy fabric to caress her skin. "So hot. So soft. I want to see you… every last inch of you."

Damn. He ground his teeth together and canted his hips away from her. He'd had no idea how powerful his toy could be. If he kept this up much longer, he would make himself come! He made a mental note to have the technical writing department add this position to the instruction sheet to be included with each device then focused on his goal—making his woman come.

His woman. He liked the sound of that. In all his years, he'd never wanted to possess a woman the way he wanted to possess this one. So prim and proper in public, she let loose in bed, and damn if he didn't want to be the last man to ever see her do it.

He ground against her again, slid the hand he'd slipped under her dress around to cup her butt. "I want to taste you."

He squeezed her ass cheek. "I want to take a bite out of your ass, mark you as mine."

Becky Jean moaned, and the sound translated into vibration nearly sent him over the edge. He backed away once more, this time promising himself he'd stay away until they got to his room. Then all bets were off.

The car came to a stop. He glanced over his shoulder, noted the floor display. Reaching into his pocket, he managed to turn the vibrator off a split second before the doors slid open to admit two couples dressed for a night on the town. They pushed the button for the rooftop lounge. Ford snaked an arm around Becky Jean's waist and pulled her in close. When the elevator stopped at their floor, he steered her past the rowdy bunch and toward his room.

"You're a wicked man, Ford Adams." Hearing the laughter behind her words, he tossed the keycard on the nearest flat surface then turned to the woman who had made him rethink everything in his life from where he wanted to live to what he wanted out of life. He'd never cared much for the plight of others, but Becky Jean's insistence on hiring local had opened his eyes to the way his decisions affected other people's lives. She made him *want* to be a better person. She made him want. Period.

"I've never claimed to be anything else," he said, stalking her. She took a step back—a halfhearted attempt to get away, at best. He stopped an arm's length from her and smiled. "Admit it, you had fun tonight."

Her face flushed with color, and her lips parted as she prepared to deny the truth.

"Turn around," he said, spinning his finger in the air. "I need to see you."

Her gaze met his for a second—long enough for him to see she wanted to continue what they'd started as much as he did. Then she showed him her back. He stepped in behind her and brushed her hair over one shoulder. "Where the hell is the zipper?"

"Oh! Here." She lifted her arm and pointed to the tiny tab. "Sorry. I forgot."

"No problem." He'd planned on nibbling his way down her spine, but this had possibilities. He grasped the zipper pull and tugged it down until it bottomed out just past the curve of her hip. He caught a glimpse of creamy skin and the band of the panties he'd sent her—and nothing else. Damn, she knew how to do sexy. He slid his hand into the gap in the fabric just below her rib cage, his palm finding soft, warm skin at the small of her back. As he guided her around to face him and took her lips with his, he instantly became a fan of side zippers.

Cupping the back of her head in his free hand, he explored the hills and valleys of her ass with the other. Becky Jean groaned and melted against him which he took as permission to continue his exploration. He'd had his hands beneath dresses before, but there was something sneaky and exciting about slipping in from the side. Like he'd found a secret entrance no one else knew about. Fuck, why didn't every dress have one of these?

Needing air, he dragged his lips from hers but continued to nibble along her jaw. Fingers still entwined in her hair, he tugged her head to the side. He kissed his way down the slope of her neck, loving the way her pulse beat out a wild rhythm, matching his own. He couldn't resist. He opened wide and bit. Not hard enough to mar her perfect skin, but hard enough to get her attention.

"Oh god. Ford." The breathless way she said his name had to be one of the hottest things he'd ever heard in his life. He bit her again, lower this time. She moaned and arched her back so her breasts pressed hard against his chest. He used his chin to scooch the strap of her dress off her shoulder. It slid down and caught on his forearm. He proceeded to kiss and nibble his way south to the tender swell of flesh. Using his teeth, he tugged the fabric lower. Lower. Her scent, magnified by the heat of her body, filled his nostrils as he slowly, slowly, revealed the top of her breast. Then the areola. Then his upper lip skimmed her nipple, and he lost it.

"Fuck, Becks." He grabbed at the dress again with his teeth—captured it and yanked like a beast tearing at the skin of a carcass to get to the meat underneath. The instant her breast popped free of the confining cloth, he attacked, nipping at her beauty, licking, and finally sucking the hardened nub into his mouth.

He couldn't get enough of her. Couldn't get close enough to sate his need. Savage. He knew it but couldn't stop. Yanking on her hair, he bent her over the arm banded around her waist. Her fingernails digging into his scalp were matches thrown on the bonfire raging inside him. Her breathless pleas, "God. Please. Ford. Need. You," were giant-assed logs that incinerated the last vestiges of his control.

He couldn't wait another minute to have her.

Pulling her upright, he took another second to admire the feel of her skin beneath the beaded dress. He'd made a mess of her hair, but what utterly destroyed him was the sight of her breast, bared for him while the rest of her remained perfectly clothed. "God, Becks. I've never seen…. You take my breath away."

"Ford."

Need. It rang in his ears, broke the spell she'd cast over him. He mentally clicked the shutter on the picture before him. Knew it would forever be burned on his brain, and no matter what happened between them in the future, he'd treasure this moment. This memory. "Take that dress the fuck off."

The shrug of a shoulder. A hip wiggle and it fell into a pool of midnight and glittering stars around her ankles. She wore the panties he'd given her and some kind of strappy sandals with heels a mile high, making her legs look longer than fuck. He had things he wanted to do to her with those panties, but they could wait. He needed to be inside her. No gimmicks. No toys. Nothing but her and him and whatever the fuck he was feeling.

"Off." He pointed at her crotch. She hooked her thumbs in the waistband and, with another hip shimmy, added the panties to the pile at her ankles.

He made a conscious effort to breathe as he gazed at the woman before him. The scent of her arousal, heavy on the air, nearly brought him to his knees. His heart kicked and his dick throbbed, anxious to get out of the starting gate. He reached for his belt buckle.

CHAPTER TWENTY-FOUR

How can it take so long to unbuckle a belt?

Becky's gaze followed Ford's hands, silently willing him to move faster. A minute ago, he'd been a wild animal, tearing at her clothes, biting her, sucking her flesh hard enough to extract the marrow from her bones. He'd switched to slow motion. She didn't know how much longer she could remain upright.

She'd been in a constant state of arousal since the moment he'd activated the vibrator in her panties in the vestibule of the restaurant. Granted, the orgasm during the concert had taken the edge off, but the reprieve hadn't lasted long. The elevator ride had put her body back to square one. She hurt. Actually hurt with her need to have him inside her.

Muscle memory. Her pussy knew the shape and size of him. Knew the delicious stretch as he entered her. Knew the regret as he slid back out. Thrilled at the anticipation of feeling the stretch as he filled her again. And had ached for it every minute of every day, it seemed.

"Let me." Carefully stepping free of her clothes, she approached, searched his eyes for a sign of the beast she craved tonight and found it. There. Leashed but straining against his cage. Holding his gaze, her fingers found the button in the center of his chest. He froze. Becky popped the fastener free then went to work on the next one. And the next, until the fabric parted. She flattened her palms on his abdomen, traced the lines of his six-pack. "You're wearing too many clothes, Kinky."

He smirked at the nickname he'd been given by one of the reporters who had interviewed him earlier in the year. Becky turned her hands, brushed her knuckles over his flat nipples. A shiver racked his body, and he sucked in a harsh breath, but he made no attempt to stop her. Her fingers skimmed lower, into the waistband of his slacks. It took nothing to release the hook closure. Less to slide the zipper down.

She read the warning in his eyes— Don't poke the animal. Too late... she already had her hand inside his boxers.

"Becks." His eyelids dropped, a muscle ticked in his clenched jaw. He groaned and rocked into her hand. Once. Twice. "Goddamnit, Becks." His fingers manacled her wrist. His eyes popped open. "Stop."

She knew she should heed the warning, but she couldn't bring herself to do it. For whatever reason, she needed it wild tonight. No holding back. Hot. Messy. Maybe brutal. Sex. She wrapped her fingers around his cock and squeezed.

The beast broke free, took her to the floor. She opened for him, but not far enough to please him. He wrenched her knees up and out. Held her there. With a feral growl, he bent and buried his face in her pussy. The scent of arousal, hers and his, wrapped around them. Becky threw her hands over her head, sought an anchor to ground her as he took her up and up toward a pinnacle higher than she'd ever climbed before. As frightening as it was, as hard as she knew she'd fall, she *needed* to fly off that cliff. Needed *Ford* to push her over the edge. No one else. Just him. Always him.

He took her relentlessly. As if he sensed her need, he feasted on her, bruising with his tongue, scraping her tender flesh with his teeth. Her body belonged to him. The beast controlled her, positioned her where he wanted, took what he wanted—and gave her what she needed.

She felt like one of those giant slingshots being stretched back. Back. Back. Every muscle in her body ached under the strain. For what seemed like an eternity, she froze in limbo. Wound too tight to let go. Wound too tight to remain still. Then he speared his tongue inside her, and the carnality of the act snapped her hold on reality.

The world she knew ceased to exist. She flew into the unknown on the wings of the most explosive orgasm of her life where pain and pleasure became one. Yet still she reached for something… something more.

Then he was there, blanketing her with his warmth, his strength—filling her. "Ford!" She rode the wave with him until neither one could stop the tide. They came together in a breathless rush. Becky held on to his broad shoulders and wished the night would never end.

~~~

With a smile, Becky greeted everyone who stopped at their booth, handing out the *KeyP Me Safe* keychain/flashlight/vibrators they'd brought along as giveaways. Somehow, she managed to answer the questions coming her way, but with Ford standing a few feet away, thinking about anything other than the night before proved damn near impossible. More than once, he'd stepped in to fill in the blanks where her brain had failed her.

The convention was their first opportunity to network with the various retailers who stocked their products. Since Adams Manufacturing had launched their own sales
~~~

platform—going into direct competition with them—maintaining a good relationship with them had to be a priority. They'd lost a few with the move into direct sales, but not all. She had a plan to bring the others back into the fold with discounted advertising on their Adult Shopping Network and the promise of exclusive product launches.

But it required her complete concentration on business—something she could not even pretend to do with Ford so near. When he whipped out a sample of his latest invention to show to a potential new client, she excused herself and went in search of someplace she could be alone. It turned out to be a stall in the ladies' room, where she closed her eyes and gave in to the memories tugging at her mind and her heart.

After screwing like mad on the floor, Ford had carried her to bed where he'd finished undressing then returned to the other room to retrieve her panties. Wearing nothing but a wicked smile, he slipped them back on her. Product testing, he'd said as he searched his phone. A few seconds later, music spilled from a small, portable speaker on the nightstand.

He removed the lapel-pin microphone and the wireless control box from his coat and set them on the nightstand before crawling in bed with her.

"I downloaded this music just for this," he'd said. Then he'd turned the device on.

Tears threatened as she recalled the way he'd touched and kissed her while the music played low in the background, converted to a tactile sensation between her legs by his invention. Then, when she didn't think she could take any more, he'd pushed the crotch of the panties to one side and entered her. It had been the complete opposite of their frenzied coupling on the floor, and where the first time had wrecked her physically, the slow, sensual mating to the strains of a symphony orchestra shattered her.

She couldn't even pretend to deny it any longer. She was in love with K. Ford Adams—the kinky bastard. He liked to pretend he didn't care about anything but the bottom line, but she'd seen another side of him.

The new HR department answered to her, so the day Ford had walked in and asked which employees had been there the longest, she heard about it. They day he called them all together and handed them bonus checks—drawn from his personal account—she heard about it.

The day one of their new employees totaled his car on the way to work and Ford went to the hospital to check on the man, she heard about it. And when he paid the deductible on the man's car insurance so he could get a new car, she heard about it.

There wasn't much Ford did she didn't know about. He was a caring and generous employer, and he cared about Butte Plains, too. *Someone* had paid to rebuild the broken-down gazebo in the square, and it sure as heck hadn't been the city council. No, the money had come from Ford Adams. Word had it he walked into City Hall one day and handed the mayor a check—told the man to fix the gazebo and anything else in need of repair. He'd said Adams Manufacturing had a reputation to uphold, and he couldn't do it if his clients saw a rundown town when they came to visit. Everyone knew most visitors to the plant never went past the town square or drove downtown to see the newly repaired antique streetlights or the fresh-as-a-daisy floral baskets hanging from them. Ford had done what he'd done for the people of Butte Plains. He cared. Deeply.

It's why she loved him—not because of the way he made her feel when they made love. Feeling loved and cherished was just a nice bonus.

Becky returned to the booth to find Ford had taken a potential client to lunch, leaving the booth in the capable hands of the staff they'd brought along. She had just finished going over the schedule for the rest of the day when her brother arrived. Colin might not think he'd *made it* yet, but judging from the reaction of the young women in her employ when she introduced him, he'd already made it big. He stood signing autographs for them and the crowd that had gathered, when the last person on earth Becky wanted to see approached the booth.

Determined to be nice even if it killed her, she plastered a smile on her face and greeted the woman. "Veronica. I didn't know you were in Vegas."

The witch smiled and tugged a man forward. Becky supposed he might be handsome, but not like Ford. Jiminy, when had she started comparing every man she met to her partner?

"Becky Jean Parker, this is Carter Hargraves. He's the—"

"I know who he is." An icy shiver ran down her spine. What in heaven's name was Veronica doing with the CEO of Toy Haven? And why would she bring him over to introduce him?

Though warning bells rang in her brain making it difficult hear, she tried her best to be civil. Becky extended her hand. "It's nice to meet you, Mr. Hargraves."

"Can we go somewhere to talk?" he said, taking her hand.

The bells clanged louder. "About?"

"Mr. Hargraves is interested in purchasing your share of Adams Manufacturing," Veronica said.

Becky removed her hand from the man's grasp and turned her attention to the woman beside him. She couldn't have heard correctly. "What?"

"Surely you know Ford is going to sell. Then what will you do? Carter wants your 25 percent, too."

A giant pit opened up inside her, her heart teetering on the edge. "Wait. Are you telling me Ford has agreed to sell to you?"

"Of course he did." Veronica laughed. "You didn't think he would stay in Butt F— Butte Plains forever, did you?"

The brakes on her personal roller coaster car failed. Her heart lurched over the crest and fell all the way to her toes.

"His home is in New York. With me." She delivered the last two words with a deadly smile.

Becky took a step back, right into her brother. "Hey, Sis. Ready to go?"

"Uh."

"Carter Hargraves," the man said. "We saw your concert last night. You're good."

"Thanks," Colin said. "Colin Parker." He leaned around her to shake hands with the woman who had just eviscerated her.

"Veronica Ramsey," she said, her voice dripping with syrup. "You and Becky Jean…?"

"Siblings," her brother said. "She never stops reminding me who's older."

"Listen," Hargraves said. "We were just going to invite your sister to lunch. Why don't you join us?"

A heartbeat later, Becky sat at a table in a swanky Italian restaurant with her celebrity brother and the two people in the world she wished she'd never met. How she'd gotten there, she didn't know. How she would get out without causing a scene, she didn't care. Maybe she could excuse herself to the bathroom and find a back exit. She had her purse. She could call a cab, go straight to the airport and catch a flight to Dallas. Judging from the looks the witch exchanged with her brother, she'd be home before anyone missed her.

A good big sister would warn Colin about Veronica, but she had to admit, she was grateful for deflecting the woman's attention away from her. If he could keep it up, perhaps the conversation she dreaded would never take place.

Attentive waiters came and went, delivering wine, bread, and plates of food she didn't recall ordering. It was as if she looked through a mirror, observing an alternate universe where another version of herself resided. This other Becky smiled and spoke when spoken to. She even ate a few bites when real Becky's stomach felt like a lead ball. She heard Hargrave's offer, but couldn't process it. The dollar amount sounded ridiculous to someone who still emptied her coin purse into a jar every evening.

Less than a year ago, the cost of this meal alone would have bankrupted her. That she could afford it, and more, staggered her. As she mentally tallied the changes in her life, she knew one thing for certain, none of it meant anything if she didn't have Ford.

Other Becky said, "Ford agreed to sell?"

"He will. He's holding out for a better price," Veronica said. "It's all about the money with him. Always has been."

Funny. Since she'd gotten to know Ford, she'd come to the conclusion the money didn't matter that much to him. He enjoyed his work. Enjoyed being compensated for it, but even when he'd thought the failing plant might eat up everything he had, he hadn't seemed particularly bereft. In fact, he'd seen his predicament as a challenge—one he'd risen to, conquered. Just as he'd conquered her heart.

"I don't have an answer for you today, Mr. Hargraves. I hadn't planned to sell. I need time to think about your offer."

"You won't get a better offer," Veronica stated. Her words were as flat as the line of her lips.

Why did it matter so much to her if Becky sold? It was Ford she wanted, Ford she needed to convince to sell. The proverbial lightbulb flicked on in her head. She knew exactly what Veronica planned. *You lying bitch.* Real Becky straightened her spine. "I've got to go." She cocked her head at her brother then reached for her purse. Colin stood and held her chair for her to rise. Star or not, he had the manners of a Southern gentleman.

"Take my card." Carter reached into his jacket pocket. "Call me when you've made your decision."

Ignoring the card he held out, she said, "That won't be necessary. I've made my decision. I'm not selling. Not unless Ford is."

The shock on Veronica's face told her everything she needed to know. Ford *hadn't* agreed to sell. They were hoping Becky would sign on the dotted line, and they could use her share as leverage to convince her partner to do the same. "Thanks for lunch," she said, knowing full well the bill had not yet arrived.

"What was that all about?" Colin asked as soon as they hit the sidewalk.

"You just witnessed Veronica Ramsey at her best." Wanting to put as much distance between her and the wicked witch of the east, she walked at a brisk pace. "As far as I can tell, no one has ever told her no. It's about time she learned the world doesn't revolve around her."

"I don't know. She seemed nice enough."

Becky stopped so suddenly the guy walking behind her had to take evasive measures to avoid knocking her over. "What? Are you insane?" She fisted her hands on her hips and glared at her brother whose familiar smile goaded her on. "Do. Not. Get. Involved. With that witch, Colin Parker. She's bad news. Spoiled. Entitled. She wants Ford!"

"And she can't have him. I get it, Becks."

"He's mine."

Colin's smile widened. "Yes, he is."

For the longest time, she stared at her brother. Then his words sank in. *Her* words sank in. She groaned and leaned against the nearest light pole.

"You should tell him, Becks."

"I know." She shifted her gaze to the flashing marquee on the casino down the street. "What if she's right and he does want to go back to New York?"

Colin shrugged. "I've been there. It's not so bad. It ain't Texas, but nothing is."

"That's not what I meant, and you know it." She'd go anywhere Ford wanted to go, even New York. "What if he wants to go back to *her*?" She used her thumb to gesture back to the restaurant they'd just left.

"Maybe he just needs a reason to stay." He cocked one eyebrow at her.

She nodded, and for the first time since Veronica had shown up at their booth, her smile came easy. "Maybe he does."

CHAPTER TWENTY-FIVE

"She did *what*?"

"Ms. Parker went to lunch," the nervous intern repeated.

"With Veronica Ramsey and Carter Hargraves?" he clarified, just in case he'd lost his mind and imagined his business partner—the woman he *loved* and *wanted to spend the rest of his life with*—had gone off to discuss selling part of their company to a man who didn't give a shit about his family's legacy, much less the people in Butte Plains.

"And Colin Parker," another intern added with a dreamy sigh. "I didn't know Ms. Parker and *Colin* Parker were related."

Ford growled. Both women took a step back, and Ford gave himself a mental shake. He couldn't blame them, they were just the messengers. He made a conscious effort to school his features into something civilized. Becky Jean would skin him alive if he scared off their help, and they had to man this booth for the rest of the week by themselves. "I'm sorry. I shouldn't have spoken to you the way I did. I'm just surprised, that's all."

"You didn't know Colin Parker was her brother either?" the ditsier one asked.

Ford grabbed control of his temper with both hands. "Yes, I knew he was her brother. I even knew she planned to have lunch with him today. I didn't know about Ms. Ramsey and the other guy."

"That was all of a sudden, I think," the more reasonable one said. *Ashley? Or is her name Amy?*

"What makes you think so?"

Ashley/Amy shrugged. "I don't know. Colin was here then Ms. Ramsey walked up. Everyone else was all, you know"—she made a whirly gesture near her temple—"over Colin, so I don't think they noticed the way Ms. Parker spoke to her. I don't know why exactly, but it didn't seem like a friendly conversation."

Knowing she hadn't had a pleasant conversation with those two helped ease the knot in his gut somewhat. "You weren't impressed by Colin?" he asked, giving her what he hoped appeared to be a friendly smile.

She shook her head. "Oh, no, sir. He's cute and all, but I have a boyfriend back home. Seth is much better looking, and he can sing, too. His band plays every weekend down at the Roadhouse."

The other girl standing behind Ashley/Amy rolled her eyes. Ford resisted the urge to laugh outright. "Seth lives in Butte Plains?"

"He has a place over on Cotton Street."

Ford nodded. As he recalled, nothing but rundown apartments lined Cotton. "Next time Colin is in town, maybe we could get them together. He might be able to help Seth. That is, if your boyfriend is serious about the music business."

Her face lit up like a Christmas tree, and she jumped and clapped her hands. "You'd do that? You're awesome, Mr. Adams!" Then she launched herself at him.

He was trying to extricate himself from her bear hug when a familiar voice did the trick for him. "Amy, how many times do I have to tell you to keep your hands off the boss?"

Amy catapulted away, muttering apologies all around.

"Amy," he said. "Ms. Parker is just kidding." He turned to Becky Jean. "Aren't you?"

"Of course I am, but let's keep the public displays of affection down to a minimum. That's not the reputation Adams Manufacturing wants to project to the public."

So, she did care about the company. He only hoped she cared enough not to sell her share, but if she really wanted out, he'd buy her out himself. Adams Manufacturing had always been a family business. Family should own it.

"It won't happen again, will it, Amy?" He winked at the young lady and she nodded.

"No, sir. Thank you, Mr. Adams," she said. "I can't wait to tell Seth what you said."

Becky Jean's head swiveled between the two of them as if she couldn't decide if she really wanted to know what he'd told the girl or not.

"Glad to help." He'd had enough small talk. He and Becky Jean were overdue for a long discussion. He reached for her hand. "Now, if you'll excuse us, Ms. Parker and I have some business to discuss."

"Call me if you have any problems," Becky Jean said over her shoulder as he dragged her away from the booth.

He would have preferred more privacy for what he wanted to say to her, but the curtained-off storage area in the back corner of the convention hall would do.

"What's this about, Ford?" she asked as he pulled her through a gap in the black drapes.

He came to a stop and spun around to face her. The color he'd noticed on her cheeks when she arrived at the booth had deepened. Images of all the places he'd seen that particular shade of pink on her body flashed through his brain like a brush fire, igniting a matching one inside him. *Where have you been all my life?*

"What?"

"I didn't— Oh. I said that out loud?"

She nodded, studying him as if he'd grown two heads or something. "Are you okay, Ford?"

He chuckled. He'd envisioned this conversation going a lot smoother. He didn't have a clue what he should say next. If he told her he loved her and asked her to marry him, would she think he just wanted to keep her from selling? And if he asked her if she planned to sell, would she think he cared more about the company than he did her? Either way, he was screwed.

"There's something I want—no, need to say to you, but I just figured out there's no good way to say it."

"Oh. My. God!" Her eyes swam with tears. "You *are* going to sell! That bitch was right!"

"No!" When she tried to jerk her hand out of his, he held on tight. "No, Becks." He got down in her line of sight and shook his head. "No. I told you. I'm not selling Adams Manufacturing. Not now, not ever."

His declaration seemed to calm her a bit, but the edge of the woods had never looked farther away. He swallowed hard and said the last thing he wanted to say. "But I understand if you want to sell your 25 percent. It's worth a lot of money. You'd be set for life, you and your mother. You could go anywhere, do anything you wanted, and never worry about money ever again." He squeezed her fingers, hoping she'd hear what he wasn't saying in the words he *was* saying. "Adams Manufacturing has always been a family-owned business."

She sniffed and wiped her cheeks with the fingers of her free hand. "I understand. You want to buy me out." The finality in her statement wrecked him. He'd done a shit-poor job of showing her what she meant to him.

"No. You don't understand at all. I don't want to buy you out." He had to get this right. Holding onto her hand so she couldn't bolt, he dropped to one knee. "I want to marry you. Becky Jean Parker, will you do me the honor of becoming my wife—my partner in life and in business—for as long as we both shall live?"

Maybe he'd laid it on thick, but he wanted her to know he understood exactly what he'd asked her to do. He'd never thought he'd marry. Never wanted to—until Becky Jean showed him what love was. His knee protested to being on the concrete, but he'd get down on both knees and beg if he had to.

"You don't have to marry me, Ford. I'll sell—"

He couldn't listen to another word about selling. Not today. "No. I don't want your share of the company, Becks. I want you. Just you. Say you'll marry me. Please, I don't know—"

"Shh." She shushed him with a finger against his lips. "Why? If you don't want the company, then why?"

It dawned on him then. He'd forgotten the most important thing. *Shit!*

"Ford Adams!" She tried to get away, but he held fast.

"Didn't mean to say that out loud," he said. He shook his head. "I'm making a mess of this, Becks." He stood and took both her hands in his. Closing the distance between them, he rested his forehead against hers. Their gazes met and held.

"I should have led with I love you. I do. Love you, I mean. More than anything. You make me want to be a better person, Becky Jean. I see you and the love you have for other people, and I can't help but want some of your love for myself. I love you. I want to have you by my side, as my wife, my lover, and my partner for the rest of our lives. I won't give up Adams Manufacturing, but I can't run it without you. You are Adams Manufacturing. The only thing you're missing is the name."

He ducked his head and brushed his lips over hers. "Please, say you'll be my wife."

Laughter—joy—bubbled up within her and came out as a hiccup. She'd always dreamed of finding a man to love her, one who respected her as an equal. She could hardly believe her ears, but *that kiss*. It had been so sweet and showed a vulnerability she'd never seen in Ford before, except maybe on the first day when he'd just buried his father then discovered his family legacy had become a concrete block tied around his ankles. She'd fallen in love with him then— or maybe it had been later, when he'd brought her a pocket sandwich and she'd seen the dismay in his eyes at what had happened to his hometown.

She'd known then his emotions ran deep. He cared, even if he told himself he didn't.

They were good together. In the office. On screen. In bed. Lord, were they good together in bed. She flushed just thinking about the possibility of experiencing the kind of passion they had together for the rest of her life.

"I'm dying here, Becks. Say something. Please."

"You're a good man, Ford Adams."

"No," he groaned.

"Of course I'll marry you."

"What?"

"Do we need to get your hearing checked? I said yes. I'll marry you."

"Yes!" He let go of one of her hands and speared a fist into the air. "She said yes!"

"Shh! Ford."

"I don't care who hears me. I want to shout it to the world." He stilled. "Let's go up to the top of the Eiffel Tower. Wait! No. Let's get married. Today. Right now." He grabbed her other hand again.

"I don't want to wait another day to make you mine. We can do the big wedding later if you want. No one else has to know we're already married. Just, please, let's do it today."

"Before you change your mind?" She fought to keep the smile off her face, but her lips had a mind of their own. Teasing Ford was so much fun!

"I'll never, ever change my mind about you, Becky Jean. I love you. I always will."

"I'll do it on one condition."

"Anything you want, sweetheart. Anything."

If she was going to get married in Las Vegas, by George, she intended to do it right. "I want an Elvis wedding."

He laughed out loud. "Anything you want, Becks. Anything you want."

"I want you. Just you."

ABOUT THE AUTHOR

USA Today Best-Selling author Roz Lee is the author of over thirty romances. The first, The Lust Boat, was born of an idea acquired while on a Caribbean cruise with her family, and soon blossomed into a five-book series originally published by Red Sage. Following her love of baseball, Roz turned her attention to sexy athletes in tight pants, writing the critically acclaimed Mustangs Baseball series.

Roz has been married to her best friend, and high school sweetheart, for over four decades. They have two daughters and are the proud grandparents of three adorable grandkids. Roz and her husband live in the wilds of New Jersey with their Labrador Retriever, Bud which is code for Big Unruly Dog.

Even though Roz has lived on both coasts, her heart lies in between, in Texas. A Texan by birth, she can trace her family back to the Republic of Texas. With roots that deep, she says, "You can't ever really leave."

When Roz isn't writing, she's reading or traipsing around the country on one adventure or another. No trip is too small, no tourist trap too cheesy, and no road unworthy of travel.

Visit Roz's website – www.RozLee.net